7th Moon

By Michael Joy

To Noah

Michael

Joy

Part 1: Rise of Heroes

Chapter 1

The soldiers gathered for their first mission, wearing their uniforms, black body suits with a subtle insignia of the number seven framed by a crescent moon, reinforced with body armor. The top soldiers out of the one hundred and eight soldiers that had been created specifically to serve the Seventh Moon were going to take out a terrorist cell in the Kanagawa prefecture.

Among the new soldiers was the first-and so far, only-cyborg that the cybernetics department had been able to produce. He was called Hidariude which means left arm and referred to the cybernetic arm he had. The cybernetics department thought only about the arm and had referred to the child by the project's code name and so it became his name as well. Now that he was ready for the field, he now had a convincing artificial skin made of latex complete with acrylic nails and hair to hide the true nature of his arm, although he was also wearing gloves as part of his combat uniform, so this time it did not matter at all. Aside from his arm he seemed fairly typical, short black hair and a body shape somewhere between a mesomorph and an endomorph, perfectly balanced between strength, speed and agility. The other soldiers did not have cybernetics, but instead drew their advantages from DNA modifications by way of specific genes from various animals that would make superior human soldiers. Hidariude's closest comrade among them was Kichiku, the brute, who had been designed simply to be strong. He was huge, over three meters tall, and heavy,

3

but pure muscle, each fiber as tough as a Hercules beetle so he could lift eight hundred and fifty times his weight, with a grizzly bear-like hump of muscle on his back and shoulders for good measure. He was also bald, not that it mattered he didn't need hair to level buildings with his fists.

The commanding officer and field leader was Gaki, the oldest soldier. He had once served in the Japanese military until the Seventh Moon provided him with gene therapy by way of a retrovirus that made him an elite soldier beyond his comrades and needed a greater challenge. He had a hand in training the soldiers, teaching them military tactics after they had been trained in basic fighting from another instructor, though he had to take over full time since the other instructor disappeared three years earlier. He had supposedly had some experience in the region, including reconnaissance before the soldiers were old enough for his training.   Then there was Renzokuken, the gunner, he was designed with the vision of a hawk and aim to match, and his muscles were built to handle the recoil of his pistols so he could actually fire continuously without losing his target. Aka was built for speed, the musculature of a cheetah and the endurance of a gazelle, he didn't have to be strong, just quick. Paku was the eater, his sharp teeth were his weapon and he was as ravenous as an entire school of piranha. Kappa was their aquatic specialist, gills and webbed fingers and toes; he wouldn't necessarily be specifically advantageous in this mission, though if anyone tried to escape across water, he would make sure they were captured. These were the best of the best and today was their time to shine for Seventh Moon by taking down the terrorist cell hiding in a farming commune just outside Tokyo.

"Remember boys," Gaki said before they disembarked from their shuttle, "There are rogues from Seventh Moon who have secrets and technology among the people we will find here. They may look like harmless farmers, but make no mistake, there are dangerous enemies here. This entire place could be full of armed militia. For our security, we must leave no survivors."

Kappa went first to get into the irrigation canals so he could quickly get into place to ambush his quarry. Next, Kichiku went to work knocking down buildings, which was surprisingly easy for him, one well-placed strike on a cornerstone and a whole two story brick building would crumble like a sandcastle. Then Aka went running, with his speed he was able to quickly catch up to and get ahead of his cohorts. He was too fast to use guns, he was actually faster than the bullets, so he just attacked any person he encountered with jabs that at the speed he was moving, had the same lethal force as a bullet. For actual gunplay of course, Renzokuken had the duty of shooting everyone with his handguns. He marched down the middle of the town and scanned quickly for anything that moved and fired.

Hidariude and Paku were there for cleanup, they were there to kill anyone their cohorts missed. Hidariude was an elegant artist of warfare, specializing in a three strike combination attack with his blades, first he used his finger blades with a palm strike, followed by a tiger claw with the blades on top of his hand, and a finish with a slice from his long arm blade. While Hidariude was elegant with his practiced rhythm, Paku was the complete opposite, greedily grabbing anyone unfortunate enough to survive the onslaught of his comrades only to cross his path and be devoured.

Some people tried to fight back, though their efforts were futile. No matter what weapon the locals used, the soldiers simply dodged or deflected the attack then countered with deadly force. Kichiku threw one attacker at the next, using the people themselves as weapons. Aka was a blurry streak of death, sneaking up to, behind, even between targets and striking each person down with a single deftly placed strike. Escape was futile; anyone who tried to run away through the fields was caught by Kappa who would drown them in the canals or rice paddies.

Within an hour the strike team had successfully killed everybody in the community. Their next task was to search for technology that might have been confiscated by the rogues. Hidariude teamed up with Kichiku to search buildings, or rather, the rubble left after Kichiku had laid waste to the village. It took time to move the rubble and check underneath, worst of all; there was no trace of any technology, not even fragments of anything that had been pulverized. If there was anything, it was dust now.

"Perhaps we should have organized the search before destroying everything in sight." Hidariude observed.

"I was just following orders." Kichiku said coldly.

"You sound so sad. Take some pride in your work."

"What is there to be proud of? These people took pride in their work, and all I did was destroy it."

"Listen big guy, I just don't think there was really anything here. Don't worry about it."

"If there was nothing here, then why did we kill all of these people?"

"Geez man, now you're way over thinking this whole thing. Maybe they sold the goods already and that's why we couldn't find anything. Whatever the case, we took out the terrorists and saved Seventh Moon. We're heroes, not bad for a day's work, especially considering it's our first day on the job. Let's go report back to Commander Gaki and head home for a victory drink."

Kichiku just stood there. He looked around the room and saw a woman lying on the floor, her head covered in blood from a fatal wound inflicted by her roof caving in on her, the handiwork of Kichiku himself. He held quiet in a moment of silence.

Hidariude walked to the door and opened it, then turned to find his comrade motionless. He closed the door and was about to say something when something else moved from under the rubble. Enough of a wall remained to create a blind spot hiding the soldiers from the view of whomever-or whatever- was still alive, but they could still see the lone survivor of the attack.

It was a child, a boy of no more than three years of age. He had been hiding in a cellar they overlooked. He approached the woman and gave her a shake. "Mama?

Mama, wake up. Come on mama, we have to get out of here. Mama…MAMA!"

The woman actually turned out to be alive, but just barely. She reached out her hand to touch her son's face and with her last breath she answered him, "Douji, don't forget, the Shrine of the Golden Dragon, Ryu…" Then her hand dropped to the floor. The boy picked up her hand as it grew cold and held it to his face while he cried.

Tears began to stream down Kichiku's face. Slowly he approached the small boy. He reached out and embraced the boy. "I…I am sorry…so sorry…"

The three shared a very somber moment. Hidariude knew his orders, but at this moment, it just seemed appropriate to let things be. Hidariude and Kichiku were close, probably the closest of any two soldiers on Seventh Moon. They knew what it was like to be alone and need somebody. Among the soldiers they were different somehow. Hidariude had grown up alone in a lab only joining the others later and everybody hated his arm-everybody except Kichiku. Despite his size and strength, he was soft hearted, kind and trusting, and the others disliked him for it, sensing weakness. The more the others ostracized the two of them, the closer they grew.

The time of reflection was broken when the door opened again. This time it was Commander Gaki. "We're almost finished; did you two find anything in here?"

Hidariude turned to face Gaki, but Kichiku remained huddled over the boy. The ruse did not work at all; Gaki approached Kichiku and looked at the boy beneath him. "Well well, what do we have here?" He got close to the boy and breathed in deep, smelling him. He had a very good sense of smell, especially for blood. He had been selected for a special task that involved information only he had been given and none of his team knew about. He was looking for someone, and this was that someone. "Okay, we're going. Bring the boy."

They left the broken building and walked back to the rendezvous point at the edge of town. As they walked, Douji saw the bodies littering the sides of the road and held Kichiku tightly. Kichiku placed his hand on the boy, fearing the worst was yet to come for the boy.

Gaki did a roll call, "Attention! Hidariude, Kichiku, Renzokuken, Paku, Kappa..." Aka was the last to arrive, showing off by setting the town on fire on the far end and then racing the spreading flames back to the rendezvous point. "...and Aka. Good, all accounted for. Did anybody find anything?"

Each soldier replied a resounding "No sir!" except of course, Hidariude and Kichiku, who knew Gaki already knew their answer.

"Well we hit the jackpot here boys. This small child your comrades located is actually one of ours, but was abducted by these renegades. Today we have liberated him so he can return with us and rejoin our ranks as he should. This mission is a success, let's go home victorious!"

The boy clung to Kichiku even tighter and cried. Kichiku couldn't stand it; he spoke out, "What is the meaning of this? We killed all of these people just so that we could retrieve one child? Did they even ever have weapons to begin with?"

"They had the boy. They were able to get this child away from our space station and evaded us for three years. Clearly they have some masterminds in their organization. Who knows what they were planning? If we had spared them today they would only make plans to retaliate later on and you'd have to kill them later. Who knows what they've put into this boy's head, who knows if we can even save him or if he's just a sleeper agent, their secret weapon all along?"

Kichiku couldn't take this, he grabbed Gaki by the throat. "No! No more innocent blood will be shed, no one else will be our victim today!" He turned to the boy, "Run!" Douji ran as fast as he could.

While Kichiku wasn't looking, Gaki bit his hand and dropped to the ground. "Aka, Kappa, after him!"

The two soldiers responded with a resounding "Yes sir!" and pursued the boy as ordered.

When Kichiku tried to stop the other soldiers, Renzokuken shot at him, but Hidariude deflected it with his blade. "He's right, no more bloodshed, especially from our own comrades!" He then attacked Renzokuken and disarmed him, deftly removing his guns from his hands and holsters with his blades, flinging them each in the air and slicing them up in midair. "You're the best with guns, but your weakness is that you're no good at hand-to-hand combat." Paku tried to defend Renzokuken by biting Hidariude, but before he could sink his teeth in, Kichiku quickly grabbed Paku and threw him at Renzokuken.

10

Hidariude looked back in appreciation. "You've got my back, and I've got yours. Get the kid, I'll take care of these guys."

Kichiku ran after Aka, who he knew would already be making his return trip with the boy in tow. He found Aka coming back, slowed down just slightly by the boy's weight because he wasn't quite as strong as he was fast. He was just slow enough for Kichiku to see where he was and stop him with a well-placed palm strike to the solar plexus. Kichiku tried to help the boy up when Kappa surfaced from a nearby canal and tried to grab him, but Kichiku was able to kick him off as well. While Kichiku was fighting Kappa, Aka got up and grabbed the child again, and then Kichiku grabbed him, gesturing to Douji to flee, only to find Kappa in his way again. Desperate, Kichiku spun around slinging Aka into Kappa, then picked up Douji and ran for his life. At this point, the fire Aka had set at the far end of town crept up on them and Kichiku used the flames as cover, appearing to dive straight into them while holding Douji tightly to protect him from being burnt. Aka couldn't do much, but Kappa swam under the fire and tried to locate the escapees in the chaos, but the smoke blurred his vision and Kichiku had really knocked the wind out of him. He returned to Aka who helped drag him back to the others.

When they got back, Hidariude was facing off against Gaki. Hidariude was trying to avoid using his blades, but still used his same style of palm strikes, punches, and strikes that were normally slashes, but now amounted more to hammering his opponent with his fists and forearms. Even without blades, he had flawless form from constant practice and a metal arm still hurts as a blunt weapon even if it doesn't draw blood. Gaki was a more experienced fighter, but also older and not quite as strong to begin with, and his fighting style was much less refined than the younger generation's training. The only thing keeping the commander alive was that Hidariude was holding back so as not to kill him on purpose.

Paku got back up and tried to attack Hidariude again. Hidariude could hear him coming and turned around to fend him off. Gaki tried to attack but Hidariude was able to deflect each with one hand. Renzokuken knew he was useless so he just stood there. Aka took Kappa over to Renzokuken so that they could protect each other. While Hidariude was busy fighting his two voracious foes, Aka quickly got behind him at full speed and struck him down before he even knew he was there.

"Thank you Aka." Gaki said.

"You're welcome, sir." Aka replied, "I'm afraid Kichiku got away with the child. He jumped into the flames and we lost sight of him." His words quickly turned Gaki's opinion of him from appreciation to disgust.

"Everybody get back on the jet." Gaki ordered, "Don't forget to bring Hidariude. The traitor needs to be held accountable."

Hidariude was still conscious enough to know what was going on even if he couldn't do anything about it. He could feel himself being picked up and dragged back onto the jet. As he got dropped in the corner, he thought about how he had heard that Kichiku and Douji got away. At least the beating he took wasn't in vain, they got away safe.

As the world seemed to blur away from Hidariude's senses, everything else about the day was becoming clearer in his mind. Why did they come on this mission? Why did they kill these people? Why didn't anyone fight back? Why didn't they find any evidence of stolen technology? Why that child was so important that they were all going home covered in blood and bruises? Why did he just lose his best friend for asking the one question no soldier was supposed to ask?

Why?

Chapter 2

When the team got back to the Seventh Moon, Hidariude was escorted to the brig. It was a little known dungeon used for disciplining insubordinates. There was nothing there, nothing to describe, just four walls and a toilet. Hidariude was charged and sentenced with treason and would be kept here until President Han Toromi could decide his final fate. This imprisonment included wearing a magnetic glove that restricted his use of his blades so that he couldn't use them to hurt anybody, which presumably reduced his overall fighting ability since most of his skills involved using the blades. Unfortunately it also interrupted the whole circuitry of his cyber arm, so he effectively only had one arm, which added to the punishment.

While Hidariude waited for his former comrades to get out of the infirmary and decide his fate, he sat there in the brig, thinking about what happened. The boy's name was Douji and his mother had said something about the Shrine of the Golden Dragon and someone named Ryu. He had no idea what the shrine was, but Ryu, he recognized was the name of a trainer he had once. He tried to remember the last time he saw the man, three years ago on his fifteenth birthday. He had just gotten his complete cyber arm, and he was meeting Ryu for a training session to test it out. The cybernetics team wanted to make sure everything was in perfect working order before sealing his arm in a synthetic skin, the tedious final touch, but as soon as he showed it to Ryu, he walked off and never came back. Could this be the same Ryu? What was he doing on Earth? Why had he abandoned his trainees at such a critical time?

The door finally opened and a cat girl walked in carrying a tray with a bowl of tofu and a glass of water. Instead of normal human ears, she had pointy feline ears on top of her head, sticking out through her thick long hair. She also had a tail that reached just below her knees when fully extended, though she seemed to keep it curled up. She was slender, yet curvy, with very full breasts, and wore nothing but the fur which was another side effect of her feline DNA. The patches of fur didn't cover much, some fur across her large chest, and also around her pelvis, it made her look like she was wearing a sort of fur bikini. Otherwise she looked like a normal girl, not that Hidariude had ever seen a girl before. She set down the tray and said "Here, eat, you have to keep up your strength. We don't want to lose our best fighter."

Hidariude let out a small laugh. "I'm the best fighter? Then why am I in here?"

"You were outnumbered. Rumor is you took on five soldiers alone. You're in trouble for fighting against your own comrades, but the fact that it took five of them to bring you down has to count for something."

"And I didn't even have to use my cyber blades. Yes, I'm dangerous, which begs the question what are you doing here? Isn't it dangerous for you?"

"It doesn't matter. I'm just a slave. You were made to fight and I was made to serve. Right now my service is to feed a prisoner and if I die, they charge you with another killing and replace me with another."

"Aren't you at least afraid of me for your own sake?"

"No. This isn't the worst assignment I've ever gotten, you don't scare me. In your case, I admire your strength, I can't tell you how many times I wish I had the strength to fight five men, but I gave up on that a long time ago." She turned to leave.

"What's your name?"

"I am called Keisei. What's your name?"

"They call me Hidariude."

"Well, Hidariude, I hope you get out of this one."

"Right back at you Keisei."

Keisei smiled at Hidariude, then left the room and closed it behind her. As Hidariude watched her leave, he could see the shadows of guards outside the door. He stayed still until the door shut. When he was done eating his tofu and drinking his water, he felt surprisingly reinvigorated. He felt the weight of his cyber arm and knew Keisei was right about him keeping up his strength, his left arm was heavy and he would have to work that much harder to make sure his right arm kept up with the weight. He slung his left arm behind his back and began doing one-handed pushups. He counted about a hundred, and then just kept going until he passed out.

*   *   *

Kichiku ran from the village. He ran into the forest beyond the village. He ran towards the mountains. He ran until he couldn't run anymore. He set Douji down and then collapsed from exhaustion. As he caught his breath he looked up and saw a streak across the sky. It took him some time to recognize that the streak was the jet that had brought him and his comrades to earth and now they had left. His second clue was that Aka was no longer following him. "Good, the fire wall blocked them and they retreated, just as I had hoped. I just hope Hidariude is okay. Stay safe my brother, may we meet again someday."

Douji lead Kichiku to a mountain in the distance and directed him toward a trail so they could hike up the mountainside to the shrine. It was long and boring and uneventful. Every now and then Kichiku would stop and look around. There was a great view from the mountain, but not much to see. Beyond the forest there were the still smoldering remnants of the village, thankfully the fire had been stopped by the water in the rice paddies. Aside from that, there was nothing but the overgrown ruins of older villages in the distance, which actually just appeared to be more forests and mountains.

Douji was surprisingly adept at moving up the mountainside, and Kichiku had a hard time keeping up. It took all day to get up the mountain, and around sunset, just when Kichiku was ready to give up, they finally reached the gates of the shrine. Douji knocked on the door, "Sifu! It's me Douji!"

The gate creaked open and out came a somewhat elderly looking man, but three years hadn't changed him so much that Kichiku couldn't recognize him. "Master Ryu...it's me Kichiku! Where have you been?"

At first Ryu had reached down to hug Douji, but then suddenly he looked up at Kichiku. "Kichiku? What are you doing here?"

Kichiku hung his head in shame, "Master, I would rather not discuss this in front of the boy, I'm afraid it's too soon."

"Come in then, come in." Ryu ushered in both of his guests and closed the gate. Ryu directed them to his house within the shrine grounds. It used to be an administrative office, but since Ryu was the only administrator left, it became his home. He made a dinner for them, tea with rice and daikon, a white radish-like vegetable unique to Japan, served with a bowl of cherries for dessert. Ryu had questions, but knew far better than to ask them in Douji's presence. He encouraged them to eat quietly and then put Douji to bed. There were three rooms, one for the priest of Kyutsume, one for the head monk, and one for the miko. For now, Douji would sleep in the miko's room.

Ryu returned to see Kichiku. "As I'm sure you've noticed, the village was visible from here. I saw the burning. I would have gone to help, but I'm afraid I'm too old to do much good and by the time I could see it, the situation was far out of my control. I prayed for Douji and his mother to survive and bring any others here. I'm afraid my prayers were not completely answered. When I left three years ago, I wanted to protect Douji, I was afraid I was too late for you and my other students. I know what was going on, my only question is, what happened with you to separate from the others and come here."

Kichiku could barely speak, he was overcome with such shame facing his master. However, Ryu's tone had set him enough at ease that he was able to answer, "I killed his mother. I destroyed his home and secretly hoped nobody was inside. Then I found his mother in the wreckage, and he crawled out from somewhere safe and began to cry over her. She told him to come here, and then our commander found us and said he would take Douji back to Seventh Moon, but he also said that he would need to be tested to be sure he wasn't a threat. I didn't know what that meant, but he was already scared."

"Listen, I still have one more room. You may sleep there tonight, and you may stay as long as you want. I just have one condition, I am an old man and it has grown harder for me to take care of the field behind the shrine where I grow tea, daikon and rice, could you help me with that?"

"Yes sir."

"Good, then it's settled. Now go get some rest, we have a lot to do tomorrow."

Kichiku went to the last room. It was empty except for a sleeping mat and some saffron robes that looked like they had been sitting there for a long time. He pulled off his uniform and put on one of the robes. He found it surprisingly comfortable. In fact so comfortable that he gave in to physical exhaustion and fell asleep.

The next morning Kichiku awoke to the smell of freshly brewed tea. He came out to the common room to find that breakfast was more rice and cherries. It occurred to him that Ryu had not mentioned any other crops and so it would stand to reason that this would be his entire diet unless Douji could forage up some good food. Thinking of Douji, he couldn't get the images of the raid out of his mind. He sat across the table from the boy and ate his breakfast in silence.

After breakfast, Douji went out to play and Ryu took Kichiku around the grounds to learn about his new home. There was one large shrine with three smaller shrines built in front. Ryu explained the significance of the shrines, "The large shrine is the Shrine of the Golden Dragon, Shinryuu. Around eight hundred years ago, the dragon appeared in this very spot, and by chance his appearance was witnessed by three travelers, a samurai, a ninja, and a monk named Nyudo. Nyudo had been a monk at a very strict temple dedicated to Buddhist discipline. Feeling a desire to connect with his Japanese heritage, he built a small shrine to Shinto kami on the temple grounds. This was a fairly common practice, but this temple belonged to a very purist sect of Buddhism and they did not approve of how Nyudo put his worship of Shinto kami above Buddhist discipline. He insisted that he did not mean to place one faith above the other, but ultimately the leaders of the monk felt he was a bad influence and destroyed his shrine and exiled him. As he wandered Japan he found himself in the mountains and happened upon a ninja and a samurai who were also there by chance or fate as at the very moment their three paths crossed the Golden Dragon Shinryuu appeared here. Accepting the blessing of the dragon, Nyudo helped to create this shrine. Locked in the main shrine is a statue of the dragon, the Yoshiro of the shrine. Nyudo, the samurai, and the ninja held vigil here in honor of Shinryuu, praying that he may return, inhabit the Yoshiro and make it shintai, blessing this shrine and all who gather here. When the founders grew too old to perform their duties, they passed on their responsibilities to a new generation of apprentices who made sure to honor the founders by entombing them in these smaller shrines. According to the teachings of Nyudo, each of the founders ascended to become bodhisattvas to whom we appeal for enlightenment as we request the kami Shinryuu to return and meet us here."

Ryu directed Kichiku to a wall of the shrine of Nyudo. "This is where we used to put prayers to Nyudo. Unfortunately, nobody has minded this shrine in nineteen years and the old prayer slips have all worn away. Perhaps you may have some prayers you would like to post here to request of Nyudo."

Kichiku asked, "What about the main shrine to Shinryuu?"

"I sealed the shrine with the miko and the head monk nineteen years ago, before I left for the Seventh Moon. The seal can only be opened with a monk, a miko and a swordsman, and right now I'm the only one left. I imagine I could train you to be a monk, but we still need a miko, so until a woman comes to take on those duties, the shrine remains sealed."

Kichiku paused, closed his eyes and whispered "Bodhisattva, take care of my brother Hidariude. Keep him safe, and may we meet again under better circumstances than when we parted."

Ryu tried not to listen, but he did hear when Kichiku stopped. "You may make a fine monk someday, but even a monk must eat, let us go to the fields."

Ryu brought Kichiku to the back of the shrine and showed him a big field on the plateau between the mountains. It seemed to go as far as the eye could see. The farther half of the field was actually a series of rice paddies, while the closer half was a daikon field, the entire field was framed by a hedge of tea plants that also divided the two fields with bridges going over the hedges.

Ryu handed Kichiku two buckets. "First you will collect water from the rice paddies to water the daikon and tea plants. Once you have watered the crops, you will prune the tea plants and collect the leaves. Then you will search through the paddies and the field for the largest plants and collect enough for meals. There are three of us and each plant should be enough for each of us for one meal, so collect nine daikons and nine plants worth of rice. Go ahead and get started with the watering, and then come and get me when you have watered the whole daikon field. I will be on the far side of the fields attending to the cherry trees."

"We have cherry trees?"

"Three. I grow them myself, and as long as I live I will never be too old to attend to them." Ryu said with a wink and a smile and walked off toward the cherry trees.

Kichiku spent the entire morning watering the daikon. At first it seemed easy enough when he was pouring water from the nearest paddies to the plants on the other side of the hedge, but when he realized he needed to water the daikon farther from the paddies and that he would need to collect the water from the paddies farther away from the daikon field, it became more difficult. Finally he got smart enough to go to the farthest paddies first so that he could reduce the distance he would have to carry the water to the nearest dry daikon. Ryu peeked through the cherry trees and smiled when he saw the strategy that Kichiku was employing.

Just a little after noon, Kichiku came to get Ryu. "So you finished watering the daikon? Now we move on to the tea plants… But first, lunch! Let's go get Douji, he should be back at the house."

They took the long walk back to the shrine grounds and entered Ryu's house where Douji was getting the table ready for lunch. Again, rice, daikon, tea and cherries, Kichiku was definitely noticing a pattern.

As they were eating, Ryu asked Douji about his morning. "So, Douji, did you find anything interesting this morning?"

"Not really." Douji answered, "I just chased some bunnies around the side of the mountain. I couldn't find any good herbs or anything."

"Well we wouldn't want the rabbits to starve because you collected all of their food foraging." Ryu said to Douji, "Perhaps you could share daikon with your furry little friends."

Kichiku simply ate in silence, looking down at his food. When he was done eating, he took his dish and cup to the wash basin and went outside. Ryu grabbed some shears and a basket and followed after Kichiku. Ryu approached the tea plants and started trimming. He was very careful and deliberate about what leaves he trimmed, only cutting the outliers, keeping the hedge neat and straight, only placing the finest leaves in the basket. He made sure Kichiku noticed his method, gesturing to the leaves as he cut so that he could see. After a few plants, Ryu handed the shears to Kichiku. "Here you go, now I will hold the basket while you cut."

For a good portion of the afternoon, Ryu followed Kichiku in silence. Although Ryu said nothing, he made Kichiku very nervous, constantly fearing that he was doing something wrong. Once they had gone around the entire perimeter, Ryu declared they were almost done, "We just have to collect a few daikons and some rice and we can call it a day. But first, I want you to come with me." Ryu lead Kichiku to the compost heap, a small pile of old tea leaves, cherry and daikon stems and deseeded rice plants. There were very clearly flies buzzing around the odorous pile. Ryu instructed Kichiku to swat the flies. "Using only your bare hands, strike the flies down from the air."

"Why?" Kichiku asked."

"Because the flies are very pesky. They buzz in my ears all night and they may infect the crops. You never know what diseases they may carry. Mostly I just want to see how good your aim is."

Kichiku took a few swats, but the flies dodged every strike. He looked at his hands and he hadn't made contact with a single one.

Ryu dug up a few rice plants and daikon stems out of the heap along with a bucket full of raw compost. "I'll go harvest the vegetables for today, and I'll plant these in their place. Keep trying to hit the flies and I'll check in on you in a bit."

It took about an hour for Ryu to harvest, plant, fertilize and return to Kichiku. In this time, Kichiku continued to try hitting the flies, but completely failed. When Ryu returned, he brought with him a wooden sword. With one swing, he brought down all of the flies but one.

"You missed one." Kichiku noted.

"No," Ryu corrected, "I left that one for you. You were able to follow my lead when I showed you how to trim the tea plants, and before that, you followed my fighting training perfectly. I know you can learn, now let's see if you can learn from me now. Bring down the last fly yourself."

Kichiku continued this training until sunset. The fly was still flying. Ryu finally stopped Kichiku "He'll still be there tomorrow, you'll get him then."

They went home for dinner as the night before, and as the night before, Kichiku ate and went to bed in silence. This cycle continued for days, breakfast, prayers at the shrine, tending to the fields, lunch, fly swatting, dinner, and back to bed to start over the next day. Kichiku did not speak much, only when he had to, and he never succeeded in hitting a single fly.

Finally one day, Ryu interrupted Kichiku's fly swatting. "Kichiku, give the flies a break and spar with me a bit."

Kichiku was hesitant to fight Ryu as he seemed much older and weaker, and in any case, Kichiku knew he had natural strength far beyond what Ryu could have possibly had at his peak. He threw a punch that was steady but light. Ryu blocked it without any difficulty.

"Is that all you've got? Remember, I have trained you before, I know you can do better than that."

Kichiku threw a few more punches and kicks, hoping some speed would wear out Ryu before he got himself killed.

"More, faster, harder!" Ryu demanded.

Kichiku continued to strike faster, putting more force into his attacks. Eventually it became clear he was fighting too hard for Ryu to simply block, so Ryu started dodging. Ryu was very subtle about the transition from blocking to dodging, carefully guiding his blows away from his body.

"Come on Kichiku, focus!"

Kichiku started giving it his all striking at Ryu with full force. Ryu could sense that this needed to end, but despite the force behind Kichiku's fighting, he was missing the will to end the battle. Kichiku threw a full force kick and Ryu saw the opportunity he needed. Ryu ducked down to the ground and did a sweep kick tripping Kichiku. In the same movement, Ryu kept turning, stood up, and kicked again placing his foot on Kichiku's throat. "You are an elite warrior of Seventh Moon! You have the strength of ten men and then some! I trained you myself! You could have easily defeated me, and yet you failed. Do you know why?"

"Master, why do you want me to fight?" Kichiku replied, "I came here because I don't want to destroy anymore and that's all that I was good for. I want a new beginning."

"And I was more than willing to give it to you, but you choose to remain in the past. You could not focus on fighting me because you are still thinking of what you did in the village. If you want to put that behind you the first step is letting go of it yourself."

"But what I did was unforgivable."

"Before anyone can forgive you, you must first forgive yourself." Ryu advised Kichiku. "Douji is hurting too. He lost his mother. Every day his first stop is to go to the main shrine and pray to the golden dragon for her. After that he runs around playing, but he is alone up here. He needs someone to fill the void."

"You think that someone should be me?" Kichiku asked, "Why not you?"

"Douji already has me. I am sifu, and I have always been in his life. But he does not need a grandfather, he needs a father."

"I killed his mother, how could I possibly be a father to him?"

"You want a new beginning. You do not want to destroy. What is the opposite of destruction? Creation, nurturing, parenthood. This is the new beginning I offer you, and you already took the first step on that journey when you brought him here. You made a decision to change from the man who took his mother to the man who saved his life. And then, you stopped. You haven't spoken to him since you came here. He doesn't just pray for the mother he lost, he prays for the father he never knew, and he hopes that is you. He is scared and you are all that he has now."

These words hit Kichiku hard because it made him think of how he did not have a father either. He knew the pain and emptiness Douji felt. He still felt emptiness, and when he realized he had prayed for Hidariude every day, he realized he needed that void filled just as much as Douji. Ryu was right, they did need each other. But this was easier said than done.

As he paused in thought, Ryu tried to simplify things for him. "Now, the task at hand, is to swat a fly. Do you know why you cannot hit the fly? It is because the fly sees you coming. A fly can see behind itself. It can see forward, backward all around. You need to open your senses to do the same. You fail to hit the fly for the same reason you failed to defeat me, you lack focus. You have a lot of strength, but no idea how to direct it. When you are able to open your mind and your heart to focus on what you are doing now, instead of what you have done, then you will achieve success."

Kichiku went back to trying to swat the fly, but again, sunset came and the fly yet lived. They went home for dinner, and again Kichiku ate in silence, still unsure of just what to say to Douji.

The next morning, Kichiku awoke to find that it was raining. Ryu surprisingly had a smile on his face. "It seems you have the day off, the rain will water the crops just fine."

After breakfast, Kichiku sat by the window, watching for it to stop raining. Douji came up behind him. "Shinryuu granted my wish."

"You wished for rain?" Kichiku asked.

"I wished for you to have the day off, Kichiku-san. You are always so busy working in the field so we can eat, and then you're so tired you can't play with me. But today you are well rested and you can't go out so we can play go." While he was talking, Douji went and got a go board with the pieces and showed them to Kichiku.

Kichiku realized he didn't have anything better to do, so he sat down and started to play. Douji placed his white stone on the grid first. Then Kichiku placed his black stone on the grid. They went back and forth for a few turns, and then Douji stopped Kichiku. "You can't place your piece there. It won't have liberties and I will capture your pieces."

Kichiku tried to place the stone on the other side of the board, mimicking Douji's last move, sure that this would work. "No, ko rule, that's the same move I made and it will just be the same as last turn."

Kichiku tried one more time, "Is this spot okay?"

"Yes."

Kichiku placed the stone. Douji placed another stone. "I win!"

Kichiku looked at the board. He realized he really had no idea what he was doing. "Master Ryu, can you come here, I think Douji might be cheating but I'm really not sure."

Ryu came over and looked at the board. "I'm afraid he beat you fair and square. But the rain stopped, so it's time for you to go pick some daikon and rice for dinner."

"Aw…" Douji sighed.

Ryu laughed, "I'm sure there will be time for another game later."

The daily routines continued with Kichiku tending to the crops and then fly swatting training again. This time Kichiku closed his eyes and listened to the buzzing sound. He felt the subtle wind of the fly's wings. He sensed it's presence until he knew exactly where it was and then clapped his hands around it. The buzzing stopped. He opened his eyes, then opened his hands, and the fly flew away.

"The power to capture the fly, and yet the restraint not to kill it." Ryu said, "Now you are ready to be a monk of Nyudo."

That night at dinner Douji asked Kichiku, "Can we play go after dinner?"

With a big smile on his face, Kichiku replied, "Sure Douji, we'll play until I'm good enough to win."

"Um… How about we play until just one game before that?" Douji said, and they all had a big laugh.

They did play after dinner while Ryu cleaned up, until the candles almost burned out. "Okay boys," Ryu interrupted, "You've got a big day tomorrow catching up from what you couldn't get done today during the rain."

"Aww…" they both said in unison.

Ryu laughed, "If you get some rest you'll have time to play tomorrow too. Maybe you can take Kichiku out to chase rabbits, maybe you'll even see a raccoon dog."

As Kichiku's training began in earnest, the days went by faster. He had a newfound energy and burned through his chores faster. He spent the extra time in his day practicing kung fu with Ryu and playing with Douji. He found the emptiness in his heart finally filled, he had found a family.

*   *   *

Almost a year had passed since the raid, since Hidariude and Kichiku had been separated. Hidariude had been in the brig the whole time, serving his sentence for treason, and Keisei had been the only person he had contact with. Over the course of the past year, they had bonded, at least enough to make an escape plan. The first step was Keisei getting Hidariude some access to files on the Shrine of the Golden Dragon so he could finally sate his curiosity over the woman's dying words. They made their plan for her to get into his cell after hours and get him out while security was down.

He returned to the cybernetics lab and looked around to find the computers where they were keeping records of his progress in using his cyber arm. He thought about getting the information from Han's computer, but it was far too risky to invade the boss's office, at least here his experience made it somewhat easier to get around. Fortunately there was little security on the computers because nobody could even get to Seventh Moon without being authorized personnel, so passwords seemed to be just a hindrance to the scientists.

Hidariude did a search to see if the company had any files concerning the Shrine of the Golden Dragon. He was surprised to find that there was one file that not only mentioned the Shrine of the Golden Dragon, but actually appeared to be relevant to him as it was filed under "Hidariude" which he realized referred to the project he was named for rather than himself directly, but still, definitely a point to start at.

The file specifically stated that his blades and the exterior of his arm had been acquired from the Shrine of the Golden Dragon. The items were all relics being kept at the shrine to commemorate a samurai that helped to found the shrine. It also stated that it was Gaki who had procured the materials and that he was also supposed to investigate if there were any other valuable relics, but that this investigation was impeded by some sort of security system that kept the main shrine inaccessible. The record went on to state that the last resident of the shrine attempted to interfere with Gaki's mission and to neutralize the threat, Gaki bit him and attempted to exsanguinate him. As a result, the individual was infected with a degenerative mutation of the viral vector that had initially granted Gaki his special abilities. In the case of the individual, he become psychotic and attacked any human he came across. Gaki had successfully returned before the full results had been witnessed, though it resulted in the Kanagawa Plague of 2091 that was credited for triggering World War III. Seventh Moon volunteered to help contain the viral outbreak, quarantined the area, and treated the infected and eliminated carriers beyond treatment. As a result Seventh Moon managed to mitigate any political fallout. Unfortunately, the war itself was much more difficult to contain and had to be waited out, although the aftermath created a niche for Seventh Moon exports allowing for a virtual monopoly among major cities.

Hidariude found this to be a lot to take in. According to this document, Hidariude had been indirectly responsible for World War III. As he let that sink in, he noticed the coordinates of the shrine and hastily recorded them and the other relevant information he could find pertaining to Gaki's mission so that he might be able to follow the directions to recreate the mission and perhaps find out the truth right where it happened. He wasn't sure when this was ever going to happen, but he wanted the information in case an opportunity presented.

He went outside to get together with Keisei and head to the docking bay before anybody caught them.

Suddenly, Keisei caught a whiff of somebody and noticed Aka as he tried to attack them. She knocked him down and wailed on him until he was unconscious. Renzokuken came up behind them and tried to shoot her, but just as he cocked his gun, her ears moved as she picked up the sound and spun around and attacked him, then ran off down the corridor.

The remaining soldiers gave chase, but they seemed to lose her at an intersection. Then Paku fell to another sneak attack as she once again came from nowhere and disappeared just as quickly. They followed her again, getting closer to the docking bay. Finally they got to the door to the docking bay and they thought they had her cornered, but they could not find her. They looked up and saw her as she attacked Kappa, leaving only Gaki, who took advantage of the moment to grab a hold of her, coming from behind he put his arms under hers and then reached behind her head locking his hands.

"Gotcha." Gaki said.

"Help me, Hidariude!" Keisei said.

Hidariude extended his blade and put it to the back of Gaki's head, "Let her go." Gaki let her go and held his hands up. "Now, I know you have access to the docking bay, let us in and help us launch a jet so we can get out of here."

"Where do you think you're gonna go?" Gaki asked.

"Don't you worry about that, just get it launched."

Gaki used his access code to open the door and got them to a jet. Hidariude directed Keisei to board and kept his blade to the back of Gaki's head the whole time. Gaki started the launch sequence, "There, you have thirty seconds to board. But you'll never…" Hidariude quickly retracted his blade and hit Gaki over the head causing him to crumble to the floor. Hidariude quickly boarded the jet, closing the door and sealing the airlock with just seconds to spare, which he used to buckle in the pilot seat and Keisei curled up in the co-pilot's seat.

As they were shot into space, Hidariude tried to steer the jet toward the earth, aiming for Japan. He was directing the jet towards the coordinates he had for the Shrine of the Golden Dragon. Once he thought he had the course set straight, they entered the atmosphere and the jet started to shake. Hidariude expected this, but then he lost control of the jet. He had underestimated the difficulty of piloting the jet and the entire system locked down. The engine cut out, the jet was crashing into the Earth. "Brace for impact!" Hidariude shouted. He saw the Earth coming closer through the cockpit window, There was the island of Japan, and there was Ocean, and they were heading dangerously toward one of them, though Hidariude could not be sure which as he closed his eyes. The last thing they heard before passing out was a splash.

*　　　*　　　*

At this same time, Kichiku was praying and said "Kami, thank you for giving me my family. I appreciate them so much. The only thing that could make my life more complete is to have my brother Hidariude here as part of this family."

As he spoke these words, there was a streak across the sky as something fell past the shrine, down the mountain, to the lake below. Kichiku ran down the mountain as fast as he could, but nothing could prepare him for what he found.

A jet from Seventh Moon had crashed into the lake and just a small part of the tail was sticking out the water, the rest of it submerged. Kichiku, in his usual sense of concern for others, Kichiku dove into the water to check for anyone who survived the crash. As he pried open the door, bubbles poured out, revealing that some air had been stuck inside, hopefully buying some time for the passengers. Kichiku found that there were two people inside, a cat girl and a man he couldn't get a clear look at. He picked up the man and saw that it was Hidariude. Without wasting another moment Kichiku grabbed both of them and took them to the surface. Once they got ashore, Kichiku checked both to make sure they were breathing. Once he was sure they were alive, he hoisted one over each shoulder and hauled them up to the shrine.

Ryu saw Kichiku bringing the two people up and recognized Hidariude immediately. He saw something familiar about the girl as well. "What happened?"

"They crashed in the lake below."

"Quickly, get them inside." Ryu said with urgency, "Let's get them dry and change their clothes."

They pulled off Hidariude's clothes, dried him and redressed him in Ryu's spare kendo robes. Keisei was also dried, but had no clothes to remove, so they put her in a kimono so she could stay warm. Kichiku took Hidariude to his room while Ryu took Keisei to the miko's room.

Now all there was to do was wait until they woke up and pray that it would be soon.

Chapter 3

Hidariude awoke in a state of confusion. He found himself in a very unfamiliar room, with no idea how he got there. He was wearing a white shirt and black pants, and when he looked at his arm, he saw that his skin had peeled off and the metal was showing. He vaguely remembered just before he passed out on the jet, the console burst into flames and burned his arm. By lucky coincidence, he must have hit the water and extinguished the flames before it damaged his actual flesh. He tried to move his hand and found it was still working just fine. He tested the blades, those were fine too. "Note to lab," Hidariude said to himself, "Mechanical arm: waterproof, durable, virtually indestructible. Synthetic skin covering, not so much."

Suddenly there was a loud sound followed by rapid footsteps. Hidariude ran out of the room and was surprised to see Kichiku and Douji in the main room and someone running out the front door. "Kichiku," Hidariude exclaimed, "What are you doing here?"

"Today, saving you and a cat girl from drowning."

"You mean Keisei? She's here?"

"Was, she just ran out the door."

"Why didn't you stop her?"

"I had no idea she could move that fast. She just woke up, freaked out, and ran like mad."

Hidariude slipped on some sandals by the door and started after Keisei with Kichiku and Douji following along. They saw Keisei running toward the fields and chased her. Hidariude tried to call after her, but she wasn't paying attention, she was just running on adrenaline. She had never been outside before and had no idea what was going on, so she was panicking and excited at the same time. With her feline grace, she was able to skip across the rice paddies without any difficulty. Kichiku however, began to sink in the mud, while Douji tired and was left behind while they were still in the daikon field. Hidariude almost caught up to her, but then he got his foot caught on a rice plant and tripped. Keisei got all the way to the cherry trees, and then when she leaped up into the tree she stopped to look around. The cherry blossoms were in full bloom, and as she watched the petals flowed through the air, she tried to grab a petal from midair. She felt a strange calm come over her.

Ryu was also there admiring the cherry blossoms, seemingly not noticing Keisei and talking to himself. "Isn't this cherry tree beautiful? Indeed, nothing compares to a cherry blossom. However its beauty is fragile and fleeting, only a slight breeze is required to cast the petals to the wind and it is no more. Following the flower is the fruit, similarly sweet in its own way, yet not so celebrated in itself. From this tiny berry comes the seed from which will grow a new tree. And so despite its meek appearance, it is mightier than the blossom, yet both come from the same place. "

Beautiful cherry,
Are you a flower or fruit?
Lovely Sakura.

Ryu then turned with his eyes closed and walked back slowly. As he walked through the rice paddies, he saw Hidariude. "Hidariude, it has been a long time. I know Kichiku has missed you. I see you brought a friend too. Let's all go back and get caught up. And when you change your clothes, try to keep from getting the next set dirty so quickly."

Ryu simply kept walking, gathering up Kichiku and Douji. Though he never addressed Keisei, he knew she was following as well. Once they reached the shrine grounds, he shared the story of the shrine with the newcomers. "This is the Shrine of the Golden Dragon. A long time ago a samurai named Kyutsume, a monk named Nyudo, and a ninja named Bakeneko came upon this place at the same time and witnessed the glorious appearance of the Golden Dragon Shinryuu. The dragon told these three that it was not mere chance that their paths crossed here, he had chosen them to be his sacred guardians. The three had each come from different places and different backgrounds, but from this point on they would share a purpose, to build the shrine to the dragon and give him a divine home on earth so that he might take them to heaven at the end of their lives. One hundred and eight evil spirits tried to destroy the shrine, and each one fell at the hands of these mighty warriors. Priests, monks, and mikos came to carry on the legacy of the champions of the golden dragon. For eight hundred years, we have kept this shrine with the Yoshiro of the kami and the subordinate shrines of the champions so that they might not be forgotten. The last time we had a full three attendants was twenty years ago when my wife was miko and with a monk and I we sealed the shrine in hopes that we would return to unseal it. However the seal may only be broken when all three are present, so unless I can train a monk, a swordsman, and a miko to take up the legacy, the shrine will remain sealed and the great Yoshiro will be trapped within forever."

Ryu had been looking at the shrine this whole time, but finally turned to face the others. "Kichiku has already begun training as a monk of Nyudo. Hidariude, I offer to you to become a kensei, the sword priest of Kyutsume. Do you accept?"

Hidariude was shocked. "I don't know what to say Master Ryu. I haven't even wrapped my head around being here, seeing you and Kichiku and Douji. I need some time to think about this."

"You're quite right. I just wanted to give you some answers to some questions I'm sure you wanted to ask before you asked them and I got a little carried away offering to train you as a priest. I should offer you some tea, let your mind settle." Ryu did as he said and lead everyone inside the house for tea and rice. "Mind you, Hidariude, I won't let you get off so easily. Until you make up your mind about whether to train with me, you will help Kichiku with his chores in the field, and we are behind today."

Hidariude drank his tea with mixed feelings. On one hand he was comforted knowing he had found a home with familiar faces, but at the same time he was unsure of learning to fight again. He had a lot he wanted to talk about, but felt awkward talking about any of it with Douji.

Ryu broke the silence. "So it seems most of us know each other, but we have one newcomer who has yet to receive a proper introduction. Who is it that you brought with you Hidariude?"

"Her name is Keisei." Hidariude answered, "I do not know much about her except that she seems to need change as much as I do."

Ryu contemplated these words as he sipped his tea. "I see. Keisei, would you care to elaborate?"

Keisei almost spit out her tea. "I would really rather not talk about it right now."

"Of course, forgive me. You and Hidariude have clearly been through quite a bit. I just don't know you as well as I know the others. You see, I trained Hidariude and Kichiku on Seventh Moon when they were younger and when I left them I began to help raise Douji. This sort of leaves you the odd man out and I feel that puts you in an unfair position, and being the only girl, I wanted you to feel more welcome. But take your time, like the cherry blossom, you will open when you are ready."

When everyone was done with tea, Ryu offered to clean up with Douji while Hidariude and Kichiku went to work in the fields. Kichiku gave Hidariude buckets to collect the water for the daikon and showed him how to handle the chores. They began watering the fields as Kichiku had learned and Kichiku decided to have some alone time to catch up with his brother.

"I know this seems like a huge change, but it's actually a great life we have here. The food is a bit monotonous, although Douji tells me that soon we'll be in season for mocci and with you and Keisei here we may be able to get caught up on the crops and have enough time to gather some ingredients to make some good ramen. There are also shrine duties and prayers, but sometimes prayers come true. You should be honored that he has offered you to be kensei, after all, that is his role. He has chosen you to be his direct successor."

"He has chosen me to be a swordsman, so I can wield another blade. I am already enough of a weapon, why should I train under him when I could just tend crops with you?"

Kichiku set down his buckets. "Strike me with your cyber blade."

Hidariude dropped his buckets in surprise, "Why do you want me to do that?"

"Just do it." Kichiku pointed to his forehead. "Right here."

Hidariude did as his friend requested, extending his blade, raising his arm and bringing it down on Kichiku's head. To his surprise, the blade stopped just as it touched Kichiku's head but before it cut his skin and drew blood. The blade stopped because Kichiku held it between his hands.

"I could bend your blade by simply turning my hands. A little more force in another direction and I can snap it in two. But I will do neither, because all I have to do is hold the blade where it is to keep it from cutting me.

This is what Master Ryu can teach you, restraint. I know this because it is what he taught me. I was also hesitant to train with him. Like you, I remember the raid and feel very guilty about what we did. But Ryu has more to teach than what he was allowed to on the Seventh Moon. Martial arts are not just about fighting, it's about knowing when to fight and why, and when it is better to hold your strength back. It is not all about destruction, it is about mastery of one self. If you wish to escape the control of Seventh Moon, you must learn to control the power they gave you and claim it for yourself." With this, Kichiku let go of the blade and picked up the buckets to return to his chores.

Hidariude contemplated what Kichiku had said while they worked the fields. Once they were done, Hidariude gave his answer to Ryu. "Master Ryu, I have decided I will train with you. I will become the sword priest of Kyutsume."

"Good," Ryu replied, "We will start tomorrow."

The next day after morning prayers, Ryu dismissed the others to their daily chores, and took Hidariude aside at the shrine of Kyutsume. "This is the most unique of the three subordinate shrines. The main shrine is Shinto for the Golden Dragon kami, the other two are solely dedicated as Buddhist memorials to the founders, but this is the only one that serves equally for Buddhism and Shinto. You see, Okazaki Kyutsume lost his arm in battle, actually when he was about your age. While his remains are interred here as his soul awaits rebirth in this world, he also left his gauntlet and a collection of blades as Yoshiro, holding the belief that the spirit of his severed arm, as well as those of the swordsmen he'd slain in battle, would come here and that the kami would reunite with the bodhisattva and become whole once again."

"I'm confused," Hidariude replied, "Is Kyutsume bodhisattva or kami?"

"Perhaps both," Ryu answered, "In those days, the beliefs mixed freely, Buddha was Kami, and Kami was Buddha. It was part of why the founders got along so well. Nyudo was a Buddhist monk, but when Bakeneko became a miko, she proved to be more Shinto, and Kyutsume hadn't been spiritual at all until he witnessed Shinryuu. And yet, as with so many other things, the three found common ground and were able to build a shrine that represented how each of them felt about their shared experience spiritually without contradicting or offending one another."

Hidariude was still confused, but now about something else. As he looked closer at the shrine, he noticed it was empty, but there were traces that something had been there. "What happened to the Yoshiro that you said was here, the gauntlet and the blades?"

"They were taken many years ago, between when I left and when I returned." Ryu paused in thought. Hidariude had only seen him take pause like this twice, the first time he'd met him when he was a child, and the last time he had seen him on Seventh Moon on his fifteenth birthday. Ryu seemed to have something to say and yet not know how to say it or if he even should.

The moment passed and Ryu took Hidariude back to the house, where he had kept two wooden swords. "These are training swords. The only metal sword we have is sealed in the shrine, so until we can unseal the shrine, these are the best we can do. These swords may be lighter than metal but they have been carved of sturdy cherry wood and shaped to have the same aerodynamics as the Masamune. For now it will have to do and it will."

"Why do I need a sword at all?" Hidariude asked "I already have blades."

Ryu simply countered, "Show them to me." Hidariude extended his blades. "Impressive. Now how about the other arm?"

"I only have them on one side."

Ryu took his sword and slapped the flat of it on Hidariude's right arm. "Seems like room for improvement to me. The point of kenjutsu is learning to make your sword a part of you. Yes, your cyber blades are literally a part of your body, but are they are part of your soul? If they were, you would have parried my strike with them. One thing I hated about Seventh Moon was no spirituality, just technique. You have learned to use a weapon, but not how to make it yours. Your name comes from what the lab called your arm; the part they worked on. You grew used to it because you knew no different, but you never took to identifying with your arm, letting it be a part of you. You are incomplete, I knew this the whole time I trained you. You have a unique situation that I cannot relate to as it is, but if you practice the art of the sword we can find common ground. Learn to make a sword a part of yourself as I once did, then I can teach you what you really need to know. Now, first we will start with form and stance. Follow my lead."

They spent the day working on the basics of swordsmanship. Hidariude felt strange about the whole situation. He had spent his entire life perfecting his fighting with his cyber blades, a unique fighting style that made him elite among elite. Now suddenly, he was starting over with a brand new style and a brand new weapon, but the same teacher, it felt like he was a child the first day of training with Ryu at Seventh Moon. It felt degrading, yet at the same time, strangely comforting, for a life where training with Ryu and Kichiku was the closest he'd ever known to family time, this was oddly nostalgic.

After a few days of basic stance and basic sword swings, Ryu determined that he was ready for sparring. It was somewhat slow going, Hidariude did not appear to be comfortable with dueling with Ryu. Ryu showed patience in spite of this, allowing Hidariude to get more comfortable with his sword. Once Hidariude picked up his form, and got his handiwork under control, Ryu decided to raise the bar by moving their sparring to a log bridge across a stream on the trail up the mountain to the shrine. It was more difficult because now he would have to watch his footing not to slip off the log. Hidariude was not so good about this, and it took days for him to improve his footing so that he could go all day without falling off the log. At this point, Ryu changed training to plum flower posts, small stakes in the ground that were just tall enough and spaced just close together enough that one had to stand with each foot on a different post, balancing on the ball or heel. This practice of balance was very trying and left Hidariude with sore feet for many nights, though the pain still came second to the fact that Ryu seemed to experience no pain at all. Every night Hidariude had to have his feet soaked and wrapped with an herbal poultice, though Ryu measured progress by how much less he needed every day.

Eventually, Hidariude started to get better balance and didn't need to heal his feet at all. Now that he had perfected his footwork and balance, he could focus on how he moved his hands and sword without having to worry about falling down or throwing himself off. The more his form improved, the more Ryu tested him. He began to feint to open Hidariude to strike him from behind. As Hidariude adapted to these attacks, Ryu began spinning to strike at Hidariude's opposite side when he focused his defenses on one side to prepare for the feint and the real attack. Finally Hidariude realized he didn't have the speed to block Ryu's spinning strike and the next time Ryu feinted on his right, he extended his cyber blade to parry the spinning attack.

Ryu smiled, "Now you understand, all reflex, reaction and instinct. You are finally learning to use both blades as a part of you. Now we can begin training in Gishudo, the way of the artificial arm."

"What does that mean?"

"It means I need a second sword to keep up with you." Ryu went to get the sword and came back showing off a few practice swings. "Two swords is the style of

Miyamoto Musashi. This may be a little awkward for training though, you have a different angle on your cyber blade, and it comes straight out instead of being held perpendicular to your hand. Oh well, there's not much we can do about it, you can't bend your blade and I don't have any weapons with a comparable angle. We'll just have to accept the challenge and rise to it."

"Like the plum flower posts?"

"Exactly." With that Ryu began with a double strike at Hidariude.

Two blades was indeed a difficult challenge, Hidariude needed to not only move two hands in two different directions at the same time, but he also needed to maintain his focus in two different directions. Ryu was much more used to this style, his old sparring partner used two weapons, one in each hand, and he had learned to use peripheral vision to watch for attacks from opposite sides of his field of vision. Hidariude was much more used to looking in one direction and focusing only on his one hand, so Ryu had to keep away from his center to force his student to learn the same.

After days of practice Hidariude was still not getting the point. He would strike towards the center and leave himself open on the edge. He became frustrated. "What is the point of all of this? When will I be good enough? We've been at this for months, what are you trying to prepare me for?"

"To be as good as Kyutsume, only then can you act as his priest."

"Maybe I don't want to. I've put forth my best effort, but if it means I have to keep getting knocked on my ass, I just want to go back to tending crops and quit this kenshi or kensei thing, or whatever."

"You don't have a choice you bear the Yoshiro, you have been chosen, and it is my duty to either make you worthy or take the Yoshiro from you."

"What are you talking about?"

"Your arm." Ryu answered Hidariude. "You asked me about what happened to the Yoshiro of Kyutsume when I first showed you his shrine, and I told you they were taken. The Seventh Moon took them and made them into your arm."

It finally hit Hidariude, he had been so excited by reuniting with his old friends that he had completely forgotten that he originally came here to find out about the record of his arm including materials that had been acquired here. It had never occurred to him that his arm would actually be made of sacred artifacts. Then his thoughts turned in a different direction. "Is this why you're pressuring me to be the priest of Kyutsume? Just because I happen to have the Yoshiro attached to me?"

"Yes and no." Ryu replied cryptically. "Remember what I said, Kyutsume's soul was split between a kami connected to a Yoshiro and a bodhisattva subject to reincarnation. I do not believe that you 'just happen' to have the Yoshiro attached to you, I also believe that you are the reincarnation of Kyutsume himself. This is not coincidence, this is fate, you have been chosen to serve Shinryuu, and you are not the only one. Kyutsume would

50

not return alone, the cycle would also bring back the monk and the kunoichi."

Hidariude was taken aback by this. He sat on the ground while he took it all in. Ryu gave him time, he had more than three years to wrap his mind around this, Hidariude deserved at least a few minutes. When Hidariude put it together, he checked with Ryu, "So… you're training Kichiku to be Nyudo?" Ryu nodded. "And does that mean Keisei is Bakeneko?"

"Yes. I was trying to let each of you come in your own time, but as I have already said, you have a unique situation. I couldn't take the chance that something would happen to you before I could prepare you, so I had to show my hand early. Since your spirit is divided, there was a chance the kami would inhabit the Yoshiro and possess your arm before the bodhisattva was reawakened and ready to accept it, so you needed to be trained. Keisei does not have the background of training as a fighter with me, so we must be patient and wait for her to come around in her own time, but when she does, we'll be able to open the shrine and hopefully the Golden Dragon will make everything clear then."

Hidariude dropped his sword. "I think I'm done for today."

Ryu understood. He said nothing, but just let Hidariude walk away.

That evening, Hidariude was very quiet during dinner, so quiet that it seemed to swallow everyone else's conversation. He went to bed still lost in thought. As he slept that night he had a dream. He was standing alone on flat barren ground.   A bolt of lightning struck the ground. The electricity crackled and came towards him, taking the form of a beast. As it got closer, it appeared to be the size of his arm. It had nine tails, each the length of one of his blades. It seemed pretty obvious what the creature was, as he looked at his arm he realized it wasn't there. He also noticed as he looked at himself that he was dressed differently, in some sort of armor he didn't recognize. He found himself coming out of his body, watching everything from the outside.   He watched himself as he started swinging a sword with his one hand, an ornate metallic sword much fancier than the wooden training swords he had been using to practice with Ryu. As his momentum increased, the beast began to move in synch, as if it were dancing with him. As he reached the climax of his kata, the beast attached itself to him and became his missing arm, grasping the sword, still crackling with electricity, and in one fluid movement, it spiraled around the blade and extended the strike beyond the length of the blade. It was the most impressive attack he had ever seen.

The next day he was much more upbeat, and he seemed very enthusiastic for training.   After morning prayer at the shrine of Kyutsume, he asked Ryu, "I thought of a new technique, but I will need a target to train with. I'm afraid it might be too dangerous to test on you."

Ryu could sense something about Hidariude today, he couldn't put his finger on it, but somehow, he knew he had to trust his student. He found an old training dummy and set it up just outside the shrine. Hidariude held his sword with both hands, holding focus as if his arms and the sword were a single limb, trying to focus his energy from the elbows out. He took a few practice swings to make sure his form was proper. When he was confident he had the right movement, he held his sword high, leaned the blade towards the right, and sliced down to the left as he had seen himself do it in the dream. As he anticipated, a lightning bolt flowed from his arm, along the blade and struck the training dummy from a short distance away.

Ryu was very surprised at first, but then he smiled with understanding. "Yes, you have come into your own and surpassed me. You have a natural ability to produce electricity, but by training to unite body and soul, you have unlocked spiritual power to surpass your limits."

Hidariude's heart was beating fast, he was excited to see what he was capable of.

"However," Ryu continued, "You will need to train on your own some more. You have a new power, but you must learn to control it. This dummy appears to have taken some rough damage, with focus I'm sure you can make a much cleaner cut. You were right, I can't help you much with this, but I will expect you to practice this technique until you can trust yourself not to hurt anyone with it. Just don't overdo it today, I can tell that although your spirit may amplify and direct the lightning, your body is producing it from the same muscles that operate your arm. If you overdo it, you may lose use of your arm. You have come far, my boy, now the lesson you must learn is restraint."

Chapter 4

The man approached Keisei. She knew what was coming, the same as every other time. He touched her, gently, at least at first. He moved his hands down her sides and held her chest, then one hand reached lower. He wasn't holding her tightly, yet it felt too tight to Keisei. She knew that once she fought, it would get worse, so she tried to hold still. He turned her around to face him and kissed her, putting his tongue in her mouth. She definitely didn't like this, it felt slimy and she could taste his breath. She couldn't take it anymore, she bit down on his tongue, very hard. "Feisty, I like that." He said with a sneer and a wicked laugh. He spanked her bottom and threw her down. She hated when they enjoyed pain and mistook her defensiveness for playing for their pleasure. She kicked back, hitting him hard in the one area she knew he wouldn't enjoy. She turned and jumped on him hitting him until he couldn't move. Just before he gave in to the pain, he pressed a button calling for help. Just before she struck what would be the fatal blow, the chain around her neck would yank her back, and someone would drag her back to the dungeon where she would cool off until someone wanted her again. The door closed behind her and the lights went off, but she welcomed the darkness.

Keisei awoke in a sweat in her room at the house at the shrine. It was just a nightmare, a memory of the past. Now she slept in the miko's room, alone and safe. But she was not ready to go back to sleep just yet, for fear that the nightmare would come back again. She got up and walked outside. Her favorite spot was a pond just outside the shrine grounds where lotus grew. From here, there was a great view of the stars and the moons. She could see Seventh Moon from here, and it amazed her when she saw it to see that the place where she had spent the first eighteen years of her life suffering at the hands of one man after another, all seemed to be so small it could fit in her hand. She liked that reminder that it was far away and couldn't hurt her anymore.

Tonight as she approached the pond, she noticed she was not alone. Hidariude was there too. He held up his hand with his index finger and thumb in front of him as he looked at the sky. "What are you doing?" she asked him.

"Pretending I was crushing the Seventh Moon between my fingers." This got a laugh out of Keisei, she wished she could actually crush it too. "So you couldn't sleep either?"

"I had a nightmare."

"Me too. I had a flashback to something bad I did."

"Anything to do with Seventh Moon?"

"That obvious? It seems like everything bad is tied to that place. The more I think about it, the more it seems like even the good things about it are all here. I hate it, and I'm so glad I left. I just came here looking for a few answers, I didn't realize I'd find a new beginning."

As Keisei listened she understood everything he was saying and absorbed every word. However, lost in thought she hadn't moved a muscle since she noticed Hidariude, and now he noticed too.

"Are you just going to stand there all night?" he patted the ground next to him, "Come sit down."

Keisei was very cautious as she sat down, keeping a little distance between her and him. They stared at the sky in silence, feeling the night breeze on their skin. Eventually it got cold enough that she began to shiver. Hidariude noticed and reached over to hug her and help keep her warm, she pulled away.

"Is something wrong?"

"No, it's nothing." Keisei said suddenly very flustered. "I'm sorry, I think I'm a little more tired than I thought, I'm going back to bed.

*   *   *

The next day after morning prayers when he dismissed the others to chores and training, he approached Keisei. 'You wear the robes of a miko, sleep in the room assigned to the position, and pray at her shrine, but do you know who she was? Bakeneko was a ninja, her name meant magic cat, because the few times she was seen in action, she had the grace of a cat, and her skills seemed to be like magic. She had once been a geisha known for performing the dance of the fans. Once she was hired to perform for a lecherous feudal lord who tried to take advantage of her. She tried to fight back, and by chance, she was rescued by a ninja assassin, for the noble was known to not be noble at all and one of his enemies had commissioned the assassination. The assassin realized that if he left the geisha behind she would be blamed, and the little he saw of her fighting showed potential. He trained her to use her fans as weapons and to use the flames of the candles she would set up for ambiance. Using kayakujutsu, she could turn tiny flames into deadly weapons, and she could kill without a trace of how she did it. She became the greatest kunoichi of her time, seducing her victims under the guise of a geisha. Then she happened upon the golden dragon, the peaceful monk, and the one-armed ronin. She had tired of killing for hire, finding it every bit as distasteful as the lie she perpetuated as a geisha that she had been using as a cover. She decided to retire from both professions and become a miko, using her skills only when necessary in service of the dragon, to protect the shrine and her friends. She passed her responsibilities on to her daughter, and so on and so forth for generations. The last of that line was my wife Sakura, bless her soul."

Ryu paused for a moment for a silent prayer for his late wife. Keisei thought about what Ryu said, and she found herself relating to the legend of Bakeneko, finding many parallels between their lives. She found herself wishing she had that strength. Ryu finished his prayer and noticed Keisei was still lost in thought. "You know if you'd like, I could train you to take up the mantle of the shrine maiden. My wife shared with me all that she knew. I haven't practiced any of it myself, but I can teach you the basics and then you can study on your own."

Keisei nodded in agreement.

"Good. We will start with calligraphy. The walls of these shrines used to be covered with ofuda, slips of paper with prayers written on them. The miko is responsible for writing these prayers. You must learn the kanji for each of the kami so that you may invoke their blessings. You must also know the kanji for your own name, as ofuda require a signature of both the kami and the representative of the shrine writing it."

Keisei looked confused. "I thought you were going to teach me to fight, using fans and fire."

"Yes, I will, but trust me, this is the first step. It's not very difficult, there are only a few kanji you really need to know, at least for this stage of training and I trust you should be able to write them by the end of the day. First I will show you how to write them, then you will copy them until you can write them from memory." He went to the cupboard where he kept the training weapons and picked up a bottle of ink, a brush, and a small stack of paper. He then sat down at their dining table, dipped the brush in the ink and scrawled the following kanji:

神竜　　　入道　　　玖ツメ　　　化け猫　　**形声**　　**火**

"The first kanji is Shinryuu, the second is Nyudo, the third is Kyutsume, the fourth is Bakeneko, the fifth is Keisei, your name, and the sixth and final kanji is fire." Keisei's eyes lit up when she heard him say the last kanji was for fire. "Yes, for the kunoichi's miko to use fire, she must be able to write it on an ofuda. Practice writing the kanji, and when you can be trusted with the precision to write all of these kanji properly, I will teach you how to conjure and manipulate fire with kayakujutsu."

Keisei eagerly began practicing her calligraphy. Her first draft was rough and she missed a few strokes. When she remembered all the strokes, some were too long and others were blurred together. It took her all day and the entire stack of paper she had been given to achieve perfection.

"Good," Ryu said at last, "Now tomorrow I will show you how to use this for kayakujutsu."

Keisei was so excited she could hardly sleep that night. When she did, she had sweet dreams, now when the men came for her, a wall of fire would rise up between them and protect her.

The next day, Ryu got the ink brush, but then he brought out a different bottle of ink and a different kind of paper. As yesterday, he wrote the kanji on the paper, then held the slip of paper between his index and middle fingers and recited an incantation, "Kayakujutsu ignite!" The paper lit up and he flicked his hand throwing a small fireball as he did.

Keisei clapped her hands and smiled with delight.

"The key is the ink, it contains vitriol. When you use it to write on this cotton paper it creates flash paper, which will ignite when it dries. Honestly the kanji are more for artistic flair, though it has been the traditional medium of this school of kayakujutsu. Since it's so volatile, you need to be able to write quickly. Precise timing with writing is incredibly important to make sure you throw it before it ignites, yet give it enough time to dry so you don't throw it too soon either. The real challenge of this art is getting that timing down. If you don't, well you burn your hands. It's a discipline that teaches itself."

Keisei proceeded to practice throwing fire. She did burn her fingers the first few times, but eventually she got a good rhythm down.

"Good, you've got the timing to not burn yourself, now for the really hard part, learning to direct it. It looks impressive at first, but for our purposes, you need to have complete control so you can put the flames where you want."

Keisei continued to practice fire throwing. Ryu continued to watch her progress. He could tell by how sharply she flicked her hand, the line of her arm, the steadiness of her stance, and most obviously, how loud she grunted when she faltered. He had a plan to get her form corrected, but first, he needed to see how far she could get without assistance.

The next day, Keisei was eager to continue her training in kayakujutsu, but Ryu had other plans. This time, instead of gathering the ink, paper, and brush, he got her a pair of fans. "Today you begin tessenjutsu, the art of the fan. Your form needs work and learning to fight with fans should do the trick." Keisei looked skeptical. "I used to train with my wife and she used fans to duel with my sword. It does take some skill, even more when you use kayakujutsu at the same time, but it is very possible, and I suspect there is some satisfaction to be had when you can hold your own against a steel blade with a pair of paper fans."

Keisei practiced form with Ryu all day. It really didn't feel as powerful as throwing fire, and it seemed like a step backward to her. Most of the time it just seemed like she was dancing, which seemed very weak.

"Is something wrong Keisei?" Ryu asked when he noticed her frustration.

"I feel so weak doing this. Are you sure this is a fighting style?"

"You feel that way because you're not doing it right. Hold your arms more firmly. Feet flat, back straight. You need to move those fans as if the wind could knock down mountains. But if you need a visual aid, I have another training method. Stay right here." Ryu walked away for a moment and returned with an armful of candles and set them up around the perimeter of the training ground and lit each one. "Stand in the center and blow out the candles using only the fan. When you master that kind of force, then I will move you on to the next stage of training."

Keisei found it to be more difficult than she thought. With the wave of a fan, she could make a flame flicker, but not blow out. She waved more forcefully, and finally with a good stiff and firm wave, the first candle went out. Repeating this feat was also harder than she thought, because she was getting tired from the effort she had put into the first one. It was sheer determination and force of will that allowed her to accomplish anything. In the end she was strong enough to put out each of the candles, but she was exhausted.

"That will do for today, tomorrow we will use lanterns."

"What's the difference?" Keisei asked, exasperated, sweating and out of breath.

"Larger flames, so you'll have to have to put more force into your fan."

Keisei still faced training with a lot of enthusiasm, though she started to understand how Hidariude had felt during his plum flower post training. She was tempted to use both fans to get more force, or lean closer to make it easier, but every time she did, Ryu would catch her, remind her to correct her posture and relight the lantern.

"The point isn't to put out the flame, it's to get form correct." he reminded her, "The flame is merely a measure of progress. If you cheat, you are getting nothing out of the training."

Keisei sighed, shrugged, and went back to practice. It took her until sunset, but as the last red ray sank below the horizon, she fanned out the last flame. She was thoroughly exhausted and her arms were so sore, she didn't think she could lift them at all. In fact, she found she couldn't even lift her chop sticks to feed herself dinner. Hidariude had to help her, feeding her himself. Part of her felt really bad about this, but she was too exhausted to care, or for that matter to even understand why she didn't want to be fed by someone else. Ryu even felt so bad, he gave her a day off, allowing her to rest while everybody else handled chores.

By noon, Keisei felt good enough to get herself out of bed and drag herself down to the lotus pond. Sitting by the pond helped her relax. She felt the breeze and listened to the rustle over the lotus petals. It was very subtle, too quiet for normal people to hear, but just on the edge of the range of her feline ears. As she settled into a meditative state, she heard footsteps behind her. It was Hidariude, and he had brought rice cakes.

Keisei was startled and asked him "What are you doing here? Don't you have chores to do?"

"Yes," Hidariude answered, "But it's lunch time, so I made some rice cakes so we could eat together down here. I figured you were hungry and I could use the break. Here, have a rice cake." He handed her one with his right hand while eating one with his cyber hand. Keisei was hesitant, but she took it anyway and sat an arm's length away from him. He raised an eyebrow at her, and sat down in a huff. "It's not poison." He stared out over the water, trying to find the same Zen feeling Keisei had a moment ago. Keisei stared at him while they ate, and he continued to look away. When he finished his rice cake, he clapped the crumbs off of his hands and stood up to walk away. "Have a nice day."

Keisei spent the rest of the day contemplating Hidariude. She knew he wanted her, but he was acting different than every other man she ever knew. Everyone else seemed to just come and get her when they wanted her and do what they wanted and she hated that they never considered what she wanted. But he didn't seem to be the same way. He didn't seem to know what he wanted, he just showed up and when she flinched, he stopped. She liked that he didn't come on too strong, but it confused her too. She had no idea what to do with a man who wanted her enough to be near her, but not enough to do what he wanted. The whole situation made no sense at all, it made her very uncomfortable.

The discomfort was an issue that had to be faced the next day, because Ryu's next step in training was to have them train together. "I used to spar with my wife, the old shrine miko. She would use her fans and I would use my sword. It was very effective training for us, and I suspect it will be good for you too." He handed them their weapons and told them to begin.

Hidariude took his stance, holding his sword with both hands at a forty-five degree angle to his body. Keisei responded by mirroring his feet and holding one fan directly in front of her to defend her midsection so she could easily block higher or lower without leaving either top or bottom too vulnerable, her other fan held back perpendicular to the other so that she could follow a parry with a strike. Hidariude could see how she was positioned and that a direct strike would fail, so he feinted. She took the bait, swatting his sword away with one fan and striking him with the other. However, he had been careful to draw her block high and brought his sword down under the first fan so he could block the second. Seeing that her primary attack was foiled she improvised by striking with the first fan that he had let go of to block her. He had to swing his sword back and forth to parry her fans as she went constantly alternated her defensive and offensive hands.

Finally, Hidariude figured out how he could draw her fans low, dodge the offensive strike, spin his sword around to hold both fans down, twirl the blade around underneath the fans to lift them high and then quickly bring the sword to point at her neck. "That's one for me."

They went back and forth like this for the rest of the day. Surprisingly neither of them got tired, even though they put forth full effort, they relied almost entirely on adrenaline. That night, they found it difficult to sleep, still hyped up from the duel. Both went out to the lotus pond, though they had not intended to meet there. Keisei was surprised to see Hidariude, and she stopped and stayed back before he saw her, but it didn't work. "I know you're there, you can come out. I promise I won't hurt you."

"How did you know I was here?" Keisei asked, very surprised, "I tried to be as quiet as possible."

"After spending all day with you, I can sense your presence. It's how I fight, a sort of sixth sense, I feel you coming."

"Great," Keisei joked, "Now how am I supposed to get any alone time?"

"Why do you want to be alone?" Hidariude asked.

"What do you mean? Aren't I entitled to some me time?"

"Everyone else here is trying to stick together and you're the only one pulling away. I'm learning to fight because it's tradition and it makes me part of something bigger. But when I fight you, I can tell you are actually trying to repel me away. You fight with the goal of defeating me, and by focusing your fighting on that, you fail to see my weaknesses. I focus on the battle at hand, instead of being distracted by the goal, I see you. When we were back on Seventh Moon, you seemed to like me, but ever since we left, you seem to be running away, trying to get away from me. Why?"

"It's not you specifically, I'm just trying to get away."

"Get away from what?"

"It's really hard to talk about. I just did some really bad things back on Seventh Moon, things I didn't want to do, but I had to, they made me. You wouldn't understand."

"I wouldn't understand?" Hidariude echoed, "I killed people. For as long as I can remember I was trained to fight all day every day conditioned for one purpose, all leading up to the day I helped slaughter a village with Kichiku. That was the day we met Douji. We watched him cry over his mother as she died. We listened to her last words as she drew her last breath. We were covered in the blood of everyone he knew and cared about. Ryu trained us to do that and it wasn't until we saw Douji cry that we realized the price we had to pay for Seventh Moon. That's why we're here now, that's why we pray every day, to cleanse ourselves of the sins of Seventh Moon. Believe me, if there is anyone who can understand what it's like to regret the terrible things you did for Seventh Moon, it's the three of us. I don't know what you did, and I'm not saying it's not as bad as what we did, but I can't imagine it's that much worse."

66

Keisei hung her head, her ears lay flat against her head, and her tail drooped. She approached the water and sat down on the edge. "I was a whore."

"What?" Hidariude asked. "I've only been educated on matters of war and, since I got here, spirituality and balance. I am not familiar with the concept of 'whore'."

"It means I was used for pleasure. The perverts who created us thought it would be fun to make us look like animals because they were into that sort of thing, and for our whole lives, we were used as they saw fit. They touched us, whether we wanted it or not, and we usually didn't. They touched us girls in places...inside." She gestured toward her pelvis and started to cry. "It hurt. A lot. The more I fought them the worse it got, the more I suffered, the more they enjoyed it. That was my life, and I hated it, I hated myself."

"And I remind you of that?" Hidariude asked, "Do I make you think of those men?"

"Yes." Keisei muttered, "You were an escape. You weren't much and I had no idea what you could possibly do, but I was desperate."

"I understand. I really do." Hidariude said as he sat down next to her, "It hasn't been easy for any of us to adjust here. If you look over the horizon you can see what's left of the village we destroyed. All we think of is how we are killers... were killers. We practice fighting because it's all we know, but thanks to Ryu, we now know we can use that power to protect those we love instead of hurt them. Still, trusting that we can be near someone else safely... It's kind of the opposite problem, but now it makes sense why we have been here for almost two years and it hasn't been until now we are actually having a conversation. We're both scared of each other, and ourselves. But you need to understand, I'm not like those guys at Seventh Moon, I'm like you. They treated us like things, but we're not just things, we're people. We both need to let go of the past and get a fresh start, let's have that start together."

Keisei looked at Hidariude and saw him stare across the water like he had done the day before. Now that she had opened up to him and heard what he had to say, she understood. He wasn't approaching her like the other guys because he wasn't thinking like them. He didn't understand doing anything for his own pleasure, like her, he was conditioned to fulfill duty. He actually wasn't sure what to do with her because he literally did not know what to do with her. So now she decided to show him.

She took his cybernetic hand in hers, and kissed his elbow, then kissed the top of his arm four more times as she worked her way down to his hand, then kissed his hand three times, once on each of the retracted blades, and finally, sucked on his index finger, holding his hand up so that she could look him in the eye. The entire maneuver was meant to disarm him, rendering the most dangerous part of him absolutely harmless, and she could see from the bewildered look on his face that it worked. As she pulled his finger out of her mouth slowly with one hand, she smiled, took his other hand and put it on her chest.

"I feel your heartbeat, it's racing."

She couldn't help but laugh at this. As she laughed her breasts bounced in his hand and he found he enjoyed this, though he had no idea why. She suddenly realized, he really wasn't going to hurt her. She didn't know until this very moment, not every man got pleasure the same way, and maybe he could enjoy her company without being a threat. She kissed him on the lips and rested her head against his chest.

Hidariude felt himself seem to slip into a bit of a trance and without even thinking about what he was doing, he reached his right hand behind her head and scratched her right between her ears. It felt good to her, for the first time in her life, she felt pleasure, and she actually felt comfortable with a man. She felt so good, she began to purr. Hidariude laughed and she blushed. "That's… that's cute."

They fell back on the grass and looked at the stars. They saw Seventh Moon up there, so far away, and a cloud passed over it blocking it from view. In this moment of peace, finally relaxed, the rigors of the day caught up to them and they fell asleep right there.

The next morning, they awoke with the sunrise. They suddenly felt flustered, though they had no idea why, and rushed back to the house for breakfast. When they got there, Ryu saw them and could tell what they had been up to. He said nothing and let them sit down to breakfast and handed them each a bowl of rice and a cup of tea. He smiled and laughed a little. "Young love." was all Ryu said.

"Love?" Hidariude said, completely confused as he had never heard the word before. "Is that what this is?"

Keisei, with her women's intuition, was a step ahead of Hidariude. She responded by holding his hand and smiling, "Yes, love."

"Love." Hidariude smiled back.

*   *   *

After that night, Hidariude and Keisei were inseparable. They ate together, prayed together, did chores together, and slept together. When they trained they were more in sync too. Ryu could see that they could anticipate each other's actions and defend, block, parry, and attack with flawless form.

The next day, Ryu called everyone to the main shrine after morning prayers. "Keisei, you have made great progress in your training as a miko, just as Hidariude and Kichiku have come along in their training. As such, we now finally have a full trio of shrine attendants and we can unseal the main shrine. Hidariude, Kichiku, Keisei, come here and place your hands on the door and repeat after me: 'Oh Shinryuu, great Golden Dragon, we present ourselves as your champions. Let us enter your home.'"

They did as they were told and the door opened. Inside they saw a statue of a dragon made of gold standing as tall as Kichiku. It held a sword in its hands. Ryu pulled a rope with three pieces of zigzagged paper hanging from it out of his robe and placed it around the dragon's neck and took the sword. Ryu turned around and handed the sword to Hidariude. "This is the Shinryuu Masamune, the sacred sword of the Golden Dragon. With this, I pass my legacy on to you."

Chapter 5

Ryu went out to the cherry blossom orchard while his students practiced. Three years had passed since Kichiku had brought Douji to the shrine, two years since Hidariude and Keisei had joined them. They had made considerable progress, but only Ryu knew how long this journey truly was. It had all started twenty two years earlier right here.

Back then, Ryu was a young student of kenjutsu, wielding a Masamune tachi, the perfect sword in the hands of the perfect swordsman. He practiced his skills, perfecting the art of the sword with every waking moment-at least those moments he wasn't attending to other duties at the shrine of the Golden Dragon with his wife Sakura. Sakura was a beautiful woman, like her husband she was dedicated to the martial arts to hone her body to perfection. Unlike Ryu she did not practice the art of the sword, but rather tessenjutsu, the art of the fan, and kayakujutsu, the art of fire.

One day while sparring in preparation for the daily rituals, a helicopter arrived just outside the grounds. Seeing the approach, Ryu and Sakura went to greet their apparent visitor. A man stepped out wearing a suit and sunglasses, his prematurely graying hair slicked back. He removed his sunglasses, "Take me to your leader."

Ryu and Sakura lead the stranger into the shrine grounds and brought him to the head monk, Muramasa Sasuke, who was in meditation in front of one of the branch shrines. Ryu called out to the monk "Muramasa

San, we have a visitor." The monk stood up and greeted his visitor properly with a bow.

The stranger removed his sunglasses. "Konichiwa. I am Han Toromi, founder and CEO of Seventh Moon Biotechnology and Cybernetics. I have come here with a business proposal. I have need of some good guards and I have heard this shrine has produced some of the greatest fighters in Japan."

"Han San," replied Sasuke, "I appreciate your interest and praise, but as skilled as we are in the martial arts, we practice them for ceremonial purposes. We must hold vigil here at the shrine and I cannot spare anyone for your company."

"I think you misunderstand me, I don't want your people as mere guards, and I want them to train my security team."

Ryu's interest was piqued, but Sasuke remained uninterested. "We must hold vigil for the Golden Dragon; that is our duty at this shrine; that is our reason for training."

Han simply stared at Sasuke, as if he could change his mind at any moment. There was an awkward silence, all that could be heard was wind through the trees. Finally Han simply turned to look at the auxiliary shrines. He noticed that one of them contained a gauntlet, and nine blades; a sword, and two sets of knives, three larger blades, and five smaller ones. All of these items were sealed hermetically under glass. The other two branch shrines were empty. "Hmm. How come there's nothing in those two?"

"Each of these shrines is dedicated to the ancestral kami of our founders." Sasuke explained, "One belonged to a monk who had no earthly possessions due to a vow of poverty. One belonged to a kunoichi turned miko whose possessions were all ephemeral and did not stand the test of time. Only the shrine to Okazaki Kyutsume, the one-armed dragon, contains any possessions of the ancestor because he was a samurai. He collected those blades as trophies, commissioning each one from Goro Masamune to celebrate his victories. In his first battle he managed to kill three major officers and had a tachi made for each one. In his second battle, he managed to kill five more officers, and wanted five more tachi to commemorate them, but could only afford the same amount of metal, so Masamune had to make them smaller. Then in his next battle his left arm was severed, ending his career as a samurai. He kept the tantos in his kote which he kept attached to his arm to hide his secret from all who did not know. These Yoshiro are all that remains of the personal effects of our ancestors."

"And how much are they worth?" Han reached out to touch the container of the blades.

Ryu drew his sword and swiftly placed it between Han's hand and the case. "Only a priest of Kyutsume may touch those items, and then only for ceremonial maintenance which hasn't been needed to be done since we had them hermetically sealed. Please back away."

Sasuke put his hand on Han's shoulder. "You are done here. Leave."

Han Toromi realized that he had no chance if he were to fight three trained fighters, Ryu alone had demonstrated his deadly skill with one swing of his blade. Sasuke was right, he was done here. He put his sunglasses back on, turned around and walked out of the shrine grounds back to his helicopter.

After a moment of thought, Ryu ran after Han. Just as Han was about to set foot in his helicopter, Ryu called to him, "Wait, Mr. Han!"

Han turned to Ryu, "Yes?"

"I wanted to know more about your plans to have us train your security team."

Han smiled. "How very bold of you to reconsider doing business with me after you almost cut off my hand."

"Only almost. Had I actually intended to do such harm, believe me, you would have one less hand right now."

Han laughed, "I'm sure, and that is why I want you. Deadly power, yet precise control. My company is based on the Seventh Moon, the orbital space station, which is secure enough considering that I own the entire station and there is no way anyone can get there without authorization. However, most of our business is exporting back to the planet so I will still need security to handle shipments and see to it that everything I send out gets to my clients without any interference. After all I do have cutting edge technology, the lengths other companies will go to get their hands on my company secrets are a large part of why I moved out into space in the first place. This is where you come in, trying to arm my security with higher technology weapons only exacerbates my problems, the only answer is to prepare them to fight by using martial arts, low tech, high efficiency, catch the enemy off guard. So why are you interested?"

"Kenjutsu seems to be a dying art." Ryu explained, "I came to the shrine of the Golden Dragon because it seemed to be one of the few places where my skills would be appreciated. However, I am curious about your plans for me. Perhaps through your company I can reach out to more people and spread my knowledge. It is very important to me to keep my legacy alive, and I think perhaps I can do it better with you than I can here. At its height, this shrine had dozens of priest in attendance, now, it is only us three, and we may be the last."

Han smiled at Ryu and pointed knowingly, "You're ambitious. I like that. I'll give you one hour to collect your things and meet me back here."

Ryu turned around to go back and get his things. Sakura was standing there, staring him down. "I heard everything. What are you thinking? I thought our life was here."

"My hope is that I can scout out some more disciples, at least three to replace us here when we grow too old to attend to the shrine. Then I will return with them here."

"That's not quite what it sounded like to me. I had always hoped our children would inherit our positions. You do still wish to make a family with me, don't you?"

"Yes, but then what? Our children could be the last generation. Mr. Han is the only visitor this shrine has had since I arrived years ago. If our legacy is to continue, we need new blood. Someone has to leave and recruit new followers."

Sakura sighed, "I suppose you are right. Go get prepared, Mr. Han will not wait forever."

Ryu hugged Sakura, then hurried back to his quarters to collect his things. He really didn't own much of anything, just a few changes of clothes, white robes, black pants, and black sashes to tie the robes closed, sandals and tabi, the traditional garb of the practitioners of kenjutsu. The only other possessions he had were not really his own, but items he had been trusted with as a priest, the sacred arms of Kyutsume, the gauntlet and nine blades kept in the shrine and the Masamune Shinryuu, the sword of the Golden Dragon which alone, of all of the blades kept at the shrine, was allowed out of the shrine for ceremonial use. This sword was also made by Goro Masamune, commissioned for the honor of the Golden Dragon during construction of the shrine. Like the relics of Kyutsume, it was made of nie crafted steel, martensitic crystals embedded in pearlite matrix, with an ornate jade handle depicting the Golden Dragon and the image of the dragon etched into the blade and inlaid with gold. This was the blade that Ryu had trained with for his whole life, and it was certainly the most sacred treasure to him. He took the sword out to the shrine of Kyutsume and prayed "Sacred kami Kyutsume, you have helped me become a master of the blade, give me guidance in this matter of my future as a swordsman."

As Ryu was deep in meditation, Sasuke approached him. "Ryu, Sakura tells me you have gone against my decision and chosen to go with Han Toromi to the Seventh Moon. Is this true?"

Ryu took a breath and replied to Sasuke. "I feel that the kami have sent Mr. Han as a sign that our future lies outside of this shrine."

"Now you put your ambitions on the kami? Very well, Ryu, you may go, but the blades stay here, all of them, even Shinryuu Masamune. Put it back in its place in the main shrine."

Together the priests opened the doors to the shrine. Inside was the statue of the Golden Dragon. It stood about as tall as Ryu, with an equally long tail curled behind it, it's hands held out for the sword to rest in. Ryu placed the sword in the sacred hands of the Golden Dragon. "Thank you, divine one, for allowing me to use your sacred blade. May you guide me on my journey that I may return to your service once again." He bowed and left the shrine. Once they were outside, Sasuke, Ryu and Sakura gathered together to lock the shrine's door, reciting a special prayer known only to the shrine attendants, a special charm of warding that sealed the shrine and protected any who were unworthy from entering. It was customary for this prayer to be recited whenever one left so that it could only be opened when three returned to unseal it. The seal had never been broken by any other means than the sacred entrance of a miko, a monk, and a swordsman who had been chosen by the Golden Dragon, it was believed to be an impenetrable defense.

Ryu then gathered his things and prepared to leave. Then he noticed that Sakura was wearing a backpack, carrying a satchel slung across her shoulder, holding a bag in one hand and a cherry bonsai in the other. "What's this?" Ryu asked Sakura.

"You weren't planning to leave without me were you? I'm your wife, where you go, I go."

Ryu suddenly realized he hadn't thought that far ahead. His plan was to assist in training for a short time, then once the security operations were up and running, he would return with a few select students. He never thought Sakura would come along with him to the Seventh Moon. But now that he thought about it, they had not been apart since they had married, no matter how long or short he would plan to be away, he could not leave her behind. "Of course. Let's go."

Together, Ryu and Sakura walked out to meet Han at his helicopter. "Fifty-nine… not a minute to spare. And I see you have brought another?"

"She's my wife." Ryu replied. He noticed Han looking unimpressed and added "…and my sparring partner."

Han lit up, "Ah, well then, the more the merrier. Let's go shall we?"

They boarded the helicopter and it flew to a more level airfield. There was a large jet in the center of the immense launch pad. The launch pad alone looked larger than the entire shrine grounds, Ryu and Sakura's home could have fit in the corner with plenty enough room left over for the jet to still take off. Ryu and Sakura were speechless, they had not seen anything man-made that was so large, they had both grown up in small villages not far from the shrine.

As Han got out of the helicopter he roused his passengers, "This is just the layover. If you think this is impressive, wait until you see the view from outer space." Some attendants picked up their luggage and carried them to the jet. Now that they were on the ground they could see that the jet was roughly the size of the main shrine back home. They couldn't believe anything that size could move let alone fly. They boarded the jet and got in their seats. "Make sure you're buckled in tightly, it's going to be a rough ride, especially the start."

Sure enough, a few moments later the jet took off and the entire jet shook with the force of the necessary propulsion into the stratosphere. For a while they could feel the Earth's gravity pulling them back against the interior of the rising rocket. Then, suddenly, they escaped the gravitational pull of the planet and weightlessness set in, their seat belts were the only thing that held their bodies in place. Sakura's long flowing hair began to fly around wildly, they looked down at their clothes, and saw that their belts, sleeves, and every other loose fold were floating as well. They looked out the window and saw the Earth below, Japan was now just a speck in the ocean.

Han laughed at the expressions on their faces. "I looked the same way when I first went into space. Don't worry, the Seventh Moon has ample gravity, or rather simulated gravity from the centripetal force of its rotation, so you won't be floating around like this when we get to our destination. Speaking of which, do you know anything about my company?" They shook their heads. "I thought as much. Seventy-seven years ago, my grandfather started a prosthetics company, and it did very well. When I took over, I invested in a growing biotech company and when I had a large enough shareholding, I arranged a merger between the two companies. Meanwhile, space exploration turned to space colonization, and private companies were encouraged to get involved because governments couldn't afford to subsidize space colonization themselves, and I saw another business opportunity. The Seventh Moon is my sovereign territory, aligned with no nation geographically or politically, I am not bound by any laws that restrict scientific development on Earth and we are free to develop technologies far more advanced than anything on Earth. We are the way of the future; crops that can withstand drastic climate changes, gene therapies that can treat almost any disease, and cybernetics that can replace tissues damaged beyond repair that can operate such energy efficient processes that the energy crisis and all attached to it could be solved. Of course, everyone wants credit for saving the world, so there many people who would like to steal my exports to decipher my secrets and claim them as their own, undermining my company and my reputation in the process, so I need good security, the kind where the people moving my goods can single handedly defend my shipments with any weapon, or even no weapon if need be. This is where you come in, I need you to train my security team. But first, let me give you some time to settle in. We should be arriving soon."

Ryu and Sakura let everything Han said sink in while they continued to stare out the window. As clear as the night sky had been from their shrine, it paled in comparison to the grand expanse of space they were in now. The mesmerizing view was broken only by the Seventh Moon itself as they were docking. "And we're here. All of your things will be taken to your quarters; in the meantime, allow me to give you the grand tour."

As they disembarked the shuttle and entered the orbital station, they found it mostly to be the typical sterile looking walls of a space craft, though above head the ceiling consisted entirely of a glass window tinted to the blue hue of a clear sky on Earth. Han lead them through the corridor past empty halls where it appeared some renovations were still underway. "As you can see, this area is a work in progress, I'll explain later. Up ahead is the residential area, that's where you will be living, and we'll be getting to that later as well. After that we'll be reaching the labs where all of our research and development is done. Half of the labs are dedicated to cybernetics where they analyze human anatomy and motor functions to better replicate them with machines. We're also looking into artificial intelligences, but unfortunately that is our company's one weak spot and we have made little progress there, though the few researchers in that department claim they are only a couple of decades away from something special. The other half of the labs are for various biotech experiments. And the far half of the station is used for farming the crops we're engineering." At this point they had passed the labs and exited to what appeared to be the outdoors, but was in fact a massive greenhouse. As far as the eye could see, there were wide open fields full of every kind of vegetable, broken up only by orchards of fruit trees. The tallest trees just barely touched the glass dome overhead, bending the top boughs and leaves, the only sign that it was not a normal sky. It was surreal, almost unbelievable.

Han then redirected them back indoors to his office. It was a somewhat typical office, and yet very elegant. The walls were painted a dark green and were decorated with fine art; paintings, tapestries and statues. All of the furniture was made from mahogany or black cherry, including bookcases filled with business books and classical literature. The floor was covered with a silk rug, and silk was also used for the couches and seat cushions. The ceiling was glass like the rest of the station, but for once it was not tinted, and allowed outer space to be seen unaltered. There was an artificial waterfall that poured into a small koi pond, lined with lanterns that provided some ambient light to the room. Han gestured for his guests to take a seat. He sat down behind his desk, rested his elbows on the desk, and folded his hands under his chin. "Earlier I told you about how some parts of the station closer to the dock are under construction. The reason for this is that the area closest to the dock is to be used for training, the area where you will be working. Now you may be wondering why I'd have you here when the training area is not ready yet and the answer is rather simple, your students have not been born yet. Truth be told, we're still a few years away from actually being able to export any goods and I'm planning on having the most elite force of guards for my business. So, I'm going to make them myself from scratch. In the biotech labs we're genetically engineering the next generation of our station's residents. As they grow you will be training them, so that from the youngest you will be able to shape them into the perfect fighters. In fact, as long as we have the two of you here, we were wondering if the two of you would be willing to contribute. Do you have any plans to have children of your own?"

Sakura answered "Yes. But I'm a little confused, what are you talking about?"

Han answered her "If you would see our fertility specialists, they will run a few tests on you, then...facilitate conception with perfected DNA."

Sakura was stunned silent. Ryu took over for her, "This is a lot to take in sir. Perhaps we should sleep on it. Can we be shown to our room?"

"Of course, it has been a long day. You may not be able to tell from the sky here, but relative to your home it is well after sunset. We won't be doing anything until tomorrow anyway, you should get some rest." Han took them to the residential area and showed them to the room where they would be staying. He swiped a card to unlock the door, then handed the card to Ryu. "Enjoy your stay."

Inside the room was decorated to look like home. The walls were covered with bamboo and tapestries. The lights were old fashioned lanterns. Everything was set up to remind them of home and make them as comfortable as possible. Ryu found their things and began unpacking.

Sakura finally broke her silence. "I don't know about this Ryu. Genetic engineering... I've always wanted children, but not like this."

Ryu paused, "I'm not sure either. Honestly, I think it might not be so bad, but I love you and I don't want to force you to do something against your will. Tomorrow, we will tell Mr. Han we have decided not to be a part of his program."

Ryu and Sakura could not find Han Toromi the next day and had to wait until the following afternoon to get a meeting with him. "I'm sorry I took so long, though I trust you used the time to fully consider the situation here. So are ready to join our program?"

"No sir, I'm afraid not. We made a rush decision to come here, and we do not think we actually want to be a part of your business. We would like to go home."

"I'm afraid that's not possible. Just last night a biological weapon was released in the Kanagawa prefecture. The entire region is uninhabitable and estimates are they will remain that way for about fifteen years until the biological agent finally dissipates. I cannot in good conscience send you back there."

"What? Our home was attacked? Why? What's going on back on Earth?"

"Well, you may not be up on worldly affairs, but there's been a lot of tension between the nations. Ever since the asteroid shower that left the new moons in orbit affluent nations have been investing heavily in research and colonization in hope of getting new resources to compensate for how depleted the planet itself is. This has angered the less affluent who have demanded that the wealth be shared on Earth instead of being wasted in space. Everyone has been readying for war for years, but there hasn't seemed to be enough of a tactical advantage for anyone to make a move. It seems someone finally decided to make the first move, though nobody knows just why yet. In any case, our best bet is to wait things out up here until the conflict blows over."

Ryu and Sakura were stunned. Their home had just become ground zero for World War III. For the next several months, they just went through the motions of their lives, going along with whatever they were told, feeling they no longer had any choices or control. All they had ever known was gone, they were prisoners of the Seventh Moon, even if nobody said so explicitly. The one thing that seemed to make Sakura happy was finding out that she was pregnant. This revelation was bittersweet though, because her children were conceived through the company's biotechnology. She was happy she was going to be a mother, but saddened that they didn't quite feel like they were her own children, she wasn't even sure they were her children or if something else entirely had been put inside her. Ultimately this despair reached its conclusion when she died in childbirth. Ryu was told that his children had not survived either.

Ryu had nothing left except to train the results of more successful experiments. Without Sakura, it was nothing but routine training. He lost his spirit and his faith, he just went through the motions of training. The days turned into years and the years turned into one big blur.

Then one day he received a new student into his class. The new student was a cyborg. He was mostly human, normal flesh and blood, except for his left arm that was obviously mechanical from the elbow down. He wouldn't get a full arm until he was older and reached his full size, but to get used to it he was equipped with a skeletal version. All of the mechanisms were visible, mostly small hydraulic pumps acting as muscles and a few cables to act as nerves, and some extra devices that looked like claws, one in each finger, three in the hand, and one set along the forearm. The whole arm was powered by the boy himself; the stump of his elbow had been injected with genes from an electric eel, specifically to make electro plaques that allowed him to generate charges sufficient to power the electronic limb. As special as all this was, the most interesting thing to Ryu was how much this boy looked like himself as a child, but Ryu was sure he was just losing his mind.

Then came the day the cyborg received his full arm. Ryu was shocked, the arm looked like a Genji gauntlet, the Yoshiro of Kyutsume. "Show me your blades boy." The cyborg was excited to show off his blades now that he had finally gotten his real blades. He unleashed all of the retractable blades. Sure enough, Ryu could recognize them, their shape had been altered, but there was no doubt in his mind, no metal sparkled like the blades of Kyutsume. He heard the boy mention that it was his fifteenth birthday, and he realized, this was also the fifteenth anniversary of Sakura's death-and the birth of their children. Could it be, was this his child, who he had been told was stillborn? He saw Sakura, buried her, he knew she was dead, but he never saw the children. Had it all been lies all along?

Ryu went to the commissary to get some tea and gather his thoughts. While he sat there in reflection a woman came over to sit with him. "Is something wrong sir?"

So many things went through Ryu's mind all he could get out was "What has been going on all these years?"

The woman thought he was actually asking her the question and answered, "We've been supplying the world with food and medicine ever since World War III."

"What? When did the war end?"

"The war only lasted a few months. There weren't enough resources on Earth to sustain the war. No fuel for vehicles, no ammo for weapons, even food was barely available for civilians, there was nothing to be spared for soldiers. Everyone simply abandoned the war and started scavenging. If it weren't for the Seventh Moon providing food to the biggest cities, they'd all be savage cannibals. Oh," the woman made a strange face, "My baby kicked."

Suddenly Ryu was roused out of his funk and became aware that this woman was pregnant. It brought back memories of when Sakura was pregnant. He reached out to touch her belly, "May I?"

She smiled, "Of course. I feel very honored, this child carries the perfect genome, the best of unadulterated human DNA with no other species spliced in. This is only the second time they've tried it, only one was ever born but there was an error and the child was born missing his left arm. He was turned over to the cybernetics department so they could fix it the best they could and the biotech department has been working for fifteen years to correct it, and now I'll have the first child that will have no defects and peak fitness."

Ryu was sent reeling again, he put it together and realized history was repeating itself.

The woman continued while Ryu was still lost in thought. "I just have one more trip to deliver some goods to Tokyo, and then I'm on maternity leave."

"Deliver goods?" Ryu echoed.

"Yes, I'm a pilot. I take food shipments to Earth. But I'm getting paid good to be a surrogate, so I get to take a break for a few months."

"Who may I ask is the father of your child?"

The woman made a nervous giggle, "Number sixteen. I don't know really, I just got my baby by in vitro. I don't know how things worked in your day, old man, but these days we need money any way we can get it, and for me the best options are pilot and surrogate mother."

Ryu came up with a plan. He picked up his only remaining valuable possession, Sakura's bonsai, and went to the dock and waited until the woman came to pilot her final flight. While she was engaged in pre-flight checks, he sneaked on board. He meditated in the cargo hold until they arrived on Earth. Once he felt the landing impact he got up and approached the pilot. "Listen to me young lady, this trip is one way for you, and you can't go back to the Seventh Moon." The woman looked confused. "Fifteen years ago, I lost my wife as she gave birth to our children. The Seventh Moon took our children and has trained them to be soldiers. I am sure that they are up to something, and I believe that they were also behind World War III."

"World War III started with a terrorist attack in the Kanagawa prefecture. Apparently it was some sort of protest from priests from a Shinto shrine."

"I don't suppose you were told that it was the shrine of the Golden Dragon? That was my home before I was hired by Han Toromi. That shrine was full of pacifists and we did not have the resources for a biological weapon, the shrine was the target. Toromi burned that bridge to prevent me from going home and leaving the company."

"But why would they go to so much trouble to destroy the world?"

"You said you were delivering food. How much of the Earth does Seventh Moon supply to since the war?"

A look of realization came upon her face. "Seventh Moon has a virtual monopoly, except for some small independent organic farming communities."

"Undoubtedly the next targets once the soldiers are ready. And your child will be one of those soldiers if you go back. Is that the legacy you want? For your children to usher in World War Four? It seems it's already too late for my children, but you can still save your child."

"And where am I supposed to go?"

"You said there were some independent farming communities. You might be safer there. Do you know where the nearest one is?"

The woman shook her head, but they started looking around the city to see if they could find any information. As they traveled through the markets they found some people talking about resettling the Kanagawa prefecture now that the threat of the biological weapon had passed. Ryu and the woman went along with the settlers and helped rebuild the community.

By the time everyone was settled in the new village, the woman gave birth. Ryu was there to witness the healthy boy come into the world. The mother asked Ryu to name the baby since she would most likely have never seen the child if it weren't for him. "His name will be Douji."

Ryu looked up to the mountains and knew he must face his past. He bid farewell to the woman. He drew a map to the shrine. "If you ever need help, come here to find me."

Ryu made the long trek up to the shrine with nothing but Sakura's cherry bonsai. Indeed, the shrine stood as he had left it, nothing changed except the broken shrine of Kyutsume. He went to sit at the shrine of the kunoichi and set the bonsai down, preparing to plant it within the shrine walls. First though he sat in reflection.

And so he returned to the present, remembering what he had thought when he had come here all those years ago. "Sakura."

Chapter 6

Hidariude was holding his stance with his sword up and his eyes closed. He was waiting for an attack, but did not want to detect it in the traditional ways, not by seeing or even hearing, but by feeling it with his sixth sense. It wasn't the first time he had done this, but he knew it would work. He also knew that his attacker knew and was feeling him out the same way, it was a matter of who was better, if she could beat his senses and reflexes. When the attack came, he parried with his sword just in time, blocking Keisei's fans. She somersaulted over his head to attack him from the other side. He quickly turned around to continue the duel. As he turned to block her fans, he found that Keisei was simply holding still. He knew immediately what was going on and in one movement he turned to look behind him to see the paper bomb she had left and jumped out of the way as Keisei said "Kayakujutsu detonate!"

"Stupid, I should have seen that." Hidariude scolded himself as he watched the explosion.

He didn't have long to think about his mistake as another assailant came from his other side. He blocked Kichiku's fist with the flat of his blade just in time. Keisei gave no quarter as she continued her attack and Hidariude had to block with his cyber blades, using his long blade to parry one fan and then twisting his claws to push the other out of the way. Hidariude then brought his cyber blade to cross with his sword and unleashed an electric attack on

Kichiku. Kichiku started his jump as Hidariude's attention returned to him and just barely dodged as lightning struck the spot he stood on only a second before. As he landed from the jump, he punched the ground, causing a tremor that split the ground. Hidariude jumped out of the way before the splitting ground caused him to lose his balance, but Keisei wasn't quite so lucky. She didn't dodge by jumping, but still had the grace to perform a split, maintaining balance on either side of the fissure. She drew another scroll and threw a fireball at Kichiku. Rather than dodging, he blocked the attack with his bare hands.

"Show off!" both of his sparring partners said to him in unison. They shared a laugh before resuming sparring.

Ryu watched from a safe distance and smiled. He left them to their sparring and walked off toward the cherry trees.

He sat between the cherry trees and spoke to them, speaking really to the spirits they represented to him, Sakura and Sasuke. "It took me twenty years, but I made good on my promise to bring back new recruits for the shrine. And not just any recruits, our children and the chosen ones as well. Oh if only you could see them, their power is awesome. Less than three years I have been training them and already they surpass all of us in martial arts. Even more impressive, they have indeed awakened as espers. Not only do they have extrasensory perception, they each have discovered other abilities as well. Hidariude can use electrokinesis to manipulate the electricity he can produce naturally, though he only seems to be able to channel it properly through blades; fortunately he has plenty of those. Keisei has pyrokinesis, and she has mastered kayakujutsu, she can delay the burning of a paper bomb and can bend the flames to her will, making the tiniest spark into a great conflagration. Kichiku has geokinesis and can crack the earth and close it just as easily as if he was molding clay. But I believe the one with the greatest potential is little Douji, though I don't think he realizes it yet."

Ryu was interrupted when he heard footsteps behind him. He turned around to see a familiar face. "Oh Hidariude, I didn't know you followed me out here." Those were the last words Ryu spoke as a cyber-blade went through his chest and pierced his heart.

*   *   *

Douji was chasing rabbits outside the shrine grounds as usual. Today his chase had led him to a field of wildflowers. What was unique about this time was finding a girl about his age among the flowers. It had been a full three years since he had come to the Shrine of the Golden Dragon and in that whole time, he had not seen another child. There had been other children in the village, but as far as he knew, they had all died during the raid, and this girl did not look at all like any of the girls from the village, so she was most certainly not a long lost survivor. She had blond hair that was tied into pigtails and was wearing a blue dress with a white kerchief tied around her neck and shiny black shoes with buckles on her feet. This was an unusual look he had never seen before, but at the same time, he found he was overcome with joy at the sight of another child.

She saw the rabbit he was chasing and grabbed it. "Oh what a cute little bunny! Is he yours?" she asked him.

"No," Douji answered, "I'm just chasing him away from our vegetable garden. Sometimes I get carried away."

"I'll say, you're really far out here."

"Not for me, I live around here. And you're one to talk, I didn't know there was anybody anywhere around here. Who are you?"

"My name is Hime!" the girl answered cheerfully, "What's yours?"

"I'm Douji, what are you doing out here?"

"I'm just having a day out with my friends." She stopped to look around. "Oh my, where did they go? Will you help me find them?" Without even waiting for an answer, Hime grabbed Douji by the hand and dragged him off.

*   *   *

Hidariude, Keisei, and Kichiku came to a three-way draw in their sparring match, Hidariude was blocking Keisei's fan with his sword while striking Kichiku with his cyber blade, Kichiku was holding Hidariude's cyber blade with one hand and punching Keisei with the other, and Keisei was blocking Kichiku's attack while striking

Hidariude and closing the loop. It was right at this moment while they were struggling to break each other's guard while at the same time struggling not to be the first to give in, that they all felt a sudden void form on the peripheral of their senses. They all turned and looked beyond the fields toward the cherry trees. They didn't even need to speak, they each knew what the other was thinking and broke their stalemate to run and check on the scene, all hoping that they were wrong.

Sadly, they were all right, their senses had not failed them, Ryu's body was lying on the ground in a pool of blood. Hidariude sprang forward and held his master. "Ryu! Please, master, speak to me! Don't die!"

For just one second, Ryu got to see the three of them as they approached. He wanted to tell them how much he loved them, how proud he was of them, just one last time let them know how proud he was that they inherited his legacy. But this would not be, his body was giving out and he did not have the chance to say goodbye. His very last thought was reuniting with Sakura in the afterlife.

Hidariude's words fell upon the unhearing ears of the dead body of the man he regarded as a father without ever knowing the truth of that sentiment. Keisei joined Hidariude, and thought about everything Ryu had done for her and that there was nothing she could do now that he really needed her. Kichiku joined them as well, solemnly saying the unfortunate truth which all refused to face, "He's gone."

This solemn moment was broken by another familiar voice. "Long time no see guys."

The three mourners turned around to see three figures, one a bunny girl with blonde hair, bunny ears, a puffball tail and white fur covering her breasts and pelvis much like Keisei, and another a relatively scrawny uniformed soldier, the third a shadow behind the other two. Keisei recognized one, and her friends recognized the other. They exclaimed in unison "Baz! Aka! What are you doing here?"

Aka answered them, "We're looking for traitors, and I think we found them."

The espers took their fighting stances with weapons drawn and fists up. Hidariude spoke for them, "You're not taking us back!"

Aka gave them a quizzical look, and then laughed. "We're not here to take you back."

"We're here to replace you." said a voice that sounded identical to Hidariude. To the surprise of the espers, the shadow stepped forward and revealed himself to look exactly like Hidariude.

"What the hell?" Hidariude exclaimed.

"Meet Seichei, your upgrade." Aka answered. "More blades, less betrayal. You see we don't need you, we can just make more."

As Seichei extended the cyber blades in his left arm, Hidariude realized the truth. "You killed Ryu! You'll pay for that!" The two doppelgangers attacked each other, Hidariude's sword against Seichei's cyber blade.

Keisei and Kichiku came to Hidariude's assistance, thankful Hidariude was still holding the sword as it was the only thing that could differentiate him from his opponent. However, before they could connect, they were intercepted by Baz and Aka respectively, who pushed them away from the battle that had already started.

Kichiku was forced to fight Aka at one corner of the cherry grove, where Aka literally ran circles around him. Kichiku was trying to fight back, but Aka was just too fast. "You may be strong, but you can't hit what you can't catch and you can't catch what you can't see!" Aka taunted.

Kichiku thought back to his training with Ryu, to the exercise tracking the fly. He closed his eyes and allowed his sixth sense to find Aka, not where he was, but where he was going to be. He took a few more hits from his streaking foe, but each hit only made him more certain of his opponent's location. Once he had a good trace on Aka, Kichiku punched the ground creating a fissure that tripped Aka and sent him flying in Kichiku's direction. Kichiku perfectly timed a palm strike into Aka's solar plexus and thrust him into the trunk of the nearest tree, hitting so hard, that the whole tree shook and bark broke off around Aka and left an imprint. Aka collapsed on the ground in a crumpled heap.

Meanwhile, Keisei and Baz fought on the other side of the grove. Baz tried to tear off Keisei's clothes while Keisei batted at her with her fans. She had some good angles on Baz and kept her off, giving her some good paper cuts at least. Baz was a lot fiercer than Keisei had remembered. Keisei had always been the only girl with attitude. She remembered a few girls that had some edge, though only because it was what their masters had wanted, and Baz was not one of them. The two of them had been in Han's service for a while, and Han liked submission from his girls, which is why Keisei hadn't held that position for very long as she didn't like to submit. But Baz was the complete opposite, she just wanted to please her master and never fought back, which made her the perfect replacement for Keisei, as she would always be more loyal and could never be swayed to leave Seventh Moon. That still didn't explain why she had become a fighter, unless she had resolved this as just another way to serve her master.

Baz gave up on deflecting the fans and managed to disarm Keisei by getting them out of her hands entirely. Baz then resumed wrestling with Keisei, trying to throw her against the tree. "Why did you have to run away?" Baz asked while pinning Keisei's arms down, "If you had just been a good girl we could have stayed together on Seventh Moon and we wouldn't have to fight now."

"I'm not a good girl and I didn't want to stay there. I didn't belong there, I belong here."

"It's too bad, Han would love to see us like this, if I could take you back, I'm sure I could go back to my cushy job at Han's side."

"Not my problem!" Keisei said while head-butting Baz which got her to back off. Baz stumbled back and put her hand to her head and felt paper stuck to her hand. She looked at her other hand and found another slip of paper on that one too. Keisei had managed to stick paper bombs to Baz's hands during the struggle. Keisei threw another one at Baz's stomach. "Kayakujutsu detonate!" The paper bombs went off burning Baz's hands. "I'm not going back, and neither are you."

Hidariude was still fighting Seichei, the doppelganger keeping up very well with one blade. Hidariude assumed Seichei was an exact copy and extended his cyber blades to try to attack while keeping Seichei's blade blocked with his sword. Hidariude was quite surprised to find Seichei blocking with a cyber-blade from the other arm. "More blades." Hidariude echoed Aka's statement from earlier. They continued to duel, not that it threw Hidariude off that much. He was used to fighting two people that could handle both of his blades at once, so one fighter with two blades was nothing. What concerned him was that if he didn't end this soon, someone else would die. Hidariude pulled back and charged up an electric attack to unleash on Seichei. It connected, but it didn't do much, Seichei was still standing.

"Okay that just pissed me off!" Seichei screamed back. He looked to the corners of the grove, seeing his comrades down and Kichiku and Keisei were coming to Hidariude's aid. "Let's finish this!" Seichei extended all of his blades while somehow retracting his skin. He appeared to double in size, tearing off the clothes he was wearing in the process. The espers now looked upon bladed death, and they knew it would take everything they had to stop this unstoppable monster.

Kichiku came in carefully, using two fingered strikes to try to hit the robot between his blades. Normally, Kichiku's strength was enough that even these small blows would be very damaging, but this robot was made of titanium and was quite sturdy, so it took more than Kichiku thought. He kept poking Seichei, trying to find a weak point while also trying to put in more force so he could do more damage all while deflecting Seichei's own slices. Hidariude continued to try to duel with Seichei around Kichiku. To an onlooker this would have appeared dangerous, but Hidariude and Kichiku had perfect synchronicity, not only were they used to each other, but with their psychic bond they could read each other's thoughts and fight as if they were one person with four hands.

Keisei also joined the fight with her fans back in her hands. The fans were getting torn by Seichei's blades, but Keisei was still able to make every blow count by deflecting slashes in a subtle yet effective fashion. If Seichei had been programmed to laugh, he would have, so confident in his ability to fight these three. After a few rounds of fighting though, everybody pulled away.

"Giving up already?" Seichei taunted, "I was just starting to have fun!"

Keisei put up one hand with two fingers, "Kayakujutsu," Keisei began. For a second between her breaths, Seichei was able to look himself over and notice that every almost every blade on his body, save only those on his forearms mirroring Hidariude's, were adorned with paper bombs. After this brief second of horror for Seichei, Keisei completed her incantation, "Detonate!"

Seichei was consumed in a fiery explosion. Each of the blades that had been marked had been weakened ever so slightly by every carefully placed strike in the four way battle, and Keisei had perfectly burned each one off at the precise melting point of titanium, just enough to level the playing field between him and Hidariude as now he only had the nine blades in each arm mirroring his. However, the sheer force of the explosion was more than Seichei's body could take and he collapsed.

Seeing their foes fallen, Hidariude, Keisei and Kichiku took a deep breath. Slowly, they returned to Ryu's body. They just stood there, looking at him. Truth be told, they really had no idea what to do. Hidariude and Kichiku had been around dead bodies before, but not people they knew and cared about, and either way, they hadn't stayed around to find out what happened next. Even if they knew what to do, they couldn't bring themselves to do anything at all. They just stared and cried.

Hime was still dragging Douji by the hand when they came upon the somber scene. Hime shrieked, "What happened to my friends?" Hime jumped on Seichei, trying to reactivate the robot. "Where are Baz and Aka?" She looked over at the corners of the grove and saw them lying on the ground. "Who did this? Was it you, you big meanies?" she said accusing Hidariude, Keisei and Kichiku.

"What are you talking about Hime?" Douji asked.

"These were my friends, Seichei, Baz and Aka, but now they're all hurt." Hime answered. She quickly ran over to Baz and put her hands on her wounds. There was a dim glow coming from Hime's hands and Baz stood up. Hime ran over to Aka and did the same to him. "Now you aren't going to take this lying down are you? You show them how tough we really are!"

The espers realized they needed to be ready for battle again, took their stances and engaged Baz and Aka again. As they did, they revealed Ryu's body still lying on the ground. Douji ran over to Ryu and held him. "Sifu! NO!" His friends may not have known what to do in this situation, but Douji was all too familiar. Suddenly that day three years ago came back to him. He had been in shock at the time and went straight from shock to living with Kichiku and Ryu, he had never processed it. In some way, he had just forgotten about death. But now, the sight of one he loved, fatally wounded and lying in blood, it took him right back to that horror of the massacre of his village. Burning buildings, everyone he knew and loved lying dead around him. He felt his world falling apart and great despair as he was left all alone, then Kichiku came out of the chaos to protect him. He looked around now seeing the only three people he had left fighting for their lives to protect him, including Kichiku, this stranger who had taken him on as his own, and once again the worst part was that he was still so small and powerless to do anything about it. He saw Kichiku and thought of his mother, something deep inside him stirred, "No, no one else will die, I will not lose any more friends today!"

Douji's body began to glow bright yellow. The glow grew and changed shape, forming into something else. His three friends could not believe their eyes as they gazed upon the divine spirit possessing the small boy. It grew long and huge, with four legs each ending in three claws as long as Kichiku was tall. The head towered above the trees, the face looked like an alligator with two deer-like antlers, each with three branches, the middle branch forking three times, and the branch on the end forking five times. Indeed, as the behemoth roared, there was no doubt, it looked just like the statue in the shrine only larger, and Douji had become Shinryuu, the Golden Dragon.

Shinryuu grabbed Baz and Aka, one in each hand, and squeezed them tight, crushing their bones, and then slammed them together in midair and dropped them from above the trees and they landed with a deep thud as they formed a crater in the middle of the grove. The dragon roared again.

Hime watched all of this with a bizarre gaze. Her eyes began to glow, and then the glow spread across her body and began to expand until she also appeared to be a dragon looking just like Shinryuu only a deep purple hue instead of golden. She roared and attacked the golden dragon. As the dark dragon tried to bite the golden dragon, the golden dragon bit back. They recoiled and then bit each other again. They went back and forth a few times before they were driven to enough to hold their bites and grapple. Once they realized they weren't getting anywhere, they released their bites while still locking claws. They reared back their heads and unleashed fiery blasts at each other. Again, this test of strength seemed as futile as those before, the fires meeting in center and holding firm with no give either way, a draconic tug of war.

As this was going on, Kichiku realized there was only one way to stop this madness. "We need to get the shimenawa from the shrine." His friends followed him to the shrine to help him open it. Once they got there they opened the door together and Kichiku entered the shrine to collect the rope from the neck of the statue. He then ran back to the dueling dragons who were now thrashing in the rice paddies. Kichiku leapt upon the back of the golden dragon and threw the rope across the dragon's throat and just barely managed to grab the other end with his other hand, arms now encircling the dragon's neck rather tightly. He now chanted a sacred mantra, "Om Mani Padme Om!"

The dragon started to writhe in pain, but not enough to stop. The golden dragon continued to fight with the dark dragon, blasting each other with fiery breath again. This time as the blasts pushed against each other, Hidariude and Keisei realized they needed to help Kichiku and chanted with him, all three repeating in unison "Om Mani Padme Om!" As they chanted, the blast from the golden dragon actually appeared to get stronger, pushing the dark dragon's breath farther and farther back until it finally pushed all the way back into the dark dragon's mouth. In an explosion of light, the aura of the dark dragon receded, leaving Hime falling from the air down into the rice paddy. Still the espers work was not done, they needed to do something about Douji. As they continued to chant they prayed for Douji to come back to them. With a final roar, the aura of the golden dragon receded, leaving Douji with the shimenawa around his neck, his body now limp with exhaustion in Kichiku's arms.

"Who knew such a small body could contain such enormous power?" Hidariude remarked.

Douji's eyes opened after a moment. "What happened? Where's Ryu?" The others were surprised for a moment, and then they realized, Douji was still young and untrained, he couldn't control this power and was completely unaware of what the dragon had done while it possessed him.

Kichiku carried Douji back to the shrine while Hidariude and Keisei went to get Ryu's body. They knew nothing of burial ceremony, so they improvised. They placed Ryu's body in the arms of the statue of the Golden Dragon, the same way the sword had been oriented when Ryu first opened the shrine for them. "Master Ryu, teacher, father, you served us well and made us proud, we can only hope you felt the same about us. Now may your soul rest with the kami in the hereafter."

They sat in silent meditation remembering everything he had done for them. They remembered how they had all been brought together here, how he had made them better people. Masamune Ryu had made them more than just a cyborg, a cat girl, a brute, and a boy, cast together by a twist of fate, he had made them a family. He had not only taught them how to fight but gave them something to fight for.

When they had finished mourning Ryu, Hidariude broke the silence. "We cannot stay here. Seventh Moon will find us again. We must go, and we must find out who else is being hurt and bring this to an end once and for all."

The others simply nodded. They stepped outside and closed the door to the shrine, together performing the rite of sealing. "Until our spirits are gathered at this shrine again, may this door remain unopened and this seal remain unbroken."

With that, the four espers, Hidariude, Keisei, Kichiku and Douji left the only true home they had ever known and began their journey into the unknown reaches of Japan.

Part 2: The Revolution

Chapter 7

Days passed as the four espers traveled through the Kanagawa prefecture. It was an empty wilderness now, nobody had lived in this region since the raid three years earlier, and that settlement had been the only one after fifteen years of abandonment. There was nothing left of that settlement now, it had been mostly burned down and the ashes had already been overgrown by weeds. All the same, they stopped there for a while to pray for the lost souls, that they may find rest in the next life.

As they continued on, they found more old buildings from over twenty years ago, but they were all covered in weeds and breaking down, inhabited by bugs and other wildlife. This was not entirely unexpected, they would stay the night in the most stable looking structure and eat vegetation that Douji would forage for with Kichiku's help. Hidariude would hunt for small game, and Keisei would cook the food. When morning came, they moved on and repeated the routine as they crossed the countryside in search of civilization.

Some nights they heard strange sounds, howls and scratching at the door. They had no idea what these sounds were until one night they were attacked by what appeared at first to be a person. Hidariude drew his sword in defense of the group, "Stay back!" The creature did not respond except to jump at Hidariude who had no choice but to skewer it. Upon closer inspection he realized what it was. "Gaki."

Kichiku recognized the name and asked Hidariude "What about Gaki?"

"My last night on Seventh Moon, I found a file about me and the Shrine of the Golden Dragon that mentioned Gaki." Hidariude explained as he used a rag to wipe the blade clean. "He came here and spread a disease a long time ago. That's why nobody's here, everybody became like him, only worse, they have no minds left. Most of them either killed everybody around them or got killed by Seventh Moon to contain the disease and prevent the spread before they had to admit blame. Damn, this is why we have to fight and put an end to Seventh Moon, to prevent any more of this, assuming we aren't already too late."

It was a somber thought to go to sleep on. Fortunately, the next day they finally found a sign of hope, over the horizon they saw the silhouette of a city. It took until sunset for them to reach it and lights started to go up in the buildings as it got dark, and the buildings were so tall they seemed to touch the sky. There were still people all over, walking down the streets. The people gave them strange looks because they were noticeably different and stood out like a sore thumb, but the four were so awestruck by the first time they were actually in an Earth city they didn't notice the looks people gave them.

At least, they didn't notice anything until a stranger said, "Hey, you got a moe ho! But I thought they were all bat girls, I didn't know they had any cat girls. Are you new?"

Keisei realized the stranger was talking about her. She turned to him "I'm sorry, we are new in town; may I ask you about these...what did you call them again?"

"Moe hos, from the Moe club in the Harajuku district. Don't tell me you don't know?"

Keisei started to get impatient. "How do we get there?"

"The fastest way would be to take the train." He pointed down the street. "The station is down that way. If you get on there, you'll be on the Yamanote line and the third stop northbound would be Harajuku. Once you're there, just look for the bright neon sign with a batgirl that reads 'Moe Club'."

Keisei tore off for the train station. Kichiku picked up Douji and he and Hidariude followed after her. When they got there she tried to board a train. A man stopped her, "Excuse me, ticket please."

"What?" Keisei asked.

"A ticket, you need a ticket to board the train, if you want to board you need one and if you don't have one go get it from the ticket window. We leave in five minutes, so be quick!"

She led the group back to the ticket window where a woman asked them for seven hundred yen per person. Of course, none of them had any yen, they hadn't even been educated on money. They heard an announcement for the southbound train leaving the station. Keisei got desperate and ran off until she could find a way to the roof of the station. She faced the northbound exit of the station and looked at the train as it started to leave.

Hidariude suddenly realized what was happening. "Keisei, tell me, you are not thinking what I think you're thinking." She leapt off the roof of the station and landed on top of the train. Hidariude and Kichiku followed suit, with the latter holding Douji tightly. "Okay Keisei, what exactly are you so interested in that you are willing to risk our lives for?"

"The man mentioned bat girls. There were four on Seventh Moon, Aikou, Tenshi, Okesa, and Einji. If they are here, I want to see them and find out what they are doing here. Either they need our help, or they are part of the problem. Either way, it's our first lead."

Now that Hidariude understood, he helped her count the stops and as they approached the third, he looked for the sign the man mentioned. He had a hard time seeing anything, he was blinded by the bright lights from all of the neon signs. One giant sign was actually a screen that played an ad for "New World Enterprises, making a new world that's better for everyone! Food, fuel, and pharmaceuticals!" The ad featured Han Toromi and it took them a moment to realize that this was the name the company was operating under on Earth. They all thought the same thing, the company was lying to everybody, and for good reason, nobody would do business with them if they knew the truth, that the same resources that went into food, medicine and energy also went into a private army to literally kill the competition.

As the train entered the Harajuku station, they jumped off the train and landed in an alley. They stepped out to the street and saw the sign from the club they were looking for. They walked up to the front door to enter.

A bouncer saw Douji and stopped them. "Whoa, that kid is way too young to come in here. In fact it's way past curfew, you should be in bed young man." Then he looked at Keisei and his expression changed as he noticed her ears and tail. "You may enter."

Keisei started to go through the door and Hidariude tried to follow, but the bouncer stopped him and demanded he pay a cover charge. Keisei interrupted, "He's with me." The bouncer let him through.

Hidariude turned to Kichiku. "Are you coming?"

"No, I have to stay with Douji." Kichiku replied. "I wish you luck."

Inside they found the building seemed to be one large room that was rather dark and it took time for their eyes to adapt to the dim light. There were two lines of neon lights that ran around the walls just above their heads. The only other source of light was the square white stage in the middle of the room that seemed to be lit up from beneath. The stage was surrounded by chairs and tables where men sat with drinks or cigars, sometimes both. The smell was a mix of smoke, alcohol, and some other smell that reminded them of the cherry trees back at the shrine, but not in a good way. Music played but seemed to come from nowhere. It was loud and crude, and reminded Keisei of some of her worst nights on Seventh Moon.

The stage had four brass poles, one on each corner. As they looked at the poles at the corners of the stage, they saw shadows slide down them. The shadows had forms that somewhat resembled Keisei, only instead of tails, they had bat wings and they also had shorter hair. They were hanging upside down on the poles, wearing nothing but their scant fur. They seemed to slither down the poles and as they reached the bottom they pulled themselves up, and then performed a split as they dropped to the ground. They crawled to the edge of the stage where they would stand up, running one hand up their shapely bodies while the other hand gestured to men to come closer. Those men that approached them dropped yen on the stage at the girls' feet while the girls got within an inch of the men and danced in an erotic fashion. The girls would also toy with the men a little by kissing their necks, and occasionally, they would bare their fangs, implying that they would like to do more.

Keisei sauntered up to the stage, making her presence known with every step. The girls saw her and recognized her. They stopped entertaining the men and approached her. The men watching whistled and hollered as they the bat girls put their hands on the new girl and appeared to stroke and caress her and try to disrobe her. All of the regular customers knew this was not part of the usual show, but they were curious where it was leading. Two of the girls noticed Hidariude still behind Keisei and pushed through the crowd to get to him.

"Don't touch him." Keisei warned the girls coldly.

One girl took Keisei's face in her hand and turned it back towards her. "Don't worry, Aikou and Einji will take good care of him. Let Okesa and I take care of you."

"We could use you," Okesa continued, "This place is getting busier, and Tenshi and the rest of us could use another girl to handle all of the men."

"What are you doing here anyway?" Keisei asked. "Why aren't you on Seventh Moon?"

"Our masters thought we could do better work here." Tenshi answered. "We did such a great job of pleasing them that they wanted to share us with Tokyo."

As they carried on this conversation, they had been subtly pulling her robe off and left her wearing nothing but her fur on the stage. Keisei actually didn't mind being naked, but she kept her fans and her ofuda in the robe and being without them made her feel more vulnerable than being without the robe itself. Soon the men started whistling and hollering at her. She didn't like these sounds, it reminded her of the way she had been treated on Seventh Moon. Then the men started to reach out and touch her and the bad memories really started coming back. She started kicking the men away.

"Feisty!" The men shouted. "We like that!"

Keisei had a sudden flashback and panicked. She shook her head to try to get it out of her mind and looked at Tenshi and Okesa who held her robe giggling the whole time. She saw her ofuda in a pocket of her robe and lined up two fingers in front of her face. "Kayakujutsu, ignite!" The ofuda lit on fire and the fireball rose out of the robe strangely without even singeing it, then splitting in four directions, aimed primarily at each of the bat girls, but also flaring out at the men in the audience. She lunged at the robe to fetch her fans and took a defensive position.

Hidariude had been waiting for Keisei to handle things on her own, but once the flames went for the two girls trying to distract him, he realized she needed him and leaped up to the stage to take a defensive stance at her back.

At first the bat girls were scared of the fire, but they were agile enough to avoid it as it hit the walls. Once they realized Keisei had used up her fire power and would be fighting only with fans, they got braver and approached her. The patrons, on the other hand, were not nearly as brave and started a stampede for the door. As the fight continued on the stage, Hidariude's blades did scare off the girls, who moved to surround Keisei. Hidariude kept his eyes on the girls, ready to defend Keisei.

After a few seconds of a cautious standoff, Einji tried to take on Keisei. Keisei blocked the attack repelling her against the wall. This created an opening that Okesa tried to take advantage of by attacking Keisei while her side was open, but Hidariude quickly blocked the attack with his sword and she just barely managed to stop herself and pull back, only suffering a small cut as the tip of his sword glanced against her. She fell back holding a hand to her wound. Aikou and Tenshi were enraged by seeing their sisters getting hurt and jumped in the middle, seeing that Hidariude and Keisei had both left the space between them open when their attacks went outward. As the girls bought into the feint, Keisei struck down one of them with her fans while Hidariude knocked the other down with the pommel of his sword bringing the bat girls down between the two of them. With one foot and weapon each on Aikou and Tenshi, they looked back toward the other girls, holding up their defense for a second round of attacks. Einji and Okesa got back up and looked hesitantly at the scene, torn between helping their sisters and getting themselves in more trouble.

The momentum of battle got cut off as another person stepped out of the back room. He was clapping his hands slowly, saying "Bravo." Hidariude recognized him, it was Gaki. "Somehow, I figured if we set up shop here, eventually you'd show up."

Hidariude looked at his former commander with disgust. "So this was all a trap for us?"

"Well, yes and no." Gaki answered. "The company just wanted to have some people in Tokyo, and this seemed like a good set up. In the outlands we have our own governors minding those who do not or cannot enjoy the pleasures of city life, but it's harder in the cities because we need them to at least have the illusion that they still have sovereignty. They have their own government, we just have an economic influence, a large influence, but still limited. We can't just walk the streets claiming we are the head honchos because that would piss them off, and we prefer their cooperation. That's where our power comes from, making sure everyone else who is powerful is on our side. They probably couldn't do anything if they wanted to, but just to be safe we run this little club. More powerful and important people come through here than you'd realize and they don't want everyone else knowing that they are here, so we make a deal, they cooperate with us and we keep their dirty little secrets."

"You'd know all about dirty little secrets wouldn't you?" Hidariude accused Gaki. "How many people have you killed? How many villages have you burned?"

"How many women have you sold?" Keisei added.

"I don't really keep track of how many. These four girls are the only ones I pay attention to, although I've heard we've got a few more going out here and there. As for the killing and burning, I lost count years ago." Hidariude lunged at Gaki with rage, but Gaki just waved a finger as he snapped his fingers with his other hand. "Look behind you." Hidariude turned around and saw the bouncers bringing in Kichiku and Douji. One held Douji with a blade to his throat, a retractable cyber blade like Hidariude and Seichei. "I believe you recognize the bouncers, a new line of robots designed in your image. Model...some number or other, we just call them slashers. They have malleable features so they can look like whatever or whoever we need them to be. Here they act as bouncers and whatever else we need. Right now they're hostage takers."

Hidariude reluctantly retracted his cyber blades and sheathed his sword. "What do you want?"

"We want the boy. Remember that girl you encountered back at your shrine? The one who turned into a dragon? Well, she's not doing too good since then. The boy seems to be in more stable condition despite the fact that they both suffered the same ordeal. I don't suppose you have any idea why she would be transforming every time she wakes up while he appears to remain in control? Has he transformed at all since then?"

Hidariude shrugged. "Support from his family. We used a Shinto charm to restore him to normal in the first place, and he's been normal ever since. Maybe if you guys were more spiritual you would be able to handle her better."

Gaki laughed. "Spirits! Ha! If you won't take this seriously, then we'll just do this the hard way." Gaki shifted his gaze from Hidariude to the slashers around Kichiku and Douji. "Bring me the boy, kill the rest."

The two slashers who were holding Kichiku extended their blades and attacked him. Kichiku reacted quickly and grabbed them by their hands and slammed them together so hard that they collapsed on the floor. The other slasher picked up Douji and ran towards Gaki. Keisei tried to stop the slasher but Okesa leapt in her way and knocked her to the floor. In one swift move, Hidariude drew his sword and sliced the robot's head off then extended his other arm to grab Douji before he hit the floor. Gaki's expression didn't change, he just waited for the bat girls to get up and block the exits. It was hard for them to get around Kichiku though, his only weakness was Douji and as long as Hidariude had him safe, Kichiku had no problem using his full strength to protect himself and his friends. Aikou made an attempt to stop him anyway, carefully approaching him with her chest puffed out to try to distract him. Usually this technique worked, but Kichiku was different, and as soon as she tried to attack him off guard he defended. He tried to be merciful and not hurt this girl too bad, but she and the others were more afraid of Gaki at this point and continued to fight.

Okesa continued to tumble with Keisei while Tenshi attacked Hidariude. He tried to fight one handed, using his cyber arm with blades fully extended while trying to hold Douji with the other hand, but Tenshi was pretty good at dodging and managed to attack Hidariude with carefully placed kicks as she cart-wheeled around Hidariude. He was at a disadvantage fighting this way but he was afraid to let go of Douji again. Without him realizing it, Tenshi managed to get him close enough to Einji for her to grab the boy from behind and run off after Gaki.

Hidariude glanced at his comrades and gave them directions telepathically. Kichiku grabbed Aikou and threw her in the middle between the others. Keisei mustered as much strength as she could to throw Okesa as close to Aikou as possible and then ran after Einji. Hidariude brought his sword around to Tenshi's opposite side from the others and unleashed an electric slash toward all three girls, stunning all of them as they fell into a pile on top of each other. Kichiku hurried up to join Hidariude and Keisei as they chased down Einji, Gaki and Douji.

Gaki had run out the back door into an alley. Einji stopped to try to slow down their pursuers but Kichiku was impatient and hit the ground opening up the ground beneath her trying to stop her. Unfortunately, her wings were functional and she simply flew above the fissure and dive bombed her opponents. Keisei was also losing patience and guided Einji's body between her fans into the club behind them and closed it after her.

While Keisei and Kichiku were busy clearing out the last of the batgirls, Hidariude continued to chase after Gaki who was jumping up fire escapes to the roof. Hidariude was undeterred and leapt up right after him. They leapt from rooftop to rooftop across the Harajuku district until they got near the Meiji shrine. For some reason, the kami seemed to favor Hidariude here somehow and for no apparent reason Gaki lost his footing and slipped and fell, dropping Douji. Hidariude was on Gaki in a flash with his sword at his throat.

"Go ahead, put me out of my misery." Gaki said with cold resolve.

"What are you talking about?"

"I know the file you were looking at the last time you were on Seventh Moon, the one Keisei mentioned, you know about the Kanagawa plague and my role in it. What you may not know is that wasn't the first viral outbreak I was involved in. A long time ago, before you were born, there was another experiment in altering the DNA of adult soldiers. They infected us with retroviruses that were supposed to give us all the same special abilities you and your cohorts have. Only there was a problem, the viruses still had enough of their original genetic programming to be dangerous. They mutated in our systems and we became unstable, psychotic even. Nearly half of Seventh Moon was quarantined while they tried to come up with a cure. In the meantime, we turned against each other, killing each other. By the time the cure was ready, I was the lone survivor. The worst part is the cure wasn't really a cure, it was just a treatment to stabilize me; they didn't want me to lose my powers that they had so heavily invested in. In order to get this treatment and keep my sanity, I have to do whatever they say. Without it, I am overcome by a thirst for blood. If I don't kill the people I feed off of, they become infected and degenerate even faster and worse than I do. They have made me into a killing machine, I have no choice, in order to survive, I must destroy others, either to feed my own hunger or to serve the whims of my handlers. Before you ask me again how I could do what I've done, why I'm such a monster, know that this is my answer, I have no choice, this what they made me. I envy you and your friends for escaping, but I can't do anything, because even if I did try to help you, it wouldn't be long before I was turned against you by my own madness. So if you want to kill me, go ahead, you'll be doing me a favor and I won't have to worry about any of this anymore."

Hidariude didn't know what to say to this, he held his sword at Gaki's neck trembling, angry at him and pitying him at the same time. He thought about the creature they had encountered the night before outside the city. That monster had once been a human until it got infected with the same thing Gaki had. If he allowed him to live, he would have to face becoming like that. If he didn't get his treatment, he would be that eventually and then Hidariude would have to kill him anyway. But was it right to kill him when he was no more responsible for his sins than Hidariude and Kichiku were?

As the sun rose, Gaki laughed a melancholy laugh, "Another side effect of my disease is that it causes a severe allergy to sunlight. I have to stay indoors all day, I haven't seen a sunrise in over twenty years. This will be my first, and my last." His skin began to turn red and blister. Right before Hidariude's eyes, Gaki melted in the light of the rising sun. His bones even turned black and crumbled from the infection.

Keisei and Kichiku caught up just as the last of his remains blew away on the morning breeze. Keisei asked "Where is he?"

"Gone." Hidariude replied.

Chapter 8

The four were exhausted from their first night in the city and crawled into the shrine for shelter while they rested. Once this shrine had been revered as an honor to the emperor, but it had been many years since there had been an emperor and recently the faith of the people faltered and the shrine had been all but abandoned. There were still some people who came by the shrine to pay respect, but mostly it was people who were so desperate that they needed some ray of hope and praying to forgotten gods was all they had left. There were also priests and mikos, but they were more for show. The espers remained undisturbed by the grace of the sacred ground that protected the only pure souls left in the city.

In the afternoon they finally woke up, starting with Douji, "Kichiku san, wake up I'm hungry." The hunger caught up with them since they had not eaten since lunch the previous day. They really had no idea how they were going to get food, there wasn't anything on the shrine grounds, so they headed out to the street in hopes of finding something. In the daylight the neon signs were not so bright and they were able to focus more on the people. Everyone looked strange, wearing various colorful outfits. Some people looked like them, dressed in more traditional garb, others were dressed in suits like Han Toromi, and still others were completely different and showed no similarity to either end of the fashion spectrum.

It wasn't the sense of sight that led them to their destination though, but the sense of smell. They were drawn to the smell of a restaurant. They walked in breathing in the sweet aroma of noodles in a broth of vegetables. "What is that wonderful smell?"

"The best ramen in Tokyo!" Said a man behind the counter wearing all white and a tall hat with a big smile on his face. "Want a bowl?"

"Four please!"

The chef ladled out four bowls of ramen and handed them the bowls with chopsticks. They weren't sure about eating the noodles as they had never had ramen before, but they had used chopsticks to eat rice back at the shrine so they made a go of it. They found the noodles were much easier to eat than rice and the broth tasted better than daikon. Just as they were happily finishing their meal, the chef slapped down a slip of paper and said "That will be three thousand yen!"

They looked at him with a quizzical look. "What is this 'yen' everybody keeps talking about and why do you all want it so much?"

Suddenly the chef went from smiling and happy to very angry. "You mean you don't have any money? What kind of joke is this? I don't have time for freeloaders!"

Just then another man interrupted. "It's okay, I'll pay for them." He put down a stack of colorful paper much like what had been placed on the stage in front of the girls at the club the night before. The chef counted the money and once he was satisfied that it was all there he turned around and went back to work on making ramen for his other paying customers.

The four looked at the stranger who helped them. He looked somewhat unkempt, with oversized denim overalls, a yellow shirt and an orange cap. It took them a moment, but they recognized this man, he was the same man who told them about the Moe club the day before. "We saw you last night, have you been following us?"

He looked a little embarrassed at having been caught. "Can we talk about this somewhere else?" He gestured for them to leave with him. The five of them went outside and walked down the street. As they passed an alley Hidariude pushed the stranger into it with his cyber blade against his throat. "Who are you?"

"This is a nice thanks for someone who just paid for your lunch." The stranger answered. Hidariude moved his blade enough to let him know he wasn't messing around. "You may call me Shuurikou. Yes I have been following you. In case you didn't notice, a cyborg, a cat girl and a giant dressed like clergy kind of stands out. I mean here in Harajuku, not so much, but you were sticking out like a sore thumb walking in from Kanagawa. What were you doing out there anyway? That place has been off limits for three years, I honestly didn't even know there was anybody still out there at all."

"Before we answer that, tell us, why are you so interested in us?" Hidariude asked.

"Well, at first I was just curious about how out of place you were. Then I saw you jump on top of that train. It took me a little time to catch up, but when I did, I saw you fighting the New Wave Elite. Nobody fights them, at least not head on and live to tell about it. Honestly, I think you should tell me how you did that, because getting that answer is why I'm here right now. Clearly it is better to have you as an ally than an enemy, so it's your turn to talk."

Hidariude retracted his blade. "New Wave Elite? That's what they're calling themselves now?"

"N.W.E., same initials as New World Enterprises. You'd think the Seventh Moon would be smarter than to leave a trail like that. But they have everyone under their thumb anyway, the only people who could do anything are only so healthy and wealthy because they bow down to the company in the first place. They cut off anyone who tries to oppose them and the few communities that survive independently get taken down in raids."

Hidariude and Kichiku both felt their hearts sink when they heard about the raids. With a very shaky voice, Hidariude asked "Just how many raids are you talking about?"

"There's got to be one every few weeks, maybe more. It's hard to keep track, communications about those sorts of things are kept on the down low. You have to be there to know, if you're too far away the news gets lost in the shuffle, messengers get killed, transmissions get intercepted. New World Enterprises may say they're all about food, medicine and energy, but they have their hands in everything. What they don't own, they leverage. What they can't influence they destroy, like Kanagawa." Suddenly, realization dawned on Shuurikou's face. "You're the ones they sent to Kanagawa aren't you?"

Hidariude hung his head in shame. Kichiku answered for him. "Yes. It was our first mission and our last. When we saw what we were actually a part of, we left and hid at a shrine. It was wrong to be a part of that raid but we had no choice. They raised us for one purpose and we had no way to escape. All the same, we do have blood on our hands, and to redeem ourselves, we must stop things like that from happening."

Keisei took over. "If you know anything about what the company is up to, let us know, and we'll be more than happy to take care of the problem."

Shuurikou smiled. "That's why I'm interested, I need someone who can fight. I'm part of a resistance group. We can't do much, none of us are strong enough to fight. Mostly we just hide in the outlands trying to salvage what we can from abandoned towns and grow food so we don't have to be tied to the company. I came to the city to pick up a few tools and spare parts for some projects I was working on, but finding you, I think I hit the jackpot! The nearest base is pretty far away and we'll probably encounter some N.W.E. soldiers along the way, hell we'll probably run into one before we leave the city. I'd appreciate if you could escort me back there and if we make it, you should prove yourself plenty en route to join us. But first, we have to get you some new clothes, and something for you too." Shuurikou gestured at Keisei and Hidariude. "The arm, the ears, the tail, if anyone is looking for you, and I'm sure they are looking for those features. They really stand out in case you hadn't noticed. You need to cover those up. Fortunately I still have some money and we are in the best shopping district in Japan."

As they followed Shuurikou to a shop, they took another look at the people around them. They realized he was right, not one person had cybernetics, and all of the women had normal human ears. Hidariude knew he was the only cyborg on Seventh Moon and it occurred to him that he may be the only one that existed at all, and based on the assumption that Keisei worked at Moe, it seemed that it was not typical for females to have animalistic features. First Shuurikou picked out clothes for Keisei because she was naked. Her fur covered everything important, so she looked like she was wearing a fur bikini, but she could only get so far before it gave somebody the wrong idea. Shuurikou found her a red kimono with room for her tail and a hair band to cover Keisei's ears, though it took a while to get one that fit comfortably. To hide Hidariude's arm, they got a black hand wrap from an athletics store. Hidariude thought it looked stupid and was comfortable with his arm showing, but to make sure nobody looked at them weird, he agreed to wear it.

With everyone set, they headed back out across the city. As they walked along they noticed that the city seemed to be so big and full of people and energy, the complete opposite of the world outside the city. When asked about this Shuurikou explained, "After World War Three, most of the world had used up their resources and couldn't go on. New World Enterprises arranged to have new alternative energy sources set up to keep the status quo in major cities. The problem is, it's just not feasible to keep up every city like Tokyo. The very wealthiest cities in the world have managed to get deals like this where everything just keeps going like the war never happened, the other ninety-nine percent gets the shaft. As soon as we get out of the city, things are going to start looking a lot more like Kanagawa. Out there we have two kinds of people, salvagers like me and scavengers. Salvagers try to make do with what's out there and help make the ruins and settlements livable. Scavengers on the other hand, just seem be really pissed about how twenty years ago, everybody lived like this, and now they've got nothing, so they just try to take what they can from other people. The problem is there's so little, scavengers generally have to fight and sometimes kill to get what they want. Nobody really does anything about it except to keep them out of cities and salvagers try our best to protect ourselves and our settlements. It's really not easy because whenever we get anything going and working, the New Wave Elite show up."

"Sounds like you'll need us a lot." Hidariude said with a laugh.

"Now you understand why I followed you guys around." Shuurikou continued. "I figured anyone who could survive in Kanagawa was pretty tough but I had no idea until I saw you fight the New Wave Elite last night. So you're really AWOL from Seventh Moon? I still can't quite believe it. But we are so desperate for someone who can fight back. It's just, they're so strong."

"Well, we are genetically engineered to be above normal human limits." Hidariude took over again. "I'd say

I'm probably the weakest relatively speaking, but that's not saying much. We are a tough breed."

"Genetically engineered?" Shuurikou was genuinely shocked, he had never put it together before. "You mean they actually used that technology to make you guys from scratch?" They nodded to him. "So it's not just our imagination. Well here we are." Shuurikou had led them to a parking garage near the Moe club. He had parked a truck here the night before when he had gone looking for them. It had some stuff in the back, all in bags, boxes and crates. "I was finishing my shopping when I ran into you guys last night. You guys are a lot faster than I expected, it took me a while to catch up and this is where I dropped off my truck last night. I've been trying to find you guys all day. Well now we are going to hit the road."

Just as Shuurikou was about to open the door to the truck, bullets started flying. Hidariude threw him to the ground just in time for him to avoid being hit. Hidariude rolled Shuurikou under the truck and told him to stay there with Douji who crawled in next to him. Hidariude, Keisei and Kichiku started running and the bullets followed fast on their heels. They had sensed the presence of the threat just in time and knew exactly who it was, they just needed to know where.

"Renzokuken!" Hidariude shouted. "Show yourself!"

"How did you know it was me?" Renzokuken's voice echoed through the garage, but didn't give away his location right away. "It was the bullets that gave me away, wasn't it? Well that was my foolish mistake, yours was returning to the scene of the crime. Just why did you come back anyway?" After looking around and not seeing them or hearing an answer he tried probing with a different question. "How about you just hand over the kid? If you do I'll just let you go."

"Never!" Kichiku answered with definite finality. The sound of his voice was all Renzokuken needed to get an idea of where he was and fire off another round which Kichiku narrowly dodged. Kichiku didn't mind, he was just distracting the shooter while his faster friends got closer.

Keisei had the most sensitive hearing and was able to pretty well pinpoint the point of origin of his voice. With all of her feline stealth she crept up on him and attacked. She was out of flash paper so she had to attack hand to hand. Just as she was about to land a tiger claw, Renzokuken saw her out of the corner of his eye and dodged just barely feeling the tips of her fingernails scratch across the surface of his face. He rolled across the ground and put up his defenses against Keisei. While he prepared for her next attack the ground opened beneath him as Kichiku had struck the ground and caused a fissure. Renzokuken had seen the fissure coming out of the corner of his eye and managed to jump out of the way but Hidariude unleashed an electric attack at him as he jumped through the air. Renzokuken was not sure how to dodge while in midair and desperately shot at the lightning. It didn't really help, it still hit him but he managed to take the blow pretty well as he landed on the ground. Now all three were coming at him from different angles, fully aware he only had two guns and two hands and could only shoot in two directions, so one of them would probably get to him before he could get them.

Renzokuken shot at Hidariude and Kichiku believing his old comrades to be the most dangerous threats. Hidariude deflected the bullet with his blade while Kichiku pulled some pavement out of the ground to block the bullet. Having missed with both of his attacks he desperately turned toward Keisei and braced for the impact of her attack. Keisei kicked him, angling the roundhouse to land him between Hidariude and Kichiku, allowing them to attack him from both sides. He tried to shoot back at her while somersaulting out of the way of the other two attacking. At this point his attention was divided and his aim was off and he missed Keisei as she flattened against the ground and dodged the bullets. Hidariude both redirected their attacks to follow Renzokuken and managed to hit his legs. When he landed from his somersault, he couldn't stand up on one leg which had been smashed by Kichiku and was holding the other leg that was cut up by Hidariude.

Renzokuken's heart was pounding, he was sure he was about to die. He was just supposed to shoot these people and get out, he was not prepared for hand to hand combat. Fortunately, Einji was there to back him up. The last of the bat girls from the night before had come to avenge her sisters. She had been waiting in ceiling above and landed a surprise ambush on Hidariude and began to grapple with him. Renzokuken thanked his luck because now he only had to fight two people instead of three.

Kichiku still came after Renzokuken trusting Hidariude to handle Einji.

Einji tore into Hidariude with a fury of vengeance. "They're dead, all of them, you killed them!" She was so angry she couldn't even explain to Hidariude that when she checked on her sisters the previous night she found them with one long burn scar across the three of their bodies and they were dead. She couldn't say it, but the image was stuck in her head, along with the image of him striking them with a lightning bolt from his sword that she saw as she looked back while running away with Gaki. The images were so burned into her mind, it was all she was able to think about consciously, her body was operating purely on savage instinct. With each strike, Hidariude could feel her rage, and with his sixth sense, he could see these images in her mind. He felt bad for her, he felt genuine sorrow that he had killed more people and that she was suffering because of him. However he also felt that now she would not know peace until one of them was dead and he still had the will to live so he had to fight. He just wasn't sure if he could end this the way he knew he had to.

Fortunately, Keisei jumped in to help him, grabbing Einji from behind in a headlock and pulling her off Hidariude. Unlike Hidariude, Keisei had not yet developed a sense of remorse over killing people when necessary and held tightly around Einji's neck trying to cut off her breathing. Keisei was not going to allow anyone to kill the man who had her heart, in this moment she was driven by fear that Einji would kill him, and she would turn into the same grief stricken psycho this girl was. Einji tried to repel her by extending her wings and forcing Keisei of her back, but as Keisei lost her grip with her hands, she wrapped her legs around Einji's midsection and held tightly as she flipped back to the pavement, landed on her hands, and then used the momentum to flip Einji over landing headfirst on the concrete. Einji crumpled to the ground, and Keisei closed the bat girl's eyes. "Rest in peace sister."

Meanwhile Kichiku and Renzokuken continued their duel. In their minds it was just like old times, matching punch for punch, kick for kick, and block for block. Part of them just went into automatic, letting the duel go purely on instinct, waiting for a moment where they could see a weakness in the other's defense. Of course, there was no weakness, after nearly twenty years of sparring against each other; they had fine-tuned their fighting to know every move the other could make. If Kichiku tried a palm strike, Renzokuken knew he couldn't take it directly and dodged; if Renzokuken tried shooting, Kichiku could recognize the way he was holding his hand before it got to the gun and evaded the shot before he could pull the trigger; if Kichiku tried to cause a tremor by hitting the ground, Renzokuken would jump just before impact.

Once Hidariude and Keisei finished with Einji, they came after Renzokuken, and he found himself once again desperate to find a way out. He realized there was no way out but one way that his pride had been preventing him from taking, but pride isn't any good to the dead. He pulled a switch out of his pocket and pushed the button activating robots that were on standby around the parking garage. These robots were not slashers like the one at the club, they had built in guns instead of blades and were shooting like Renzokuken, heavy fire but well aimed and focused on the espers. Hidariude, Keisei and Kichiku all had to ignore Renzokuken and start dodging bullets, a feat made possible only by their ability to sense where the bullets were coming from before they were fired.

This sense was also what allowed them to locate the robots around the garage. They started running at top speed away from where the bullets were landing and toward where they were coming from. They had no fear, just focus on where to step to be out of the line of fire and knowing how to disarm the robots when they found them. Hidariude was the most efficient, he recognized Renzokuken's fighting style in the robots and realized that as soon as he got close their defense would be poor and all he had to do was slice and dice, his first strike always being to cut off the hands and breaking the firing mechanisms. Kichiku followed suit crushing the robots and their guns in his big muscular hands. Keisei wasn't quite so well prepared to fight the robots head on, but she quickly found an efficient method of dispatching them. She'd find pair of robots and run between them drawing fire, and since her reflexes were faster than the robots they would end up shooting each other.

There were a few dozen robots and it took quite some time to stop all of them. While the three were distracted with this task, Renzokuken noticed his real target under the truck. He grabbed Douji by the collar.

"There you are you little brat." Shuurikou tried to hold back the boy and keep him from being taken, but Renzokuken's genetically altered muscles, though not necessarily a match for Kichiku or even Hidariude, were still more than enough to overcome Shuurikou's relatively meager strength. As Renzokuken hopped on a motorcycle and drove off holding Douji captive, Shuurikou felt helpless and was reminded that these people were in a league of their own.

Once Hidariude, Keisei and Kichiku finished with the robots, they came back to find Shuurikou still hiding under the truck. "Where's Douji?" Kichiku asked.

Shuurikou ashamedly admitted "He took him. I'm sorry I tried to stop him, but he jumped on a motorcycle and drove off."

"Which way?" Kichiku asked quickly, "Can we catch up with him?"

"Hop in the truck, I'll drive." Shuurikou jumped in the truck and the others jumped in the back. He started up the truck and sped the vehicle off. He was desperate to make up for his mistake, he didn't want that little boy getting hurt.

As they went down the street, Kichiku used his bond with Douji to track down where Renzokuken had taken him. When he realized that Renzokuken made a turn that they missed he told Shuurikou to make the next turn, hoping they could get ahead and cut him off at the pass. When he sensed that they got ahead, he directed another turn to intercept Renzokuken. It almost worked when they saw Renzokuken speed by just as they came to the corner. This time Shuurikou needed no directions as he turned and rode right up on Renzokuken's rear. Renzokuken saw them in his rear view mirror and started to shoot back. It was very hard to drive, hold onto Douji, and shoot all at the same time, so his aim was off and Shuurikou was able to pull away before they took too much fire.

As the truck came around the motorcycle. Kichiku jumped off the truck and landed fist first on the ground creating a massive quake and a fissure directed straight up under Renzokuken's motorcycle, which sent it spinning in the air. Keisei reached out and grabbed Douji off the bike as it went flying over the truck. Renzokuken tried to land the motorcycle upright and when he landed he turned to pursue the truck which was now doubling back to pick up Kichiku. Renzokuken began shooting back at the truck but Hidariude deflected the bullets and jumped back onto the bike knocking Renzokuken off of it.

As they tumbled to the ground, Renzokuken struggled to fight with Hidariude, doing his best to keep Hidariude's hands back knowing that they were his strong point. Fortunately for Renzokuken, his muscles were made for holding his hands steady against the recoil of a gun and that same strength helped him hold Hidariude's hands back firmly. The downside was that Renzokuken's strongest muscles were his arms, and since Hidariude had a sword in one hand and cyber blades extended in the other, he would need both hands to keep from getting sliced. Desperately they began kicking each other as they maneuvered into an alley.

"You don't have to do this Renzokuken!" Hidariude exclaimed. "You are on earth now, you could leave the company and join us!"

"You mean betray the people that made me like you did?" Renzokuken answered. "I will not be a traitor!"

"You mean you'd rather be a killer? Don't you understand what they're using you for? You're nothing but a weapon to them! They're trying to take over the world and they're killing everyone who stands against them!"

Renzokuken laughed. "What's wrong with that? We are the New Wave Elite! We have been made for this if we do not rise to our full potential as the masters of the new world, what are we then? Failures! That's what you are, you and your cohorts are all failures! You have thrown away your purpose and now you just stand in our way, and that's why we must eliminate you!"

"No, we did not throw away our purpose, we found a new purpose, our true purpose. We are devoted to this world and seeing to it that there is no more unnecessary bloodshed."

"That is why you are a failure, because this path will create more bloodshed. More people will have to die in your wake as we hunt you down, or else you will have to kill us. Either way, there will be blood."

Renzokuken pushed Hidariude's right hand against the wall forcing him to drop his sword. Renzokuken didn't need to hold up the empty hand and reached for his gun with his now free hand. At the same time, Hidariude poked two fingers at a pressure point inside Renzokuken's elbow to weaken his grip on his other hand.   Once Hidariude was free he rolled to grab his sword. Renzokuken fired and Hidariude deflected with his sword. The bullet ricocheted off Hidariude's sword, then off a garbage dumpster and right back into Renzokuken.   He took two steps forward before he felt it, the bullet hit his heart. As he pulled his hand from his wound and looked at the blood, he laughed and said his dying words to Hidariude "See, there will be blood."

Chapter 9

Shuurikou had picked up Hidariude and driven everybody out of Tokyo as fast as possible. They also picked up Renzokuken's motorcycle and brought it along in the back of the truck where Hidariude, Keisei and Kichiku were also riding. Shuurikou insisted that Douji ride in the cab with him. The back window of the truck had been shot out by Renzokuken so they carried on a conversation through the window. Hidariude and Keisei were very interested in the motorcycle and had a few questions to ask Shuurikou about it.

"It runs on biodiesel, though when we get a chance I'll convert it to a methanol-ethanol mix like my truck." Shuurikou said while thumping the dashboard with his hand. "They used to run on gasoline, but there isn't any anymore. The last of it was used in World War Three and when it ran out, the war ended and everybody had to convert to alternative energy. New World Enterprises makes a good business of selling their fuels but they only have enough to manage a few cities and the rest of us have to make do with what we can. Here in Japan, Tokyo is the only city that was deemed worthy of getting what they needed to keep from falling into ruin. The sad part is we can get by with solar, wind and hydroelectric energy, but every time we build a generator based on those sources the New Wave Elite steal it from us or destroy it. We don't have much choice though, not everyone fits in the city so some people have to live in the outlands. Every now and then somebody gets desperate and forgets the consequences of trying to improve our lives and starts building a village and then just when it starts to prosper, that's when they show up." Shuurikou sounded very angry, like he'd been that one who tried to start a village more than once and was very frustrated with seeing his hard work destroyed. The espers could sense that he was so desperate he was putting his faith in them because he would do anything to stop the destruction, even if it meant relying on a group of rogues that he knew nothing about except that they could hold their own in battle against an otherwise invincible foe. Shuurikou took a moment to let his rage subside and decided to change the subject. "So how did you guys...you know, with the lightning and the fire and the earthquakes?"

Hidariude leaned up against the back window, or at least the hole where it used to be. "We are espers, we have extrasensory perception and various psychokinetic abilities. Before you get your hopes up, we do have limits. Our ESP is uniform, we can sense what others are thinking or feeling. We can't actually read minds, except each other's, and when we're in battle, we can predict our opponent's actions, which is what really gives us the edge to achieve victory. Truth be told, the physical abilities that Seventh Moon gave us aren't enough for us to beat them, but the ability to know what they'll do and react to it before they do it is what helps us win. As for the more overt fancy stuff, I have electrokinesis, the ability to manipulate electricity with my mind. I can only use it because of an electro plaque in my arm that allows me to produce electricity to operate my cyber arm. Since the charge originates from my body it has my Ki so I can continue to manipulate it as it's leaving my body. I'm really only good at directing it through my metal blades and I have to be careful about how much I use it because there is a chance I can burn out the circuitry in my arm or injure my own muscles and then I lose the use of my arm. Kichiku has geokinesis, he can control the earth, but he has to maintain a physical connection to the ground so that he can use his powers. For the two of us, we have trained to be fighters so well, we only use it when we have to. Keisei is a little better with her pyrokinesis because she more specifically trained for it with kayakujutsu, the ancient art of pyrotechnics. She can't create fire from nothing, she needs flammable materials, but once she has the right stuff, she can ignite it and manipulate the fire."

Shuurikou was impressed, though he wouldn't have believed it if he hadn't seen it with his own eyes. "So you all have the power to manipulate a specific element of your surroundings, but you can't create it, only manipulate what's already there. So you do seem to be bound by the laws of physics, you can't generate matter or energy, only change the form it's in. And this has nothing to do with Seventh Moon?"

"No, not that we know of." Hidariude answered. "They can't make abilities like this, we learned them while training under Master Ryu at the Shrine of the Golden Dragon."

"So he's psychic too?"

"No, he wasn't. Maybe being genetically engineered beyond normal human limits gave us a predisposition to break limits like this, but we're pretty sure this isn't what they made. We only saw one of theirs that had powers like this, and she was very unstable, clearly she didn't have the same senses we have so she was unstable because she is raw undirected power."

"What about the kid?" Shuurikou asked. "They seemed to be really interested in him."

Kichiku came to the window and answered this time. "He is special. He has potential to do what each of us can do and a whole lot more."

Shuurikou whistled. "That does sound worth the trouble of hunting you down."

"Yes, but he can't use his power yet. He's too young, he's not ready to handle that much power, so he has to be trained to control it better, and he needs to get older before he's ready to take on the necessary degree of training. The real reason they want him is because the girl they made is just like him, but the environment they raised her in has made her unstable and they want to know why he's not going haywire like she is."

"Do you have any idea why?"

"Sure. On Seventh Moon we are trained from the moment we can walk. Douji was raised here on Earth like a normal child so he isn't under the same pressure. Think of all the pressure you feel sometimes, and then throw in the power to warp your surroundings with your thoughts. She's just having some nervous breakdown, if they just let her relax and play like a normal kid, she'd probably work it out of her system."

"Why don't they do that?"

"That's not their style. All of the bad things you keep saying about the company, well, you don't know the half of it. We lived there under their tyranny, believe us, we have our reasons to fight."

Shuurikou took in what they were saying and realized it was worse than he thought. He was used to understanding that Seventh Moon was cruel and tyrannical to the people of Earth, but the idea that even their own people could feel so mistreated made him hate the company even more. For a moment he was going to ask them why they had begun to trust him after Hidariude had drawn a weapon on him when they first met, but then he realized with ESP, they could tell how honest he was and that first confrontation was just from them all being on edge. Then Shuurikou decided to ask them about something else that was somewhat irrelevant, but made him curious anyway. "What was this shrine like?"

"The Shrine of the Golden Dragon was on a mountain in Kanagawa." Kichiku replied. "It was dedicated to the golden dragon Shinryuu and his three champions, Okazaki Kyutsume, Bakeneko, and Nyudo. We trained in martial arts and disciplined ourselves with the teachings of the founders. We ate daikon, rice and tea which we grew right there."

"Lots of rice, daikon and tea." Hidariude interrupted. "Nothing else for three years. There are only so many combinations you can make of that before it gets old. You have no idea how good that ramen tasted, if for nothing else than just a change. I don't even care what was in it, just as long as it wasn't daikon and rice."

147

Kichiku glared at Hidariude. "As I was saying it was a very peaceful, serene and isolated location. A samurai, a monk and a ninja built that shrine in dedication to the golden dragon. We learned kenjutsu, tessenjutsu, kayakujutsu and kung fu to emulate them and keep their memory alive as has been done for centuries."

"And we would have stayed there, except Seventh Moon couldn't let us be and they came to hunt us down and..." Hidariude choked on the words he was about to speak. "Then they killed Master Ryu."

Now Shuurikou understood, this really was personal for them. They had lost someone dear to them and they wanted revenge. The only thing about this that made them different from anyone else he knew was that they actually had the power to do something about it. This was a very sensitive subject now, calling for a moment of silence. In this silence they looked around at the landscape. Some of it was beautiful, when they were simply looking at untouched land filled with nature, trees, grasses, some lakes, rivers and ponds, and mountains in the distance. Then they'd pass through where there had been a town or village or some smaller settlement that didn't even count as a village, and it was terrifying. The buildings were broken, the windows were smashed, weeds grew up the walls and occasionally they could even see the bones of someone who had been killed and nobody had even bothered to come by and move it let alone give a proper burial. "We're still too close to Tokyo, the patrols come around too often for anyone to dare live here. It's going to be a while before we get far enough that anyone will feel safe enough to actually live."

After hours of driving, they finally found an actual settlement. It wasn't very obvious, they only knew because Shuurikou knew it was there. All they could see was an old gas station and it appeared to be abandoned. Shuurikou got out of the truck and went into the station. It still appeared that nobody was there, but Shuurikou kept looking around, moving certain things around, and thumping a shelf or counter. It took a moment but they recognized a pattern, he was signaling someone. Finally a man came out from the back room, he looked old, but it may have just been that his living conditions made him look worse than he really was. The man helped Shuurikou with the hoses at the fuel tank and filled up both the truck and the motorcycle. The attendant seemed shocked at the sight of the espers in the back of the truck, they looked very unusual, but Shuurikou assured him they were okay.

"Okay guys we're staying the night here." Shuurikou told them. "Everybody out." They got out of the truck and followed Shuurikou. He took them into the gas station and then to the back room. They were very surprised to find that beyond the backroom was an entire underground village. It was a network of sewers, subway tunnels, and collapsed buildings with a roof of trash suspended over any gaps. Light came in through sewer grates and glass windows that were fitted in amongst the trash that made the roof. "Since the settlements keep getting attacked, the only way to keep them safe is to stay where nobody can find us. We build underground, the food still comes from above ground, but we just have to farm creatively, which means a lot of gathering from amongst the weeds. We also eat mushrooms that grow down here and we also try to fish and hunt, and by hunt I mean catch rats, roaches, and whatever other vermin we find down here."

"I'm starting to miss rice with daikon."

"Relax, it's a joke, there's not so much in the way of rats and roaches now. What we do catch is ground into feed for the chickens and goats." As if on cue, a chicken and a goat crossed their path. "Chickens for eggs and goats for milk. We used to use cows but they were too big, they kept drawing attention from NWE. All of the other free range livestock have been captured or eaten or both."

At the mention of the word eaten, Hidariude and Kichiku exchanged a look. "What do you mean eaten?"

"The patrols I told you about." Shuurikou answered. "For a while it was a group of soldiers, but once they devoured so much food that they drove out most of the people, most of the soldiers got reassigned elsewhere and it came down to just one soldier and the android garbage disposals called 'eaters' he drags around."

"Could you tell us more about this soldier?"

"He's got sharp teeth and a long tongue and spits acid. He's fat, but he used to be thinner, he just eats a lot."

"Do you know his name?"

"No, his name is never spoken. He doesn't bother to speak much because the more he talks, the less he can stuff his mouth. All he seems to say is 'Hungry! Feed me!' and threatens he'll eat us if we don't give him all of our food."

"That's enough of a description, we know who he is. And we may also know how to stop him for good. Do you guys have anything spicy? Spices, herbs, peppers, wasabi, anything?"

"Yes, but we've tried feeding them to him before. It just makes him mad and then he tries to cut the heartburn by eating us."

Keisei chimed in. "But you never had me doing the cooking before!"

Shuurikou was very concerned by what she said. "What does she mean by that?"

"She means we have to help her gather everything spicy, she's got a recipe for his final feast. And we have to be ready, he'll be here soon I'm sure. We've already been attacked by two soldiers we used to know, if this is his territory he'll be put on our trail and he'll track us here. We don't know exactly when, but we'll want to be prepared when he does."

Keisei went above ground with the locals to forage for herbs. The rest started gathering the spices from the storerooms and put everything in the house where they were staying. Keisei looked over everything and started picking out certain herbs and smelling them, then setting them together by a cooking pot. She carefully added the ingredients into the pot to prepare her spicy concoction, stirring them together and grinding them a little to make sure they mixed and the aromas came out properly. The smell got stronger and stronger, and when it peaked, she added a vial of some fluid, her secret ingredient. Shuurikou and the others were mystified at what she was doing, but her fellow espers knew all too well what she was doing. This had been an experiment they worked on once when they were a little bored and wanted to test some new flavors and stumbled upon a secret that made for a most unpleasant memory but could also prove very effective against this particular foe.

Once they had the brew going, Keisei put the lid on to allow it to age, the longer it sat the more potent it would be. They ate a meal together following a prayer and then shared a few laughs over the smattering of vegetables, eggs and fish that had been provided as a meal. Then they retired to the beds that had been set aside for them. The espers only needed two beds between them, Hidariude and Keisei shared a bed as a couple and young Douji felt more safe at night in a strange new place with Kichiku. Shuurikou looked at them before he went to bed and was in awe of how they just seemed to be a family completely at peace with themselves. It seemed almost a shame that he would have to tear them away from the peace of this moment eventually, but they all knew that there were many families who needed them to take the risk for the greater good.

*   *   *

The notorious devourer of the greater Tokyo area was able to find his quarry pretty easily. This was mostly because the truck was sitting in the gas station that appeared to be abandoned, and yet there were fairly fresh tracks in the dirt that had eroded part of the pavement. It also didn't help that Renzokuken's motorcycle was clearly visible on the bed of the truck. He went to the door of the gas station and barked out his usual call "I'm hungry! Feed me!" At first it seemed there was no answer. "I know you're there, don't bother hiding or I'll just sic my eaters on you until I find you and then I'll eat everything anyway. And while you're at it, send out those fugitives you have with you. You know, they're traitors, they used to be with us, you can't trust them, they're unpredictable, they turned on us, and they can turn on you too! Of course, I can fix that situation...for a price."

Keisei came out with the first platter of food, with her friends bringing out the rest. Even little Douji carried a platter of food, it was small but still something and besides, Kichiku made up the difference with the helping he brought out. Shuurikou also brought out some food, but the server that drew the soldier's attention was Hidariude. "You seem to be the leader of this ragtag band of traitors, would you mind sitting with me while I eat?"

"Do you mind if these others join us?" Hidariude replied.

The soldier looked at the others. "Not at all. In fact, I would definitely appreciate these three joining us." He gestured at Keisei, Kichiku, and Douji. "Mind you, I'm only asking you to sit with me, I still get to eat all of this."

"You always had a big appetite Paku." Hidariude commented.

"I have a high metabolism." Paku said as he sat at the table in the gas station's old minimart café. His eaters were rather imposing and he was rather confident that his gang would keep the espers from attacking him.

"It seems to be failing, you've gained some weight."

Paku began to eat the offering of food presented to him. Between bites he spoke through a full mouth, surprisingly clearly. "You're lucky I'm famished from my journey here and need to eat or I'd kick your ass for that. As it is, you have until I'm finished to win me over, or I have you three for dessert before I take the kid back."

"Why do you eat all of this anyway? I know Seventh Moon can provide enough food to fill even your gullet, but you're taking everything these people have and leaving them to starve."

"Are you kidding? I eat a village every day or so and I'm still starving! If this is the best they can provide, I'm doing them a favor. I mean think about it, if they can't feed me, what are the chances they can feed themselves? The only way to survive is to bow down to Seventh Moon and anyone who doesn't, doesn't deserve to live. That's what we're for; we need to clear out the extras, the surplus, the overpopulated masses. What's the point of these people fighting, in the long run they won't make it anyway. You're too soft, thinking they stand a chance, it's better just to take them out quickly and end their suffering as soon as possible."

"You think making them starve is humane?"

"I'm saying it's more humane that I speed up the process so that the few who get away can either give in and seek refuge in Tokyo or give up now before they waste any more time or resources trying to make a future that's never going to happen." Paku began to sweat and burped. "These folks make it extra spicy in these parts don't they? I've developed a taste for most spices, but I don't think I know this spice. Something new, not wasabi... what is it?"

"It's just something special we whipped up for you. You're right there isn't much we can do. We really didn't realize how bad the situation was until we came out here, but now that we see it, it is a lost cause. So we're just going to give you a good meal to celebrate that we're going to join you and finish off these people before we all go back."

Paku laughed. "Well now that sounds like a good deal. You know the others all wanted to kill you, but I always knew you'd come around. It doesn't take long in the outlands to realize that this is just no place to live." By now, Paku had cleaned the first platter and started on the large one Kichiku had brought out. Normally he savored the food he ate as well as the looks of frustration on the faces of the starving locals as he ate their food, but Hidariude's words inspired him to hurry and finish his meal, so he opened his mouth wide, even unhinging his jaw and sliding all the remaining food into his mouth, downing a platter's worth of food in one gulp each until it was all gone. "So are we ready to party?"

At this point, Douji tugged at Shuurikou's pant leg and signaled him to retreat back underground. Hidariude drew his sword on Paku. "You'd better believe it!"

"Huh?" Paku looked surprised, but as he saw the other two get into their fighting stances, he realized they weren't on his side after all. "Once a traitor always a traitor. Get them!" The last words he spoke were a command to his eaters to go after the espers.

The first move they made was to rush out of the gas station to draw Paku and his eaters away from the settlement. Hidariude engaged Paku to keep his attention. Of course Paku remembered fighting Hidariude and his cyber blades and knew how to keep out of his way. Hidariude managed to get in a few cuts across Paku's belly, but he managed to avoid taking anything more than superficial wounds and just kept dodging while trying to get Hidariude in position to be taken by the eaters. Hidariude simply cut through the eaters without any difficulty.

Outside more eaters came after Kichiku and Keisei. Once Kichiku got enough distance, he turned around and pounded the ground with both fists creating two fissures that opened directly beneath the eaters dropping them into the crevices. Kichiku then clapped his hands together and the crevices closed on the eaters holding them fast in the spot where they stood. Keisei ran down the line smashing the eaters. When she hit the end of the line, Paku caught up to her and she had to spin around and retreat again.

Hidariude caught up to Paku and started striking at him, forcing him to dodge, while Kichiku tried to hit him from behind. Paku was used to this tactic too as they had done this several times when they were growing up and he knew how to dodge their attacks while looking for Kichiku's weak spot. The problem he didn't anticipate was Keisei pulling out her war fans and covering her comrade's weak spots. This made Paku desperate so he jumped as high as he could and started spitting stomach acid. The espers saw this coming and dodged the acid. Paku was disappointed that it didn't work, but it did cause them to spread out enough that he could safely land where he thought he would have an advantage. His next move was to stick out his tongue and grab Keisei's fans to eat them. After disarming her, Paku tried to do the same thing to Hidariude by grabbing his sword. However, the sacred nature of the sword made it more valuable than the easily replaceable fans Keisei wielded, and even she recognized the value so before Paku could retract his tongue, she grabbed a hold of it in her hands and stopped him in his tracks.

"What's the matter?" Keisei taunted Paku. "Cat got your tongue?"

"Vewy funny, bow wet go!" Paku screamed with a mix of anger and vulnerability.

"You first." Keisei demanded, forcing him to let go of the sword and threw it back to Hidariude. "Okay boys, now it's my turn, you'd better get out of the way." Following her orders, they both retreated to a safe distance. Keisei held up her index and middle finger on her free hand and focused her eyes on the fire kanji Hidariude had etched in Paku's belly. As she let go of his tongue she incanted "Kayakujutsu ignite!" and then jumped out of the way.

Paku had no time to react, he just felt a rumble in his stomach as the vitriol Keisei added ignited the spices in the food he had eaten. He tried to hold his mouth closed and hold it back for a fraction of a second before the flames burst forth. With a final burp of smoke, Paku collapsed. Keisei had mixed a much more potent batch than she had in previous experiments, this was a fatal amount, and his insides had been completely burned by the explosion. The fight was over, Paku was dying, and his last thoughts were the realization that the fight itself had been nothing more than a diversion to make sure he was a safe distance away before he exploded.

The espers returned to the settlement to tell everyone the good news that the eaters would not be coming back. Shuurikou went out and gathered the spare parts from the robots so that they could start using them for something before anyone came to get the parts and rebuild the eaters. After he got the final payload on his truck, he joined the celebration feast being held for the espers since now the people could farm and forage freely and would have more food to go around.

Shuurikou took the espers aside. "I'm really proud of your work, but our journey is not over. Now that you have proven yourself to this community here, I'm going to take you to our leader. There is a resistance and she's going to make you official members."

"When do we set out?" Hidariude said with much enthusiasm.

"I'll let you guys enjoy the victory for today, then we head out first thing tomorrow."

Chapter 10

The truck was now overloaded with spare parts from the robots so there was no longer room for anyone to ride back there, so Kichiku and Douji had to squeeze into the front seat with Shuurikou. As for Hidariude and Keisei, they were riding the freshly fueled motorcycle. They found it very enjoyable and freeing to be speeding down the highway, the wind in their hair. Hidariude was driving in front with Keisei holding on behind him, and there was something about holding onto her man that felt very comforting to her. She could ride like this forever, though it would have been even better if they weren't stuck following Shuurikou's truck, smelling his fumes, and worst of all, not being able to go top speed.

After a long drive, they finally arrived at their next stop, a dam. "Not just any dam, the Sakuma hydroelectric power dam." Shuurikou said as he got out of the truck at their destination. "This dam produces a significant amount of renewable environmentally friendly electricity. Under New World Enterprises, it all gets sent to Tokyo, even though it could be divided among the power grid to all of Japan."

"Let me guess, there's a soldier here making sure that doesn't happen." Hidariude said.

"Yes." Shuurikou replied. "I don't suppose you know this guy too?"

"When we first arrived on Earth, we were part of a team." Hidariude answered. "Since then, we've met all but one of them, and the last one was an aquatic specialist."

"Perfect to watch a hydroelectric dam." Shuurikou surmised. "Previous attempts to liberate this dam have met with a soldier and a group of robots that are designed for aquatic use. Be prepared."

"We always are."

All five had to go in together. They would have liked to leave Douji behind for his safety, but Shuurikou needed to go in to reprogram the hydroelectric power grid and the other three needed to go in to protect him. They crept up the path from the main road to the dam, lying low in case security was watching outside. Apparently there wasn't any security watching outside, because they made it to the entrance without any trouble.

Getting in was a different story. Shuurikou was able to hack the lock to get in, though as soon as they did, the security bots descended on them. The robots looked like soldiers wearing scuba gear. They knew the truth though, those tanks on their backs weren't for breathing; they contained water that they used for high pressure hydro cannons making them similar to Renzokuken's blasters only with slightly different weapons. Kichiku punched the ground and managed to bend the ground into a wall that blocked the water. Hidariude and Keisei maneuvered around the wall Kichiku created to flank the robots and attack as they ran past. The first wave went down, clearly not programmed to be prepared for their unique fighting style.

They continued working their way through the corridors, Shuurikou giving them directions from a map of the dam he had kept from a previous attempt on the dam. Shuurikou knew the importance of the dam and was desperate to get the electricity running back to the rest of Japan, but his previous attempts failed. Resistance soldiers drowned either by robots or by the lead soldier who dragged them into the reservoir. This time he had a team that could handle the robots, a sword slash here, a fan swipe there, and a palm strike to cleanup anything that got by, these new allies knew how to fight. They knew that Shuurikou was using them, but they knew that Seventh Moon was taking away people's free will and they wanted to stop it. They already had their mission, and they were using Shuurikou to help them with it.

At every turn there were more robots, but the espers sensed them coming and prepared with their attacks first, each robot went up in a splash of water from their tanks that they couldn't empty before being destroyed. Sometimes a robot would appear while the espers were otherwise occupied, but Kichiku managed to put up an unstoppable defense that blocked every single attack. The robots had no chance of stopping the intruders, they could only slow them down.

After a long journey through the dam to the control room, they finally found it and entered. Inside the room the soldier was waiting for them in the chair. It turned around to reveal a familiar face. He clapped slowly. "Congratulations for making it this far but it ends now."

"Yes, Kappa, it ends here, for you." Hidariude told his former comrade.

Kappa laughed quietly as a few more robots came up behind them. They didn't take the espers by surprise because they could sense the robots coming and dispatched them as easily as all the others before. Shuurikou was not so lucky though, lacking the ESP and the time to get a warning from the others as well as being in the back of the group since it seemed safest, he got captured.

"Oops, looks like you missed one." Kappa taunted. "Unless you want him to die, you'll surrender and give me the boy."

"So then you'll have four hostages instead of one?" Hidariude retorted. "Assuming you actually let him go."

"Of course I'd let him go, what do I care about him?" Kappa replied as if he really didn't care at all about Shuurikou other than as leverage. "In fact, I'd like him to go just so that he can tell everyone about how I destroyed his last glimmer of hope and everyone will know that they cannot stop the New Wave Elite!"

They tried to think about a way to save Shuurikou, but there simply was no way they could move fast enough or even use their powers to attack the robot without risking Shuurikou's life. Hidariude decided to make a bum rush and try to grab Shuurikou and take out the robot at the same time. Instead he was surprised to find that the robot simply turned and ran carrying Shuurikou along. Hidariude chased after him, knowing that there was no point in   liberating the control room if they didn't have Shuurikou to reprogram the power grid.

The others stayed in the room with Kappa and tried to fight him, but Kappa knew Kichiku's fighting style well and had been in enough group fights to know how to evade Keisei as well.   He grabbed Douji as he leapt between his foes and rolled out the door.   "Now I've got two hostages.   Try and get me!"   Kappa ran off after Hidariude and the robot carrying Shuurikou.

The abductors had an unfair advantage since they actually knew their way around and the espers could do nothing but follow.   Though they didn't know exactly where they were going, they knew exactly what the endgame was.   Kappa's advantage was that he was uniquely adapted to the water.   Not only did he have superior mobility, but since he could breathe underwater, he just needs to last longer than his opponent's ability to hold their breath.   They were going to the top of the dam so he could lure them to jump into the reservoir.   Normally they wouldn't fall for this, but they couldn't just let Shuurikou and Douji go.   They had to follow straight into his trap unless they could cut them off before they got into the water.

Unfortunately they were not so lucky, their precognitive abilities did not give them the speed they needed to stop Kappa and his robot.   The robot jumped over the edge of the dam into the water carrying Shuurikou with it.   Hidariude was about to follow but he picked up a telepathic message from the others and waited by the door as Kappa came to the surface with

Douji. Hidariude turned around and drew his sword against Kappa. Kappa almost got killed but saw the sword at the last second and dodged. In that split second he lost focus on holding Douji and Hidariude was able to grab the boy. Kappa realized he still had one hostage and would stand a much better chance if he could lure them where he wanted. "You've got one, but there's still one to go!" Kappa taunted as he jumped into the water.

Realizing they didn't have any choice they jumped in after Kappa. Here they were at a disadvantage because they couldn't use their powers; the water would extinguish Keisei's fire, they were suspended too high above the river bed for Kichiku to use his geokinesis, and if Hidariude tried using his electrokinesis he could electrocute everybody. However, they still had a plan, Kichiku went after the robot and managed to pry it's arms off of Shuurikou, setting him free so that Keisei could lead him back to the surface while Kichiku crushed the robot. Meanwhile, Hidariude desperately fought with Kappa to distract him and give his friends a chance to get away. Kappa had drawn a pair of ceramic knives to parry Hidariude's blades, which he did quite easily since the water created enough resistance to Hidariude's movements to nullify his precognitive speed advantage. Hidariude found he was running out of breath quite quickly and tried his best to surface, but now was Kappa's time to shine, he would hold Hidariude down and drown him. Just when he was about to pass out from lack of oxygen, Hidariude noticed the intake for the dam's turbine. He didn't know what it was, but he knew there had to be some way he could use it. Kappa was trying to push Hidariude through the narrow opening, but Hidariude used the last of his strength to kick off the dam and throw Kappa in instead. Hidariude relied on an adrenaline rush to push himself to the surface where he gasped for air.

Hidariude swam out to shore to rejoin his friends. Together they returned to the top of the dam where they located Douji. Then they looked over the edge to the other side and saw that Kappa had come out the other side of the dam in bad shape after being beat up by the turbine and the force of his fall coming out of the dam finished him off. His corpse washed up on shore and they knew the battle was over. They returned to the control room so Shuurikou could do his part while Hidariude, Keisei and Kichiku stood guard at the door against any remaining security bots.

""...and done." Shuurikou said when he finished switching on the circuits to the outlands. "There, now the power is up for all of Japan. Tokyo is now at half power, so there will be plenty of pissed off people back there. I hope nobody had plans to go back there."

"No, we're ready to meet your leader and formally join the resistance."

"Good, that's our next stop. Everybody, back to the truck."

The five took the long hike back down to their truck and bike, more than ready to get on the road again. Unfortunately, it was not to be. They sensed a threatening and familiar presence. There by their vehicles, Baz, Aka and Seichei were waiting for them, clearly having received cybernetic reconstruction. Baz appeared to be wearing gloves and a corset made from some sort of lavender plastic. In truth, this plastic was replacing her skin that she had lost when Keisei burned her. Aka looked normal, but under his uniform as a fully cybernetic body replacing what was destroyed when they had last met in combat. There was really no way around this, they would never reach the end of their journey without their vehicles and they wouldn't reach their vehicles without confronting their pursuers. After warning Shuurikou and Douji to stay back, the three faced their enemies.

"Well, now, there you are." Aka greeted them with a nasty hint of sarcasm. "We've been looking all over for you. You've been very slippery. I notice you seem to be missing one, where is the boy?"

"You won't get him." Kichiku answered sternly.

"Yes we will, and we'll kill you too."

"How can you be so confident when we have won every battle so far?"

"Because we're pretty sure you must be getting weary by now. Besides we are stronger than the last time we met."

With that they all attacked. Seichei did not go all out as he had before because he couldn't, and even if he could, he knew it wouldn't do any good. Extra size and extra blades just made him more bulky and less maneuverable, so he just extended his remaining arm blades and proceeded into a duel with Hidariude. Hidariude parried with his cyber blades in one hand and his sword in the other. He wanted to end it with an electric attack, but since he hadn't fully dried out yet, he risked short-circuiting his arm and he couldn't risk it, so he was stuck in the duel until it came to its natural end. It seemed to be a pretty routine fight, but what Hidariude did not realize, was that Seichei was actually learning more about Hidariude's fighting style with each battle and at some point he would gain the advantage, or so the android thought. In the back of Hidariude's mind, he thought Seichei would make the perfect sparring partner, if he wasn't actually bent on killing him.

Keisei and Baz squared off once again. Keisei felt at a disadvantage because she didn't have any fire talismans and was still wet so she couldn't use her fire powers at all. Baz however was able to use her new abilities and decided to get revenge on her by using her new flame throwers to blast Keisei. Unfortunately for Baz, even though Keisei couldn't create fire right now, she could still us her pyrokinesis to deflect Baz's fire. Realizing that fire wouldn't work, Baz switched to her icy freeze blast. Keisei tried to block this with her fans and found that her fans were frozen immediately and when she tried to strike back the fans shattered. Another pair of fans shattered, she'd have to replace them again later; in the meantime she needed to make sure this remained close combat so that the ice didn't come out again. As she grappled with Baz she focused her sixth sense on detecting the source of fire within Baz to try to use it against her. She finally was able to sense the containers of accelerant and coolant and the hoses that connected them and came up with an idea. She pinned Baz to the ground on her belly and scratched a small fire kanji on her back. "Kayakujutsu ignite!" Keisei set off the flame thrower inside of Baz. She'd already used enough fuel that there wouldn't be enough left to stop her, but there would be enough to burn out the coolant system and neutralize her new abilities. Baz was hurt, but she was much tougher now than their last encounter and she responded to the pain by lashing out at Keisei. The fight was on.

Aka came on quite fiercely, having gotten used to his cybernetic parts enough to have almost regained his speed. However, his speed was matched by Kichiku's precognitive battle senses and managed to keep up with him blow for blow. Once Aka realized his speed wasn't going to cut it he decided to bring out the big guns and transform. He back pedaled a bit then initiated his transformation. Kichiku tried to hit Aka mid transformation, but Aka was too quick and managed to become a half metallic doppelganger of his opponent, catching his punch and holding it. Kichiku tried another punch, but Aka blocked that too. Kichiku punched the ground to create a fissure quake to trap Aka, but surprisingly, Aka was able to punch the ground and divert the fissure around him, effectively countering the tremor. This was dangerous, Kichiku realized, Aka did not have precognitive senses, but between his new strength and his old speed, he could still make up the difference. They were evenly matched, and this battle would not end soon.

Shuurikou looked on with amazement. He had seen a lot of fighting in the short time he had been part of the resistance, but he had never seen anything like this.

There were powerful soldiers, but they had always easily taken out their opponents. His new allies had shown significant power, but the way they overcame their enemies just as easily. This was the first time he actually saw them with their equals, two teams of fighters that were totally in a league of their own. Shuurikou had no doubt in his mind that if any other person got involved in this they would be swatted away like a fly. This was a battle royal and he could do nothing but hope and pray that his allies would emerge victorious.

Douji was being held back so he couldn't see what was happening, but it didn't do any good. He was an esper, he was continually in sync with his family and he could feel what was happening. Even though he couldn't see what was happening, he could still feel their pain and frustration. He could feel how tired they were from their battle with Kappa and his robots. He knew Keisei was disarmed and at a disadvantage. He could feel the energy from their enemies and that their cybernetics were keeping them active and they would outlast his friends. It was only a matter of time before they gave into exhaustion. They were holding up but for how long? Douji's heart was pounding, he clenched his fists, closed his eyes and gritted his teeth. "No, not again! They can't get hurt, I need them!"

Shuurikou could hear the fear I Douji's voice and tried to calm him down. "It's okay, they'll win."

All three espers could feel it at the same, their seal was breaking. They each looked over toward Douji and saw an all too familiar glow. Once again the golden dragon

Shinryuu emerged and towered over the battle field. Shuurikou was paralyzed with fear as the fearsome apparition flew over him and began to battle with the soldiers.

Baz, Aka and Seichei remembered what happened before with Hime. This time they didn't have her to fight the golden dragon, but they did have a sedative they believed they could use on Douji. Unfortunately, they needed to be able to inject into the boy and had realized the dragon form was a projection that wouldn't respond to their chemicals. Aka took point with the sedative, reverting to his speedier form. Seichei and Baz tried to distract the dragon. Baz put her hands up to use her blasters, forgetting that they were damaged and wouldn't work. It did buy some time for Seichei to try to get in an attack, not that it did any good. Shinryuu simply swept both of them away, flinging them with his hand into the air, launching them towards the horizon. Aka managed to get on the dragon's back and tried to stick in the needle to inject him with the sedative, but what he did not anticipate was that unlike Hime, Douji had ESP and could sense his presence. Before he made contact, the dragon's tail swept him off toward the others in the distance.

The dragon roared and the entire area around the dam began to glow blue with a faint golden rim. Aka looked up. "Abort mission, it's not happening this time." His comrades agreed and retreated at top speed. The blue and gold aura actually seemed to give them a tailwind, urging them to go.

The glow around the area was something new, but the espers knew what had to be done all the same. Kichiku and Keisei each clapped their hands together while Hidariude held his sword pommel up and they all began to chant "Om mani padme om." The dragon roared again and the glow began to fade, and the dragon shrank back down until it was just Douji again, the last glimmer of spiritual light twinkling out on the shimenawa around his neck. Just like the last time, Douji was unconscious and completely unaware of what had happened.

Hidariude and Keisei got on the motorcycle while Kichiku carried Douji to the truck. Shuurikou still had not moved at all since Douji transformed. He stood there catatonic.

Hidariude called to Shuurikou. "Hey Shuurikou, come on. Kichiku doesn't know how to drive a truck and none of us have a clue where we are going. It's time for you to take the lead."

Shuurikou very slowly began to come back to his senses and uttered three barely audible words. "What was that?" The others had no immediate response and silence hung in the air. Finally, after what seemed like an eternity, Shuurikou got up the nerve to ask again. "You want me to just climb into that truck with you after what I just saw? No way! We don't go anywhere until you answer me! What the hell was that?!"

Kichiku slowly got back out of the truck and approached Shuurikou. "We came from the Shrine of the Golden Dragon, dedicated to the Golden Dragon Shinryuu. Within that shrine is a golden dragon statue, the Yoshiro of

Shinryuu. When we gather in worship that is where the spirit of Shinryuu dwells. However, it seems that after we have spent much time there, the spirit has transmigrated to Douji, he is the Yoshiromi. When he senses we are in trouble, the spirit awakens and they attain shintai. Unfortunately, he was never prepared for this and he is too young, so the spirit overcomes him. We are his guardians and it is our sacred duty to protect him and subdue the dragon's wrath and power."

"And NWE has one of these?"

"Sort of. The girl we told you about seems to be able to mirror his power, but it may not be a true dragon, or even a spirit of any kind. It may just be the psychic echo of Shinryuu."

"This is why they're after you?"

"Yes. This and because we deserted. We deserted to protect him. We are the enemies of the Seventh Moon, and they will not rest until they have him and the rest of us are eliminated."

"Well, I guess we just can't let that happen."

With that, they returned to the truck and began their journey to their destination, the resistance headquarters.

Chapter 11

Shuurikou's head was spinning. He understood there was something special about these people when he had seen them fight the New Wave Elite and win, but he wasn't prepared for this. As it was, it had taken him most of that day while they were sleeping to work up the nerve to approach them. He was ready to hear that they came from the Seventh Moon, that they were genetically engineered to be superhuman, that they were living weapons, even that they were espers with supernatural powers. But somehow, even accepting all that, he never imagined that the little boy now sleeping between him and the gentle giant Kichiku in the front seat of his truck as he was driving down the highway could in fact be a dragon. The other things, he had a scientific explanation for, he even had a hypothesis concerning the psychic abilities, but the manifestation of the dragon was beyond his ken. This was impossible, but he didn't know what he could do, they had just killed four operatives over the past few days that had previously been thought to be invincible. No matter how intimidating this situation had become, no matter how far in over his head he was, he still needed them. That's what being part of the resistance was, realizing that sometimes it really was bigger than you and you need to do whatever it took.

Shuurikou looked back at his passengers. Kichiku smiled, he was huge, twice the size of Shuurikou easily, pure muscle, and yet when he smiled, it showed his real personality, calm, warm and friendly. Douji also seemed impossibly harmless, a six year old boy barely a meter tall and only average weight for that height. And yet this tiny sleeping child had become a dragon so enormous that it dwarfed the Sakuma Dam. As Shuurikou thought about this, he realized, this gave him hope, clearly anything was possible.

After what seemed like an eternity on the road, they finally arrived at their destination. It appeared to be a forest of gingko biloba trees, but there was some sort of garage opening covered in moss. Shuurikou drove in, Hidariude and Keisei following on their bike, and they found their way into a vast parking garage and Shuurikou found his parking spot, Hidariude parked next to him. Shuurikou got out of the truck, Kichiku woke up Douji and the five gathered together for the walk out of the garage and into the great underground city where the Japanese resistance against the Seventh Moon was based. It was a lot like the previous town, only much bigger, and lit up much more brightly since the electricity had been turned back on. It actually kind of looked like Tokyo, only with a ceiling. People seemed to give them strange looks. Part of this was the way they were dressed as most people were dressed like the people in Tokyo, only much more ragged, and few if any were dressed like Shinto clergy, but mostly it was because of the usual differences, Hidariude's arm, Keisei's ears, and Kichiku's size.

"Welcome to Hiroshima." Shuurikou told his companions as they entered the city and walked down the streets looking at everything around them. "This city was destroyed in World War II nearly two hundred years ago by a nuclear bomb. It was the first time one was ever used in war time and not long after the second and last was dropped on Nagasaki west of here. In time people eventually rebuilt, but given the history, the Seventh Moon refuses to come here. My guess is they're afraid that residual radiation could adversely affect their soldiers."

"Does that mean we're in danger?" Hidariude asked nervously.

"From the radiation?" Shuurikou reassured them. "Nah. There were only trace amounts and we actually made a point of cleaning up everything that was left anyway. My parents developed technology that isolated radioactive isotopes and removed them. We can't destroy them of course, but they were stored and I found a way to make use of them, so it's really a non-issue. But the clean-up happened after World War III, so Seventh Moon doesn't know about it and we like to keep it that way."

"Why doesn't everyone live here?" Keisei asked. "Like the people in the last settlement, why didn't they move here?"

"It's a long journey, especially for people without vehicles or protection." Shuurikou answered. "There's no guarantee of food or water on the road, and even if you can find some, there are still scavengers and soldiers on patrol who can kill you. It's safer to just stay in one place unless you're forced to move."

It wasn't long before they encountered a stern looking woman wearing military fatigues. She addressed Shuurikou. "Ijirimawasu, what took you so long? And who are these people?" She was quick and cold, a personality not unlike their former superiors on Seventh Moon. She was in was in her twenties, and fairly attractive, but it was hard to tell from the way she carried herself. Her hair was tied back in a ponytail and she had an air of authority as if she were much older. The way she dressed hid her body it was hard to tell her form though she was clearly muscular.

"I was collecting some parts for the mecha and it took longer than expected." Shuurikou answered. "I ran into some New Wave Elite. Fortunately, I had some help from these people, Hidariude, Kichiku, Keisei and Douji. They are trained martial artists, Shinto mystics, and espers with psychokinetic abilities. They also happen to be rebels from Seventh Moon." The woman had given a look of mild disgust when Keisei was introduced to her, but her expression became much stronger and fiercer when she heard that they were from Seventh Moon. Before she could respond, Shuurikou quickly finished introductions. "This is Zokushou Suki, leader of the resistance against Seventh Moon."

Very quickly it became clear why her expression had changed. As the leader of the resistance against Seventh Moon, the last thing she wanted was a group of Seventh Moon soldiers in her headquarters, and that anger made her almost forget that Shuurikou had made sure to identify them as rebels on her side. The only thing that kept her from reaming him out where he stood was that in her impatience she had met him in the streets and did not want to make a public scene for fear that screaming about Seventh Moon would cause a panic.

Instead, she directed the group to follow her into a secure building where she would reprimand Shuurikou.

"What were you thinking bringing them here Sora?" Zokushou screamed at Shuurikou.

"I was thinking we need them!" Shuurikou shouted back with surprising conviction. Hidariude, Kichiku and Keisei admired his bravery, they didn't think they could have argued with Seventh Moon officers with his attitude. "They have killed three New Wave Elite since I met them, another five just before we were formally introduced, and took out their robotic shock troops as if they were nothing. We've been fighting for three years, ever since the Kanagawa Raid, and we haven't gotten anywhere. The New Wave Elite are too strong for us to fight, we need something more!"

"That's why you're working on the mecha, so we can use them to fight!" Zokushou reasoned.

"We only have two and there's no guarantee I'll ever get them to work." Shuurikou replied. "If it hadn't been for these people, I wouldn't have made it back with the parts I went for and I salvaged quite a few extra pieces from the robots they took out."

"They're from Seventh Moon, how can you be sure they're not really double agents who are just trying to get your trust and turn on us later?" Zokushou pointed out. "Do you even know the full extent of their abilities? They could be holding back to give you a false sense of security."

"I can assure you, they haven't held anything back." Shuurikou said, trying not to give away too much.

"Prove it." Zokushou demanded. "You know how to run diagnostics on them, take them to the hospital and run them through to get some hard data, and when I can be assured that I know the full extent of their abilities, I'll determine if it's safe to let them walk around freely."

Shuurikou led the espers out of the edifice and down the street to the hospital. It was a long silent march, Zokushou was so intimidating that they were all afraid to talk. Finally they reached the hospital, which actually was a hospital, though it was in a state of disrepair. Still, it was full of patients and doctors who hadn't made it to Tokyo or were left over from the war and were still desperately trying to attend to those in need for the past two decades. Shuurikou continued to lead the silent march to the abandoned neurological research wing. There simply wasn't any use for this part of the hospital, there were few maladies that could be treated here and fewer who even knew how to administer such treatment.

Hidariude finally broke the silence. "So, what was with those names she was calling you? Sora, and that long one..."

"Ijirimawasu, my real name." Shuurikou answered. "Ijirimawasu Sora. I suppose it's safe for you to call me Sora from now on. I'm sorry but Suki was right, I didn't know if I could trust you so I used Shuurikou as an alias. I couldn't use my real name because I do have a reputation as a known dissident. If you were enemies, you could have sold me out, so I had to be sure you were trustworthy. I trust you now. The truth is, I am a high ranking member of the resistance because I'm good with technology and machines and I have knowledge that can allow people to survive independent of Seventh Moon and choose to share it publicly. Seventh Moon doesn't want anyone to know about alternatives to them so they hunt down people like me and give us a choice, work for them or die. The resistance consists entirely of people who, like me, understand the truth that Seventh Moon is trying to control the world. Zokushou, which is what you should call her because she'll smack you up one side and down the other if you call her Suki, is the leader of the resistance because she knows the truth better than anybody. She was Han Toromi's daughter, but she didn't like his corporate greed and moved to Earth. She was behind the Kanagawa restoration, but she happened to be out of the village when it got attacked. She came back just after the attack and knew the truth right away. She tried to start the resistance right after that, but it wasn't until she rescued me from New World Enterprises in Tokyo that she got her first recruit. They got me when they found out I was working on converting old cars and motorcycles to run on alternative fuels and that I'd figured out how to do it without any training from their educational institutions. They are invested heavily on keeping people dependent on the fuels they make, so my work threatened their monopoly. Han Suki claimed to come back to the company so she could get near me, but once we escaped we became public enemies numbers one and two. She changed her name and we went on the run, attracting every other rebel who had enough of New World Enterprises. We travel between Hiroshima and Nagasaki when traveling is safe, but mostly we gather the resistance here and attempt strategic operations to fight Seventh Moon."

This was a lot to take in, but the espers understood the importance of Sora's confession. Every day it seemed that Seventh Moon was an even worse force to be reckoned with and they needed to do something. They made up their mind that they would do whatever Sora told them to do to prove themselves to the resistance, they needed to end this nightmare once and for all.

The whole time, Sora was collecting small electrodes, pads and wires. "These are for recording your brain waves. My theory is that I can collect some data and get a better understanding of how your psychic abilities work. I will need you to actually use your abilities to get a reading though."

"We can perform a kata." Hidariude volunteered. "It's a rehearsed series of movements that allows us to practice our skills without risking harm to anyone. We have arranged one that involves us using all of our abilities, and we have practiced it enough that we can guarantee no harm comes to anyone."

"But Douji does not know this kata so he cannot participate." Kichiku added.

"That's okay." Sora replied. "I don't want to include him anyway. I don't know how to test his powers and I'm afraid it would scare Zokushou to even attempt it. She doesn't know he has powers, so we'll pretend that all the boasting I made about your abilities only applies to you three. So, the way this will work is I'm going to stick these to your head and you will perform your kata and then I will interpret the data for Zokushou, hopefully she will be satisfied with the results. You will perform your kata in an observation room where Zokushou, some doctors and other curious members of the resistance will watch."

They nodded in agreement and let Sora place the nodes. Kichiku didn't mind too much because he was bald, but attaching the nodes through Hidariude and Keisei's hair was a little more difficult. Keisei couldn't imagine how hard it would be to clean the adhesive out her hair and was hoping she wouldn't have to cut it. Sora led them to the observation room and directed them inside. He closed the door and took Douji to the audience hall.

The observation room seemed eerily familiar to Hidariude and Kichiku, it was just like the rooms where they had trained back on Seventh Moon. This made them feel uneasy, yet at the same time, they felt nostalgic about all the training they had done and were confident they could perform without any difficulty. Keisei was comfortable enough with her sparring partners to follow their lead.

Hidariude took his stance to prepare for an attack from Keisei. When the attack came, he parried with his sword just in time, blocking Keisei's fans. She somersaulted over his head to attack him from the other side. He quickly turned around to continue the duel. As he turned to block her fans, he found that Keisei was simply holding still. He knew immediately what was going on and in one movement he turned to look behind him to see the paper bomb she had left and jumped out of the way as Keisei said "Kayakujutsu detonate!" Kichiku then came at him from his other side. He blocked Kichiku's fist with the flat of his blade just in time. Keisei gave no quarter as she continued her attack and Hidariude had to block with his cyber blades, using his long blade to parry one fan and then twisting his claws to push the other out of the way. Hidariude then brought his cyber blade to cross with his sword and unleashed an electric attack on Kichiku. Kichiku started his jump as Hidariude's attention returned to him and just barely dodged as lightning struck the spot he stood on only a second before. As he landed from the jump, he punched the ground, causing a tremor that split the ground. Hidariude jumped out of the way before the splitting ground caused him to lose his balance, but Keisei wasn't quite so lucky. She didn't dodge by jumping, but still had the grace to perform a split, maintaining balance on either side of the fissure. She drew another scroll and threw a fireball at Kichiku. Rather than dodging, he blocked the attack with his bare hands. Hidariude, Keisei, and Kichiku came to a three-way draw in their sparring match, Hidariude was blocking Keisei's fan with his sword while striking Kichiku with his cyber blade, Kichiku was holding Hidariude's cyber blade with one hand and punching Keisei with the other, and Keisei was blocking Kichiku's attack while striking Hidariude and closing the loop. At this point they had done everything they needed to do so they withdrew their weapons and bowed to each other.

Sora came back in and took them back to the first lab and removed the nodes. He then directed them to yet another room. "I'm sorry guys, but you'll have to be quarantined in here until I get the results of this test. I'll try to get this done as quickly as possible." Sora closed the door behind him as he left them. Hidariude and Keisei had flashbacks to when they were in the prison cells back on Seventh Moon, and held each other feeling comfort that at least this time they were together. Kichiku simply sat in the corner and meditated. At times like these, his Zen attitude was kind of annoying.

As promised, Sora did not take long. He returned with a clipboard after a few hours and took them back to the observation room so that he could read off the results to Zokushou. "The results as predicted showed that they do in fact have abnormal brain activity. They showed some uniformity in terms of sensory input, their brains actually seem to be detecting their surroundings by a sort of echolocation only instead of sound waves they use their brain waves. Unlike most people their brainwaves are not actually limited to their brain, they are able to generate a field that surrounds them. This level of activity peaks during combat and otherwise seems negligible. I would deduce that it is primarily sensory, and they have limited ability to affect their surroundings. As we witnessed they do have psychokinetic abilities but these abilities are extremely limited. Hidariude seems to be the weakest in this regard, his abilities stem mostly from an electro plaque in his arm that powers his cybernetics. Through rigorous discipline he can manipulate this electricity beyond its normal confines, but he is only able to use his own natural electric charge along his own metal conduits and he loses this control once the charge no longer has contact with him. What he demonstrated earlier was the full extent of his electrokinesis, and it is doubtful he has any potential to ever become more powerful. Kichiku is the next most powerful; his brain waves actually resonate with seismic waves, which allow him to manipulate the earth by extending these waves to generate tremors. However, like Hidariude, he requires a physical connection to his medium to maintain this resonance, if his connection with the ground is broken his powers fail. Keisei seems to be the most powerful, her brain waves resonate with the infrared spectrum, or heat waves. She has superior abilities because she can manipulate fire without touching the medium, but she is not able to generate fire without a combustible substance to ignite. This seems to be her only limitation though, once she has access to fire, she can manipulate it to her will by extending an electromagnetic field of a very specific frequency and amplitude. In this way fire becomes an extension of her body. This seems to be because her brain waves come from higher brain function, including the cerebrum, instead of merely the cerebellum as with the other two."

Zokushou took a moment to consider the findings. She crossed her arms, held her chin in her hand, and tilted her head as she looked at them. "Very well, Keisei and Kichiku are free to go as long as Keisei stays away from anything flammable and they both avoid using their powers. As for Hidariude, I trust him as much as the other two, but for good measure, examine that arm before you let him go."

Again they cooperated. Sora took Hidariude back to the lab and pulled out his tool kit and some medical examination goggles and rubber gloves. He asked Hidariude to sit still and put his arm out. His first step was to apply a local anesthetic for good measure in case what he did actually hurt. He used a screwdriver to pry open the arm at the seams. The chassis looped around connecting on either side of the long blade shaft. Once it came loose, he disconnected it from the wrist and pulled it back against Hidariude's elbow. He saw pretty much everything he needed to see right away. There were two metal rods in place of the bones that should have been there, the ulna was stationary while the radius was rigged to rotate around it in a semicircle. In addition to that there were cables coated with red and grey plastic that connected nerves and muscles to activate full range of motion in the hand. There were also a series of extremely tiny wires connected in a meshwork to the chassis, which Sora figured was an artificial nerve matrix that allowed Hidariude to feel through his artificial arm as if it were his real arm. He could see how the blades were connected with extra wires and these wires had caused some swollen nodes in the connective tissue at the elbow. In a normal human, this could be a problem, but for Hidariude, it was clear this augmented anatomy was a necessary adaptation. Sora took some photos and did some scans to collect some data, then explained to Hidariude. "I am a mechanic, and as long as I have the chance to look at the inner workings of your arm, I want some records so I can figure out how to repair it if it gets damaged." Then he closed the arm back up and sealed it using a very small blowtorch. His skill was so fine that it looked as if he had never opened the arm to begin with.

Meanwhile, the others were waiting outside. As Zokushou was waiting to hear from her subordinate, she looked over Keisei. She did not like this woman. She was beautiful and shapely, her red silk kimono was rather form fitting and showed off her figure quite well. She was slender yet muscular, rather busty, and yet completely balanced. She seemed too perfect, and the fact that she could fight with a giant and a cyborg as if they were equals demonstrated a power that actually seemed more significant than her pyrokinesis. Zokushou would not admit it, but she was envious, and afraid that Keisei would take her place. She was strong and she led her people, mostly men, by presenting her strength, but if Keisei could present herself as stronger she could lose her standing.

The espers might have been able to sense what Zokushou was thinking, but right now, all of their thoughts were on Hidariude. They could sense that he was okay, but still, they hadn't been apart since they'd all met for the first time at the shrine. He was Keisei's husband and Kichiku's brother, they were a family and they belonged together. Keisei, Kichiku and Douji breathed a collective sigh of relief when Sora brought Hidariude out. "I'll make a copy of the report for you later chief, but there wasn't anything unexpected, he's safe. Are they cleared to go now?"

"Welcome to the resistance." Zokushou kept her stone cold stare on them as if to say, "I'll be watching you."

Sora led them through town and showed them the Hiroshima Gokoku Shrine that had been all but abandoned since World War Three but happened to survive over the years. "You'll be staying here the night, but first I want to show you something else." He led them down the street to an extremely dilapidated building, even worse than the others. It clearly showed wartime damage in addition to decay. "This is the Genbaku Dome. It was made in memorial of the bomb drop back in World War II. Traditionally it was supposed to represent peace and should be the last place to store a weapon, but it's also the only place big enough for the mecha."

As he opened the door, they looked up in awe at an enormous robot that towered over all of them. It was over four stories tall and its foot alone was larger than all four espers put together. It appeared to have its own proportionate guns and swords. There was no doubt that this monstrosity could easily take on the New Wave Elite. "I present to you, the mecha Hiroshima."

Chapter 12

Hidariude was standing alone just outside of the shrine. It was quiet except for a strangely familiar voice chanting and praying from inside. He reached for his sword, but he could not find it. "It's okay, just come inside." He had no idea why this voice answered his unspoken question but now that he heard some specific words that he knew, he realized how impossible the voice was. Still he did as he was told and entered the shrine. He saw an old man sitting in the middle of the floor with his back to the door. Hidariude slowly approached the man, and then walked around to face him. He could not believe his eyes. "Hello Hidariude. It's been a while." Ryu greeted him.

"Master Ryu, how is this possible?" Hidariude asked with great surprise. "Didn't you..."

"Die?" Ryu completed the thought Hidariude could not bring himself to say. "Yes, I did. But now I am your ancestral kami and I have come to you through Shinryuu Masamune. I want to let you know that I am still with you and your brother, and as long as you keep this sword, I will fight with you, you are not alone."

"Isn't Shinryuu Masamune a Yoshiro for Shinryuu or Kyutsume?"

"Yes, but as we have discussed, the spirit of Kyutsume has found a new vessel, and as I'm sure you've realized, Shinryuu has as well. So there's a bit of a vacancy in this particular Yoshiro. Besides I'm also spending some of my time in the afterlife with a few other souls, such as your mother."

"My mother? You knew her?"

"Of course." Ryu suddenly realized there was something else he had never discussed with Hidariude. His appearance grew younger until he looked exactly like Hidariude. "This is how I looked when I first met your mother at the Shrine of the Golden Dragon. I am your father, and Kichiku's as well. You really are brothers, both in spirit and in blood. Seventh Moon created you but even they cannot create something from nothing. You are our children who were changed by them into something more. But no matter what, you are my sons, and I will love you even from the next life." Now his appearance returned to what Hidariude was familiar with.

Hidariude was a little stunned, yet he was so used to thinking of Ryu as his father, it didn't seem like a huge surprise. "Easy for you to drop this on me now, since you're free to disappear into the afterlife. Whatever happened to mom?"

Ryu hung his head and closed his eyes. "She passed away when you were born. In fact, I was told you did not make it either, and for many years I didn't know you were alive. When you were born without an arm, they wanted you for their own purposes. But when I saw your face, I knew you were my son." Ryu looked at his son and smiled. "Well, it was good to see you again. Tell Kichiku, Keisei and Douji that I am proud of what you are all doing, fighting the good fight. And always remember that I am with you." With that, Ryu got up and walked back out the front door of the shrine and a bright light shined out from the door.

As the light faded from Hidariude's vision, he woke up from his dream in the Gokoku Shrine, lying next to Keisei as he did every night. He looked over to his sword lying on the floor on his other side. He whispered to himself "Maybe I've been working too hard with Sora."

Ever since Sora had shown them the mecha, he had them helping him restore it to working condition, which mostly meant they hauled the spare parts from his truck to the Genbaku Dome so he could use them in repairs. Sora explained that mecha were the weapons of World War III. Every country that had enough resources to make them did make them. For energy, they used the cores of nuclear weapons, so many of them had been named after the bombs they were made from. After the destruction of Hiroshima and Nagasaki in Japan, it had been deemed irresponsible to use bombs and so they used giant robots to create the same level of destruction only more controlled and without the radioactive fallout. Unfortunately, the cost of creating these robots in haste had led to a war that could not be sustained. Every last resource of technology, materials, and energy had gone into the mecha, all with the hope that the victor would take all the remaining resources from the defeated nations. Since every nation that had any resources worth taking put those resources into their weapons, the prizes of war were also the weapons themselves put into war. The war was reduced to an elimination tournament between the robots, though no one even realized it until the last battle ended and all nations had been reduced to the same state of poverty. There was no prize to be claimed, the soldiers returned home empty handed and global civilization was doomed to collapse. It was only then that New World Enterprises had begun exporting from the Seventh Moon to the Earth. Meanwhile the mecha had been left in the outlands waiting for someone to put them back together. There were very few in Japan, but Sora was pinning his hopes on getting at least one to function again so it could be used against Seventh Moon.

Hidariude, Kichiku and Keisei were amazed by Sora's engineering skills. They watched in awe as he climbed and jumped around the mecha with tools in one hand, requesting parts as he moved, retrieving them and placing them in almost the same movement without breaking momentum. They realized that they were seeing him as he saw them when they fought, functioning on a whole separate level that simply could not be fathomed by the observer. They truly had no idea what he was doing, but they knew that he was more than aware of what he was doing. His mind was two steps ahead of his body, grabbing what appeared to be random scraps and put the pieces in place as if they were meant to go there all along. He had a sense of intuition comparable to the espers' psychic abilities.

"So it can use the swords and guns like a giant person?" Hidariude asked Sora while he was working on the arms.

"Yes, and I'm sure the swords would be better used if it were piloted by someone who actually knew how to use swords." Sora replied while looking at Hidariude. "Of course, one would also have to know how to operate the machine, so this will be complicated. As for the guns, they're no good without ammunition, and these guns were emptied in this mecha's last battle. In fact, that's probably why it lost. Anyway, I'll need to get more ammunition, and since nobody makes this stuff anymore, the only choice is for me to make it myself."

"What would you make it from?" Kichiku asked.

"From the leftover scrap I'm taking out." Sora answered while patting the pile of scrap. "Once I'm sure I've got enough parts to get this thing working again, I'll melt down the rest to make bullets. The guns will have to be a last resort, we can't just shoot everything knowing there's no guarantee we'll ever have more bullets."

"But will you get this thing working soon?" Zokushou's voice startled all of them as she walked in on the scene. The espers could normally sense her coming, but they were distracted by Sora's work and they had relaxed their senses since they entered Hiroshima. Since she had insisted they weren't a threat and the city was safe enough they enjoyed the break from the hypertension they had gotten used to.

"I really think I've actually fixed everything here." Sora answered. "I just need to make a few more adjustments and then it should be ready for a test run tomorrow." Just then something blew in the mecha making a loud noise and releasing smoke. "Make that next week." He immediately jumped back in the mecha to repair the damage.

She looked at Kichiku. "It's a good thing he has you to help him with the heavy lifting. He seems to have been making a lot more progress since he got back with you."

"I just drag the big stuff here from his truck." Kichiku said modestly. "I really think the key to his improvement is the parts he brought back, though how he knows where to put everything, I'll never know."

Zokushou nodded to Kichiku then turned to Hidariude. "He told me he got some insight from your cyber arm. He says having an actual cyborg around has inspired him and it's all falling into place."

Hidariude was also humble. "I'm glad I could help in some way, but for the first time in a long time, possibly ever, I feel useless next to him."

"I'm sure you will contribute plenty during the test runs." Zokushou assured them. "He's a great mechanic but nobody's piloted one of these things in twenty years so before this is of any use to us, he'll need to learn some combat movement. Ever trained a robot to fight?"

Keisei decided to take a turn and very confidently answered. "There's a first time for everything."

Zokushou seemed to ignore Keisei and finished her conversation with the men. "Well, keep up the good work, keep me posted and let me know when he's done."

After Zokushou left, Keisei commented on her attitude. "Did anyone else notice that she ignored me?" Hidariude and Kichiku nodded in agreement.

Sora happened to climb back out of the mecha just in time to hear Keisei's question. "She enjoys being queen bee. She started the resistance and everyone has followed her since. Most of the higher ranking members are men. You're the first powerful woman to show up and threaten that."

"But I don't want to take over her organization." Keisei replied. 'I just want to stop Seventh Moon so we can go home in peace."

"It doesn't matter whether you want to or not, in her head any strong woman is a threat." Sora explained. "Haven't you noticed the way guys around here look at you?"

Keisei rolled her eyes. "Yeah, but I can't help that. I was made for that, and I hate it. It's why I like Hidariude and Kichiku, they're the only guys I know who don't look at me that way."

Sora was confused. "I thought you and Hidariude were a couple?"

"We are, but not for the reasons you think." Hidariude told Sora with a tone that let him know that he shouldn't press the issue.

"Well, anyway, you guys may have yourselves all figured out, but she still thinks you're a distraction."

"If you understand all that, why didn't you tell us before?" Keisei asked.

"I honestly didn't think it was going to be an issue." Sora answered. "I was more concerned with you being an asset and I hoped she would see it the same way. You guys may have ESP, but I don't and for the rest of us, that's just not something we can prepare for."

Keisei thought for a moment. "I'll go talk to her. If we're going to work together, there can't be even the slightest animosity between us. Besides, Sora's doing all the real work here anyway."

Keisei went off after Zokushou. She caught up to her while she was still walking down the street. She knew what Sora had told her, but she also understood that such a proud woman would not respond to an approach that was too direct. "So I think we got off on the wrong foot, is there any way we can start over?" Zokushou kept walking, still completely ignoring Keisei. Keisei looked over Zokushou, she seemed to be an attractive woman, a very muscular build, just well hidden under fatigues and dirt she hadn't bothered to clean off. "When was the last time you had a day at the spa?"

Zokushou turned on Keisei with an unmistakably angry face. "I'm in charge of a resistance effort to liberate the Earth, or at least Japan, from Seventh Moon. I do not have time for a spa!"

Keisei actually expected this and was unfazed, then continued to talk to Zokushou. "I understand you have the weight of the world on your shoulders, but that is exactly why you need to relax once in a while. Your tone tells me you haven't had a day off since you started this organization. How long has that been?"

"Three years." Zokushou admitted while rubbing her neck with her hand. "Three long years. But the people need me."

"And they need you to have a clear mind." Keisei replied. "I come from a place where my kind works hard every waking moment. It was very refreshing to finally be free and relax for the first time when I got away from that.

It's great that you work so hard, but if you don't stop, take a step back, and take some time to just think about what you're doing, you may not be helping anybody. You're tense and it's making everyone around you tense too. Just take one day off okay? I learned some old herbalism secrets from Master Ryu that will make you feel a lot better."

It really did sound good to Zokushou, but she didn't want to give Keisei the satisfaction. "Just what do you think you can do for me?"

Keisei's ESP let her know what Zokushou was really thinking and played along. "I'll collect everything we need at the shrine, meet me there tomorrow okay." Keisei then ran off before Zokushou could say no.

Keisei went above ground to look for herbs; the things she needed wouldn't be in the greenhouses or cultivated fields, she would have to check the outskirts of town. She sensed some scavengers coming while she foraged, but she hid from them and they went on by. Or at least she thought they did. One of the scavengers was a very skilled tracker who noticed her footprints and the remnants of plants she had harvested and knew there was somebody around. They walked off a bit and then hid themselves to wait for Keisei to come out and show herself. As she stepped out to collect some more herbs, the tracker made his approach.

'Well ain't you purty?" The scavenger said before his partners pounced on her. She planted her hands on the ground and kicked both of his partners, and then bounced her feet off of them and used the momentum to kick the speaker with both feet. She gathered up her herbs and returned to the city before they could regain consciousness. By the time they did wake up, they knew better than to follow her; she really hurt them, and that was when they ambushed her, they didn't want to know what she would be like with preparation.

The next day, Keisei was preparing her herbal treatments and putting the finishing touches on her makeshift spa. Hidariude, Kichiku and Douji went off to assist Sora, leaving her alone when Zokushou joined her. "Welcome to my spa. Please put on this robe." Keisei offered an old but soft plain white robe for Zokushou to wear during her treatment, then she went to another room for some privacy to change her clothes. While Zokushou was changing, Keisei lit some candles to create a pleasant ambient aroma. A few moments later, Zokushou came back out wearing the robe and Keisei directed her to an ergonomic chair. Once she sat down, Keisei began to apply a cream to Zokushou's face. Once she was done with the face, Keisei began applying lotion to Zokushou's hands and feet, massaging them as she went. She brought out small scissors and trimmed Zokushou's nails and filed them with an emery board. After all this, the cream on Zokushou's face had time to settle in and do its work, so Keisei brought out a basin and a pitcher of water to rinse off the face mask and wash Zokushou's hair. Keisei had made some shampoo with lavender to help Zokushou relax. In spite of herself, Zokushou was relaxing and let herself go while she rolled over for a back rub.

Once Keisei had done all the hard work of getting Zokushou to relax, she had one last thing for them to share. She took Zokushou by the hand to a hot spring where they could both sit in the water and relax. Keisei went first, removing her robe before stepping into the water. Keisei was very comfortable with her body, having spent most of her life naked, but it was a very different situation for Zokushou. First of all, she was surprised to see that Keisei had fur covering her breasts and pelvis, so being naked wasn't quite the same for her. As Keisei sat in the water and let the heat soothe her muscles that were so sore from the journey she had been on for the past few weeks, she noticed Zokushou still standing by the water's edge somewhat nervous. "Come on in, the water's perfect."

"It's not the water." Zokushou said nervously. "It's um... I don't know about taking off my robe in front of you. I'm not really comfortable being...you know...naked...in front of others."

Keisei's ears drooped, she was confused. "I'm sorry, I've been naked and around naked women most of my life, I don't know what the big deal is."

Zokushou felt silly, she didn't quite know how to explain how she would look different, but at the same time, she realized Keisei really did not understand and she would just look more foolish. With a sigh, she removed her robe and stepped into the water, trying to cover herself with her arms.

Keisei's ears perked up with surprise, she really wasn't expecting what she saw. Keisei had seen naked women before, but they were all like her, with furry parts, she had never seen a woman without fur. Zokushou actually looked more like a man to Keisei because of this, and yet, the shape was still like a woman. Keisei had known for a while that she had been made to be different than normal girls, but it wasn't until now, when she saw a truly bare female form, that she truly understood how different she was.

They sat in silence relaxing and enjoying the break from the rigors of the resistance and survival in the outlands. "I forgot how good this can feel." Zokushou said. "I haven't done this since I lived with my father."

"How long has that been?" Keisei asked.

Zokushou sighed. "Since I found out he was making people to kill for him and to serve him and his cronies. I was only a teenager when my mom caught him with a girl. She was afraid I'd be next, so she took me to Earth. What she didn't know was that that same day, I saw the boys training. It was scary to see such young men being so violent. After I got to Earth I grew up in Tokyo and saw how different things were, and all because of what my father did on Seventh Moon. It made me sick to know that paradise came at such a cost, boys being raised to be killers, girls raised to be slaves. I was a part of it, living off of money my dad made running this whole thing. I had to do something, but nobody wanted to believe the truth until I met Sora. He introduced me to the outlanders who needed our help. I've never looked back."

"I understand, that's what drives Hidariude and Kichiku, the guilt that this is all somehow our fault." Keisei replied. "But we each have our own path, and once we have chosen to go against Seventh Moon and stick to our goals, it's all right to take a day off every now and then. The worst part of Seventh Moon was how weary we got from serving our superiors until we fell asleep and by the time we woke up, we were starting over again. We're fighting for the freedom not to be that way, and if we don't take a little time for ourselves every now and then, it's no better than the way things were before."

"I guess you're right, I never thought about it that way." Zokushou sighed again and stretched, almost coming out of the water.

Just then two men walked by and saw them. One whistled and Zokushou shrieked a shrill cry, blushed and ducked under the water. Keisei immediately sensed her discomfort and decided to deal with the men. She pulled herself out of the water, her wet fur sticking to her body. She leaned on one hand and using the other hand, crooked her finger in a come hither gesture. The man who whistled pointed to himself as if to ask, "Who? Me?" Keisei nodded back and he approached. As soon as he got close enough for her to reach, she grabbed his arm and in one swift movement twisted him around, holding him in a very painful position. "A gentleman respects a woman's privacy. Move along." She pushed him away and he and his comrade moved along very quickly. "That's how you handle a situation like that." Keisei told Zokushou.

Zokushou began to pull herself back up above the water. "That's what really gets me. How do you do that?

I'm so embarrassed they caught me, but you didn't skip a beat. How do you do that?"

"Well, I didn't have much choice." Keisei replied. "I first learned to fight on Seventh Moon when guys mistreated me. When I escaped, I fought five guys naked and unarmed. There's a bit of an instinct in me to fight even when I'm vulnerable. That's the trick you need to learn. I can sense you're not comfortable being naked, and I remember being vulnerable like that. But that's what they want. When I learned to fight properly with Hidariude and Kichiku, I found out that the key is to get any advantage you can. If they sense you're weak, they take advantage of that. But if you don't let it be your weakness you can catch them by surprise. Of course those guys thought I was going to be an easy target here, and that's why I got the drop on him. Turn your weakness into strength, bait them in by letting them think they have control, but don't ever give in."

"Easier said than done."

"Meet me back in the shrine tomorrow." Keisei said. Before Zokushou could respond, she shook herself dry, put her kimono and sandals back on and walked off like she did the day before.

The next day, Zokushou showed up at the shrine as Keisei had asked her to. She was surprised to find Keisei was naked. "Strip down to your underwear."

Zokushou was shocked. "What?"

"You heard me, down to your skivvies missy." Keisei pointed to the ground in a rather clear gesture demonstrating where she wanted her clothes to go. "You have an issue with confidence, you sense I'm stronger because I have an advantage, and that advantage is that I can fight naked. If you can learn to get comfortable fighting naked, it eliminates my advantage and restores your confidence. Now clearly, my naked body looks a little different than yours, so let's settle for getting in your underwear."

Zokushou found that this actually made sense, so she stripped down to a sports bra and panties. She was then surprised to be ambushed by Hidariude and Kichiku who were both wearing boxer shorts. She dodged just in time. "What is the meaning of this?"

"You're even less comfortable around men than when you're around me when you're naked." Keisei explained. "I have sparred with both Hidariude and Kichiku plenty of times. For you to prove yourself my equal, you need to have the confidence to fight all of us at once."

"But why are they naked?" Zokushou asked.

"Why not?" Keisei replied. "When we fight, we focus on the fight itself. None of us are any stronger or weaker right now than when we are wearing clothes. Look at their faces, do they look like they're afraid or concerned about being naked? No, because they are warriors, they fight under any circumstances. Clothed, naked, armored, wounded, the true warrior fights with everything they have and doesn't make excuses for being weak. If you're impressed by our psychic abilities, don't be, they are only the result of extreme training, pushing ourselves to the limit and beyond. Your only weakness is the one you put on yourself. Turn it into strength and you too can be invincible. Until you own that as a part of yourself you're no good to us or anyone else in the resistance as a leader."

"How dare you talk to me like that!" Zokushou screamed back at Keisei. She did not like Keisei's tone at all. She reached out and punched at Keisei.

Keisei blocked, "Good, that's what we need." She encouraged Zokushou to continue fighting, and as they traded punches and kicks, Hidariude and Kichiku got in on the action as well. They could have easily defeated her at any point but instead they used their ESP to stay one step behind her and let her have the advantage. It wasn't long before she figured this out, and for a second she was offended that they were letting her win. But then Zokushou realized something, these were the most powerful fighters she had ever met and they were letting her win to boost her confidence. That was saying something about their loyalty; that they respected her enough to submit to her authority. Once she realized this she became much more confident and started fighting with more force, and the espers reacted with increasing force to keep her going. They could feel a new energy in her and soon all four were moving like a well-oiled machine.

Just when it seemed like Zokushou was going to win, they were interrupted by Sora. "Zokushou I...oh sorry I didn't know I was interrupting." He held his hands up in front of his eyes when he realized they were all in their underwear. "Why aren't any of you wearing clothes?"

Zokushou looked at the others. Keisei nodded, and Zokushou understood. She walked over to Sora, and pulled his hands down from his face. She smiled letting him know she was okay with him seeing her in her underwear. He had never seen her in her underwear, or out of her fatigues at all for that matter. He had thought about it, but actually seeing it was something new and different. After a moment she nudged his head up by the chin to meet her eyes. "What's so important?"

Sora regained his composure rather quickly. "The mecha is ready to go."

"Good we'll have a party to celebrate." They were all a little shocked to hear her say this. No one, not even Sora had ever known her to be in any kind of party mood. "We need to relax every now and then. Let's go get the good sake." She walked back to the others with a bit of a saunter. Sora couldn't help watching her butt. Suddenly he realized everyone was looking at him looking at her and he found himself a little embarrassed. He blushed and ran back to the dome.

"I think he liked what he saw." Keisei said. They all broke out in laughter.

That night everyone was gathered in the Genbaku Dome wearing their best attire, which wasn't that great in most cases considering how poor most of the locals were. Zokushou was wearing a silk dress and looked gorgeous after a makeover from Keisei. Everyone was stunned by how great she looked, having been used to her wearing fatigues and keeping her hair tied back in a ponytail.

"Everyone, I thank you for joining us here today for this celebration. After three long years of hard work, Ijirimawasu Sora has finally gotten the Hiroshima mecha functional again. Today we will see our greatest weapon in the war against Seventh Moon in operation, observe now the beacon of hope for the resistance!" She raised her glass and every member of the resistance cheered.

Sora climbed up into the cockpit of the mecha and activated it. Everyone cleared out of the way as it walked out of the dome and into an area that had been cleared for test runs and demonstrations. After a few test punches and kicks, the mecha climbed out a special door made just for it to exit to the surface. As it reached the surface, the scavengers Keisei had encountered a couple days earlier were stunned by what they saw and decided to leave the Hiroshima area forever.

Meanwhile, the espers noticed a large pile of folded paper. "What's this?" Kichiku asked.

Douji answered. "Origami cranes. You get a wish if you fold one thousand of them. I wished for victory."

It seemed that right at this moment that the wind picked up the cranes and then blew away out the exit passage. It appeared that they actually flew out the passage, and for a moment, the espers could swear they saw the flock of paper cranes take on the shape of Ryu, just long enough for him to wink before the cranes came apart and dispersed into the night sky.

Chapter 13

By the next day, Zokushou was back in her fatigues with her hair in a ponytail again. She hadn't forgotten what Keisei had taught her, she just realized that she was most comfortable as a military commander and looking the part. Keisei didn't care as long as she stopped being suspicious of her and her friends.

The period of comfort was short lived however, as the resistance intelligence network brought news of two developments. First, it seemed that Seventh Moon was attempting to take back Sakuma Dam. Second, it seemed that there was a new threat coming from Kyushu Island. They didn't know much about either one, although it seemed that Kyushu had some fruit that was making the residents much stronger and they were just now coming to the Honshu and it seemed to be that their intent was to take over.

Zokushou was very quickly decisive. The mecha from Hiroshima would be taken to Sakuma to defend and secure the dam while the espers would accompany her and Sora to Nagasaki so that Sora could complete repairs on the mecha there and then investigate the matter of the fruit there. Sora gave a pilot a crash course in how to operate the mecha and sent him on his way with a small back-up force to maintain operations inside in the dam. While Sora was training the pilot, Hidariude, Keisei, Kichiku, Douji and Zokushou gathered supplies they would need for their trip to Nagasaki. By the time they had everything loaded up into Sora's truck, there was just enough room for Kichiku and Douji to squeeze in the back. As Douji tried to squeeze into his spot, Zokushou tried to stop him. "Oh no, you're too young for this, you need to stay here in Hiroshima where it's safe."

"He goes where I go. We are a family and we stay together." Kichiku responded with a tone of finality, his words as hard and immovable as he was. Hidariude and Keisei nodded in agreement as they put on their helmets and got on their motorcycle. Sora had just joined them in time to hear the beginning of the conversation and nodded in agreement with the espers. Zokushou wasn't sure why, but it seemed to be pretty clear that if she was going to get cooperation from the espers, she needed to accept Douji would come along with them. She still thought it was dangerous to allow the boy to come with them under such dangerous circumstances, but she relented.

Sora took the wheel driving his truck with Kichiku and Douji riding in the back and Hidariude driving his motorcycle with Keisei riding along following them. At first Zokushou was uncomfortable because she didn't know the others very well, but Sora was calm and focused on leading the way to Nagasaki and the others just quietly followed. Kichiku and Douji were actually meditating and communing with Hidariude and Keisei telepathically. Hidariude was trying to make sure he kept pace with Sora so he had to keep his conscious focus on driving and only passively listened to his fellow espers.

The espers didn't exactly speak in words telepathically, they weren't quite advanced enough for that. It was more a mix of shared emotions, abstract thoughts forming simultaneously in four minds at once. They had all developed their abilities together at the same time, so they were used to each other, but if someone new were able to join in, they'd probably be shocked and confused. They mostly reminisced in a dreamlike state about the shrine where they used to live. It seemed real enough, especially when they could truly relax and abandon reality, but they always knew sooner or later they would have to wake up and face the real world far from home. It did, however, remind them why they were fighting, to go back home and never have to live in fear of Seventh Moon ever again.

While the espers were passing the time on the open road half living in their own minds, Zokushou observed them with curiosity. She was completely unaware of what they were doing and it looked like the two in the truck were sleeping. "What are they doing back there?"

"I don't know." Sora answered. "Probably a Shinto ritual."

Zokushou laughed. "Shinto, what good are those ancient gods anyway? They sure haven't been helping us so far. Where were they in Kanagawa three years ago? Or twenty years ago during the plague? And what about what my father is doing? Did the kami of the moon turn a blind eye to the one trying to usurp his throne?"

Sora was a little surprised at the venom in his compatriot's voice. "Wow, you really have lost faith haven't you?"

Zokushou gritted her teeth. "It's hard to believe in god when your father is the devil."

"How do you feel about the espers then?" Sora asked. "They were created by your father. Does that make them monsters or do you believe that they are capable of redemption?"

"I suppose if the devil's daughter can find redemption, anyone can." Zokushou postulated. "Or perhaps I'm just siding with the lesser of two evils and hoping we all go down in a blaze of glory."

Sora laughed dryly. "I know you don't really mean that. You want us to achieve victory. But then what?"

"I don't want to get my hopes up thinking about that." Zokushou replied. "First let's just focus on bringing this to an end, and cross the bridge of victory when we come to it if any of us are alive to do it."

Sora did not like the negative direction this conversation was taking and decided to continue driving in silence. After driving all day they stopped with the mountains between them and Nagasaki just on the horizon. They agreed they would save the mountain pass for the next day. They were all quite hungry so they stopped for a meal. They had very meager rations, mostly rice cakes and water. They did have some dried vegetables as well, but just enough to add some flavor. After they ate they set up camp for the night. Kichiku volunteered for first watch since he hadn't spent a lot of energy riding around all day and could afford to just sleep in the truck the next day. Keisei felt she was in a similar situation and volunteered to take second watch while

Kichiku caught up on his sleep. The next morning as the sun rose, both were ready as everyone else and they got back in the truck and on the motorcycle and went off into the mountains.

At first the mountain pass was quiet and empty. The espers felt nostalgic, as it reminded them of their mountain home. However, this sense of peace gave way to a sense of dread as they detected a threat looming over them. They knew exactly what the threat was, two different assailants coming from different directions. Kichiku stood up in the truck in preparation of the fight to come and Keisei prepared to stand on the motorcycle for the other threat to come at a different angle.

A ball of white fell out of nowhere attempting to crush the truck and strand the travelers, but Kichiku jumped and threw himself into the ball sending both hurtling into the road ahead. At the exact same moment Keisei jumped on top of Kichiku while he was at the height of his jump and bounced off his back into the air. Sora swerved the truck to avoid them and was surprised to see in the rearview mirror that the white ball was actually Yeti, an NWE soldier the size of Kichiku and covered from head to toe in white hair. Meanwhile, Keisei was attacking Yeti's partner Tengu, a soldier with sharp features and black feathery wings, in midair.

Keisei and Tengu had a complicated fight. Tengu had the advantage of flight which meant that if he could shake off Keisei, she would fall to her doom, but at the same time flying was harder with her trying to attack him. He decided his best move was to try to get as high as he could and then dive bomb and twist at the last moment to land on her. Keisei sensed what he was doing and let him rise up, and then when he started his dive bomb she waited until the last moment and then jumped off just before he performed his evasive twist. Tengu crashed into the ground, though his evasive maneuver helped him to avoid too much injury. As he got himself to his feet he found Hidariude pointing a sword at him.

Meanwhile, Yeti was grappling with Kichiku. Yeti had tried to prepare tactical advantages by taking time to familiarize himself with the territory and use everything around him to his advantage. He moved Kichiku towards cracks and loose stones to throw off his balance and lose his footing. Kichiku could sense these traps and carefully stepped around the pitfalls, even manipulating his opponent to fall into his own traps. When Yeti was thrown off balance he picked up rocks and threw them at Kichiku. This was a flawed method of attack since with Kichiku's geokinesis, he simply struck the rocks with seismic force from his fists forcing them to explode back towards Yeti.

Both of the soldiers realized that they were outmatched by their opponents, but suspected that they might have a better shot if they switched opponents. Tengu desperately launched himself into the air and dive bombed Kichiku. At the same time, Yeti lifted a large rock in each hand and threw them at Hidariude and Keisei. To Yeti's dismay, Hidariude was able to slice through the flying boulder with his sword and Keisei jumped on the other rock and brought herself into the air to drop on Yeti.

He blocked Keisei's attacks and immediately turned his attention on Hidariude.

Kichiku was now busy fighting with Tengu. Tengu was able to take advantage of Kichiku's weaknesses. First, Kichiku was very heavy so when Tengu was airborne Kichiku could not jump high enough to reach him. Second, Kichiku's geokinesis was useless against someone who could stay off the ground, Tengu was immune to tremors and Kichiku could not control any earth that he was not in contact with, so midair manipulation was not an option. Tengu's fighting style was based on birds of prey that relied on high speed dives, so Tengu would rise high up into the sky and dive bomb Kichiku faster than he could react. They were familiar with each other's fighting styles from when they trained together on Seventh Moon, but since there had always been relatively confined spaces, the range that Tengu had now was more than Kichiku was ready for. Kichiku remembered the flies when he trained with Ryu, and once again, he closed his eyes and prepared to focus not on where Tengu was, but where he would be going. On the next dive bomb, Kichiku threw a well-placed punch at Tengu's solar plexus, launching him back into the air. Tengu managed to regain control in the air and kept himself out of range, but he would need a moment to recover and plan his next move.

Hidariude had an advantage on Yeti because of his sharp blades, but Yeti did have a tough hide and had learned long ago to block Hidariude's blades by carefully grabbing them with his hands as a direct blow would wound him. The hard part was defending against Keisei while maintaining focus on Hidariude, but his tough hide allowed him to endure her blows. Keisei threw a few punches and kicks before she realized she was ineffective, so she decided to try a different approach. She had managed to make more of her paper bombs from materials she found in Hiroshima over the few days she was there and now kept them in a special pouch that Sora managed to find time to make for her. She attached a few of these paper bombs to Yeti and threw a few through the air toward Tengu. At just the right moment, Hidariude and Kichiku backed up and braced for impact as Keisei put up her two fingers and said "Kayakujutsu ignite!"

Yeti had been warned that this could happen and started tearing off the paper bombs just before they exploded and managed to avoid taking too much damage. Tengu had managed to stay just out of range and the bombs exploded in midair stunning him more than anything else. By now Sora had managed to get Zokushou and Douji far enough away that they could just see what was going on, but they were still safe. Douji projected this sense of safety to his fellow espers and they took a moment to try to talk down their attackers.

"Yeti, Tengu, we don't have to fight." Hidariude said.

"This is madness, Toromi is turning us against each other for no reason." Kichiku continued.

"Toromi created us and you betray him by going against us." Tengu replied. "We are the New Wave Elite and it is our destiny to take over the world. In the past three years, we have achieved much success, and if it

214

weren't for you delaying the inevitable we'd have Japan already!"

"I have cleared out the Himalayas, Tibet and the southern rim of China by myself!" Yeti chimed in. "I killed every last Sherpa and yak in the region with my own bare hands and I'm not letting you stand in my way!" Yeti roared and lifted a chunk of the ground to throw at the espers.

Kichiku grabbed the rock and threw it back at Tengu and Yeti. The two soldiers dodged in either direction and realized it was time to call in reinforcements. They pulled out small handheld devices to call robot shock troops. First Tengu's troops arrived like bombs being dropped from the sky, landing in a cloud of dust that the espers just managed to avoid. As the dust cleared, the robots attacked the espers. By now anyone else would have been killed, but the espers could see through the dust and greeted each robot with a neutralizing attack. Hidariude sliced his robot causing the two halves to fly around him into the mountainside behind him. Kichiku met his robot with a well-placed punch that compressed the entire machine like a spring and resulted in a violent implosion. Keisei did not have the same level of strength to put on such a showy destruction of her robot, but she knew a few aikido techniques and used one to redirect the momentum of the robot towards the remnants of the robot Hidariude dispatched and crashed into the nearer half of the robot.

There wasn't a lot of time to celebrate victory over the robots because Yeti's backup caught up with them.

Tengu's flying robots had simply been a diversion while the other robots were attacking the truck, trying to kill Zokushou and Sora and capture Douji. Douji's pangs of fear alerted the other espers and they responded immediately by sprinting to their allies' defense. Zokushou and Sora pulled out their handguns to shoot at the robots attacking them, but Douji was somewhat defenseless. Before the robot that took Douji could get far, Kichiku smashed it and retrieved the boy. "Are you okay Douji?" The boy nodded back. Hidariude and Keisei finished off the other robots securing their friends.

Yeti and Tengu felt desperate, they did not know any other way to fight their enemies so they had begun climbing back up the side of the mountain where there were explosives set up to create a landslide. Once they were above the line of impact, they detonated the explosives. They were all in the direct line of destruction, so Kichiku thought quickly. "Everybody on the truck and get out of here now!" He stood between the motorcycle and the mountainside and pressed his hands against the ground. Using his geokinesis he managed to halt the landslide, but he couldn't fight gravity forever, they would have to move fast. Sora drove off the truck as fast as he could with everyone but Kichiku in tow.

Tengu and Yeti started to pursue the truck figuring they would be easier to fight without Kichiku among them. Hidariude and Keisei sensed them coming and launched a counterattack just as their assailants caught up with them, buying enough time for Sora to drive the truck over the mountain peak and down the other side of the mountain.

Kichiku sensed that they were all safe and let go of his hold against the landslide. He hopped on the motorcycle and quickly sped off trying to keep up with the truck. As Kichiku passed Hidariude, Hidariude jumped on the motorcycle to take it over while Kichiku jumped off to take over his fight with Yeti. Hidariude caught up with Keisei who hopped on the back of the motorcycle.

Sora desperately tried to keep ahead of the landslide now rushing down the mountain behind him. Zokushou turned around in the passenger seat with her gun in one hand and Sora's in the other and shot at Tengu to protect Hidariude and Keisei. Tengu tried to evade the attack, but his feathers were frayed by combat and the bullets hit his wings, finally grounding him. Kichiku and Yeti had managed to get on top of the landslide and were riding it down the mountain, but Tengu was out of luck and was now buried under the rubble. Yeti struck out against Kichiku with rage over the loss of his comrade, Kichiku dodged to leap down in front of the landslide and again used his geokinesis to hold back the landslide to protect his allies. To Yeti's surprise, Kichiku did more than stop the landslide, he actually redirected it as a tidal wave of debris back over onto Yeti. The moment played over in slow motion as the mountain seemed to swallow him up. In his very last moment, he could swear he saw the faces of every one of his victims in the wall of earth about to consume him. He saw no pity on those faces as it collapsed on him and swallowed him up.

Kichiku then began to run downhill with all he had, though he had broken the momentum enough that he was no longer in any real danger. Everybody met at the bottom of the mountain some time later. They looked back at the battlefield, amazed at how the landslide had covered the road and changed the appearance of the mountain. Again they had to face more destruction because of Seventh Moon.

Kichiku stopped and said a prayer in memory of the fallen soldiers. "Though they were our enemies, they were once comrades. They were born with so much potential, corrupted by those who created them to serve as weapons of destruction. Let them know the peace in death they never knew in life." The espers bowed in honor.

Zokushou did not feel as bad as the espers did. It took everything she had not to say out loud "Good riddance." But even though she did not say it, her feelings were palpable to the espers. They did understand her feelings though, they were almost killed. They were only sympathetic from knowing where the soldiers had come from, but part of them agreed with Zokushou. But to admit the endemic evils of the New Wave Elite was to accept it within themselves, so they chose to have mercy on these departed souls and believe that anyone could be redeemed.

After the brief memorial, they got on their way. Hidariude and Keisei got on their bike while the others got in the truck and they drove off towards the Kanmon Bridge, the last step in their journey to Kyushu and Nagasaki. They were all tired from their battle, but they were not comfortable setting up camp so close to the battle. They drove until it was too dark to see the mountain or anything else for that matter.

In the twilight they pulled out some rations for dinner before they went to sleep. They couldn't help looking up at the night sky to see the seven moons. It looked so strange since only the original moon looked like it should. The others had once been asteroids but were now covered in man-made structures and appeared to be more machine than rock. Even among the rest, the one where the espers were born was unmistakable. They all looked at it with a mix of hatred and relief at the distance.

Zokushou started to reminisce. "I remember living on the Seventh Moon as a child. I was born just a few years before the last war and the birth of the first soldiers. I didn't know much about the world where I lived then, but I remember being amazed that it was no older than I was. Everything was being built around me constantly. I didn't know any different so I didn't understand how dangerous it was to being living in a half-built space station. I was just excited by the growing world. I felt like it was a part of me and I was a part of it. Then I learned what was really going on. I really don't know what my father had in mind for me, or if he even wanted me in the first place. When I first got to Earth, I looked at the moons and I thought the seventh was the most beautiful because it was my moon. But in time I grew away from it and realized that it was an ugly place filled with ugly things. It's been six or seven years since my mother got dragged back there and I was left alone to spread the truth about what was going on. That's about seven years of running and hiding. How do you guys handle it?"

Hidariude was very quick with his response. "I just look up there and hold my hand up with the Seventh Moon between my finger and my thumb and go squish." He demonstrated as he described it, pressing his fingers together as he said squish.

Kichiku, Keisei, and Douji all said "Me too!" and followed his lead. "Squish, squish, squish!"

Sora joined in, "Squish!"

Soon they were all laughing. Hidariude continued his thought. "We're on Earth and we're free, that's half the battle. Now we just need to make sure they know it's over and leave us alone. Remembering how tiny it is in the night sky is just part of remembering that it's not impossible, just far away."

Zokushou thought about what Hidariude said and realized he was right. She smiled and felt a lot better. "I'll take watch tonight. I don't know if I can sleep after all that anyway, but I'll catch up tomorrow as we ride the last leg."

The others agreed. "If you change your mind and need someone to take over, ask me." Keisei said.

Zokushou nodded and watched as they all went to sleep. Sora sprawled himself across the front seat of the truck. Kichiku and Douji curled up in the back of the truck. Hidariude and Keisei leaned up against the bike and spooned. It didn't take long at all for the weariness of battle overtook all of them and they fell asleep. They all looked so peaceful it seemed a shame she would have to wake them in the morning. She looked back up at the moon with her finger and her thumb around the Seventh Moon.

"Squish."

Chapter 14

Sunrise and rice cakes, the morning routine was getting fairly predictable. It was everything after that concerned them. On the horizon they saw the Kanmon Bridge, and when they got across it, they would be on the island of Kyushu. This would be good and bad, good because they would be that much closer to Nagasaki and the other mecha, bad because they would also have to deal with the mutants that had been reported in the area, which meant the last leg would also be the most dangerous.

As they approached the bridge they thought about all the possible threats. Scavengers from Honshu, mutants from Kyushu, and those were just what Zokushou and Sora could think of. Hidariude and Kichiku knew the soldiers they had trained with and could think of about ninety specific soldiers that they hadn't already eliminated, any of whom could be backed up by slashers or other robots. They were all on high alert.

The one drawback of the particular brand of extrasensory perception the travelers had was that it tended to be vaguer when not in battle. They could sense people's emotions and intents, but only in battle could they get a specific enough idea to really work with. If someone was careful enough to set up an ambush that relied on traps, they could sense the residual threat the ambusher had left when he set the trap but knowing what the trap was, where it was located, or how to avoid it was not within the extent of their current skillset.

It was because they lacked the ability to sense a specific threat that they didn't know about the explosives that blew up the bridge behind them making sure they could not retreat to safer ground. They were very aware of the threat when they heard the explosion, but it was during this moment of distraction that two soldiers ambushed them. Gozu, a strong bulky soldier with a hornlike haircut, landed on the truck and Mezu, a slender speedy soldier with a Mohawk, landed between the truck and the motorcycle to divide the group in two. These two were named after gods of death for a reason, they were the elite assassination squad, their purpose was not to let anyone leave alive. Both were equipped with chained sickles that doubled as weapons and tools for moving around the bridge or preventing movement. Mezu threw his sickles across the bridge spreading the chain in Hidariude's path so that he could have him all to himself. Gozu used one hand to strike out at Kichiku while grabbing Douji with the other hand. So far the mission was a success.

Kichiku grabbed the sickle from Gozu and attempted to hold him back to prevent him from getting away. Gozu let go of the sickle and allowed Kichiku to have the weapon while he took Douji and jumped over the side of the bridge to climb underneath. At the same time, slashers came out and attacked Kichiku. Using the sickle he took from Gozu, Kichiku parried the slashers and tore them apart. Despite Kichiku's best efforts to prevent Gozu's escape, he did get away with Douji.

Meanwhile Hidariude tried to jump Mezu's barricade, but Mezu's speed allowed him to jump into the air and grab Keisei off of the bike. Mezu attempted to kill Keisei quickly but she bit his hand, elbowed him in the gut and kicked him away. Hidariude pulled a U-turn and drove straight into Mezu. Mezu would have been hit, but he had quick enough reflexes to catch the bike coming at him and throw himself into a back flip over the bike head-butting Hidariude as he did so, forcing him off the bike as it crashed into the chain across the bridge. Keisei pounced on Mezu who was quick enough to react, blocking and turning to face Hidariude who was trying to slice him with his sword. Mezu grabbed the sword between his hands and kicked back at Keisei at the same time. Hidariude let go of the sword with his left hand to let out his cyber blade to strike at Mezu. Mezu let go of the sword with his right hand to catch the cyber blade and redirected them both away from himself. Without breaking his momentum, Mezu let go of Hidariude's blades, dodged Keisei, and dashed back to the chained sickles, pulling them out of place and preparing to fight. He started swinging the sickles in the air so he could throw them at Hidariude and Keisei. Hidariude tried to parry the sickle with his sword, but the chain wrapped around the sword and Mezu pulled it out of his grasp. Keisei caught the sickle thrown at her and pulled the chain in. Mezu let the chain slip through his hand so that he could grab the far end with the sword. Mezu held the chain in one hand and the sword in the other and let Keisei pull him in with the blade pointed directly at her.

Hidariude could sense the danger and blocked the sword with his cyber blade. Mezu pulled back on the chain to bring Keisei next to Hidariude then jumped and kicked out at both of them at the same time. Keisei lost her grip on the chain and Mezu was now in possession of both the chained sickles and the Shinryuu Masamune. He laughed victoriously, but Keisei just put up two fingers and said "Kayakujutsu, ignite!" Mezu just noticed out of the corner of his eye that Keisei had managed to stick a paper bomb in the chain in the few seconds she had it in her hands and now it exploded in his face. He was stunned for a moment and Hidariude took advantage of the moment to punch Mezu with the claws on top of his hand extended, then use his finger claws to tear up Mezu's arm and finally use his long blade to slice Mezu's arm, severing his tendons with surgical precision, forcing Mezu to let go of the sword so Hidariude could reclaim it.

Now Mezu was in a bind; one arm was sliced up, and the other was burned by the explosion, which meant he had lost the use of both arms. However, he was not ready to give up yet as his best trait had always been his legs. He bum-rushed his enemies and kicked at both of them with all the fury he could muster. They both blocked, though with his adrenaline rush, Mezu was fighting harder than they could defend against, and both got knocked back. Mezu laughed maniacally and prepared for a second round. Keisei feinted into the attack to draw it away from Hidariude and he came in with both blades out to cut Mezu's Achilles tendons in mid-leap.

Now Mezu was done for, he had lost the use of all four limbs. He braced for the killing blow he was sure was coming. But it did not come. Despite all of the time they had trained to be killers, how much of their lives had been dedicated to this single task, Hidariude had lost his thirst for blood and simply passed over Mezu. Hidariude picked up his motorcycle, which was still operable, and got back on it with Keisei. They had no time for death because they had other lives to save, they set off to reunite with the others. The entire concept that someone's life could be more important than finishing the battle to the death was lost on the assassin who lay paralyzed and on the verge of death on the ground, watching his former comrade drive away.

Kichiku was still standing on the edge of the bridge trying to locate Douji. "Douji!" Kichiku cried out several times hoping he would respond. When there was no response, he closed his eyes and tried to sense his presence. Fortunately, Douji's fear caused a strong projection of energy for Kichiku to focus on. Once Kichiku had a lock on Douji's location he opened his eyes and at the same moment, Hidariude and Keisei pulled up on their motorcycle. All three jumped over the edge of the bridge and started climbing along the underside of the bridge. Up ahead was Gozu running at a good pace considering he was weighed down by the boy and wasn't as fast as Mezu to begin with. However, he did have some familiarity with the bridge as well as a head start. Kichiku considered using his geokinesis, but it was too risky, the bridge was too unstable. Hidariude and Keisei's powers were no good either because there was too much of a risk that Douji would get hurt in the cross-fire. There was no way around it, this battle was going to be a melee.

"Kichiku, help me!" Douji cried from under Gozu's arm.

"Quiet brat!" Gozu tried to hush him. "You're just lucky the boss wants you alive. If you know what's good for you, you'll shut up!"

Kichiku homed in on the child's voice. He led the way as the others followed. As they closed in on him, Gozu realized he would be at a disadvantage, he needed to hold onto the bridge with one hand and Douji with the other, which meant he did not have a hand free to fight, so he desperately jumped up to the topside of the bridge so he could at least have one hand free. The others followed and soon the battle began. They had met at the far end of the bridge, which they now realized had been destroyed as well to prevent them from escaping at either end. They did not yet know how Gozu planned to get away, but he had no intention of letting them live to find out.

Gozu immediately took a defensive stance, which now looked to the espers like a rudimentary form of Kichiku's more disciplined stance. Kichiku took the first strike against Gozu, who blocked the attack, though he was surprised to find how much more force Kichiku's punch had since the last time the two had sparred back when they were soldiers in training on the Seventh Moon. Hidariude followed up with his triple strike cyber arm combo that Gozu was familiar enough with to know how to block, but he was not prepared for the finisher from

Hidariude's sword. Keisei then followed up with her war fans out which distracted him from the paper bombs she was sticking to him. As she put her fingers up to detonate her paper bombs, he scrambled to pull off all of them, except, one that he couldn't quite reach in the middle of his back. "Kayakujutsu ignite!" The slips of ornate flash paper exploded, mostly in midair, but the one still stuck to him burned his back and threw him to the ground. He had been warned the espers were stronger now since leaving Seventh Moon, but only now did he realize how true this was.

While Gozu was on the ground, Hidariude grabbed Douji and handed him off to Keisei while Sora's truck ran over Gozu and at the same time Kichiku used his geokinesis to bend the end of the bridge into a ramp so that the truck could leap the gap. Kichiku quickly grabbed Douji and leaped into the air to land on the back of the truck as it safely landed on the far side. This left Hidariude and Keisei to go back and get their bike to follow after their friends. As they returned they found Gozu pulling himself up. The tough soldier had taken a lot of punishment but he had survived being run over. Hidariude drove his bike around Gozu while drawing his sword and cutting him down for good as he went by. Before Gozu hit the ground, Hidariude and Keisei were already safely off the bridge and reunited with the others.

Everyone was so afraid that someone could still be following them that they just kept going at full speed. As they traveled Kyushu Island towards Nagasaki, they found that there seemed to be a massive forest on one side of the highway. None of them had any idea what was going on with that forest, but it didn't take ESP to know that there was something ominous about it. Every now and then they noticed someone among the trees, and when they did, they pushed on the gas a little harder, terrified of who could be watching them. They didn't stop for anything, not even the dark of night, pushing on by pure adrenaline in spite of exhaustion. Finally, after what seemed like forever, they made it to Nagasaki.

Nagasaki seemed to be a lot like its sister city Hiroshima. The entire city was underground, the entrance being an old parking garage on the edge of the city where they parked the truck and the bike. They walked the streets, Zokushou calling all members of the resistance to meet them at the World War II museum where the mecha was being kept. Along the way, Sora pointed out the old Suwa Shrine where the espers could stay while he worked on the mecha. When they got to the museum, a few dozen people had gathered, the entire Nagasaki contingent of the resistance.

Zokushou addressed the group. "First and foremost, I must inform all of you that Ijirimawasu Sora has managed to get the Hiroshima mecha operational and using it, the resistance has secured the Sakuma Dam, restoring power to rural Japan." Everyone cheered. "Second, we have come here to restore the Nagasaki Mecha so that we can double the strength of the resistance against Seventh Moon." Again, more cheers. "Third, though not at all unimportant, we have added three new operatives to the resistance, Hidariude, Kichiku and Keisei. These three are espers, their skills are not to be underestimated. They are to thank for securing Sakuma Dam as well as escorting Ijirimawasu and myself here safely. They have defeated a dozen New Wave Elite by themselves, four of which I have witnessed with my own eyes. They are a valuable asset, and we should be very thankful for their assistance in our struggle." The espers noticed how she did not mention that they were from Seventh Moon. They understood that there was no need to make these people angry over their origins when all that mattered now was that they were on the same side.

"Now that I have stated our progress, I must ask, what has been happening in Kyushu?" Zokushou continued speaking to her troops. "We are already aware that some sort of mutant group has appeared in the area. It also seems that there is a forest growing out of control. Something doesn't seem right about this situation, I would like to know any and all intelligence on this matter."

One man stepped forward. "Lieutenant Burumba ma'am. It is called the Jinmenji. It started in Kagoshima in the southern part of the island. No one knew where the tree came from, but a stranger brought the fruit to market when there was no other food. It was hailed as a miracle fruit and everybody began to eat it. At first they were simply hungry and glad that the food was available, but soon the fruit lived up to its claims, the sick became healthy, the healthy became superhuman. There was no fear that it would run out because the more people ate it, the more the trees grew. At first it was just Kagoshima, but the rate that it's growing has increased exponentially. In less than three years, it expanded across the island, the area you drove through to Nagasaki is the last stretch that has not yet been overgrown."

"I have no doubt that Seventh Moon is behind this somehow." Zokushou surmised. "Who was the stranger that first brought the fruit to Kagoshima?"

"His name is Kodama. He still lives in Kagoshima and has claimed himself overlord of Kyushu. Though nobody knew it until he already had half the island under his control, he is indeed from Seventh Moon."

Zokushou glanced at the espers, then paused for thought. "I will need some time to plan our next move. Until then you are all dismissed." Everyone left except Sora and the espers. Zokushou turned on the espers. "What do you know about Kodama?"

Hidariude did not hesitate to answer. "Not much. We know Kodama was one of the soldiers created by Seventh Moon, but he was different. We received some training from him, but we know very little about his specific abilities. We don't know much about Jinmenji either. However, I doubt that there is any coincidence in their arrival, they are definitely connected. The properties of the Jinmenji's fruit sounds like something that Seventh Moon would come up with, but exactly how they are using this to their advantage other than making Kodama the prefect of Kyushu, I have no idea."

Zokushou sighed. "Well, we are all exhausted, we are in no shape to fight right now. Go to the Suwa Shrine to recuperate. Tomorrow we'll meet back here to work on the mecha and our battle plans."

Sora took the espers to the Suwa Shrine. "This Shrine was erected hundreds of years ago by Shogun Ieyasu Tokugawa to preserve Shinto in a time when it was being forgotten. When the bomb fell during World War II, this was one of the few structures that actually survived the destruction.   Some say that it represents the unshakable faith of the people of Japan; that we will survive no matter what. I suppose it's appropriate that the heroes of our time would stay here and represent hope and faith in the face of adversity." They paused for a moment to take in the significance of the sacred shrine. After a moment, Sora broke the silence.   "Good night everybody, see you tomorrow." Sora waved and left for the museum where he would stay until the mecha was fixed. They were all so exhausted from their journey, all they could do was eat one rice cake a piece and then they collapsed into sleep.

The next morning they found themselves slipping into the same routine they had in Hiroshima. Kichiku and Hidariude hauled spare parts from Sora's truck to his worksite while Keisei helped him with tools and Douji sort of just sat around watching and folding origami. Keisei took notice of how Douji was folding his origami since she saw the thousand cranes during the ceremony surrounding the mecha at Hiroshima.   Most had just assumed it was the wind that swept them up, but with her experience in the mystical aspects of kayakujutsu, she had realized that the cranes were actually flapping their wings.

There had been no wind, the cranes were flying of their own accord. The question was, how did that happen? They knew Douji had incredible power, but he had not exhibited any ability to actually control it. Keisei decided to see if she could learn something from Douji about his origami. "Are you going to fold a thousand paper cranes like you did in Hiroshima?"

"Yes." Douji responded while continuing to fold another paper crane.

"Where did you learn to do this?" Keisei continued.

"Master Ryu taught me. He also taught me how to fold a turtle, a kitty and a bunny." He pulled out three pieces of paper that had been folded and flattened. He unfolded them a little and set them out. "Do you wanna see a neat trick? I can make them jump!" He clapped his hands together and focused his sight on the three origami animals and suddenly they began to move as if they were alive. The turtle crawled, the bunny hopped, and the cat walked over to Keisei and started rubbing it's head against her. "They're my shikigami."

Keisei was impressed, but then she remembered what they discussed with Sora, about keeping Douji's powers a secret. "This was how the flock of cranes flew the other night wasn't it?" Douji nodded. Keisei cupped her hands around the cat and corralled it together with the other two. "How about we keep this our little secret, just you, me, Kichiku and Hidariude? We'll tell them you can do this, but don't show this little shikigami trick around anyone else okay?"

"Why not?" Douji asked with genuine innocence.

"Well, this is a special ability, like when I make fire, Kichiku makes earthquakes, or Hidariude makes electricity. When we do it we fight and we're determined to do that to protect you, but you're little and if someone finds out that you have special powers they'll make you fight too."

"They'll make me fight with origami?" Douji asked, clearly confused.

Keisei couldn't help laughing a little. "If you have enough of them, or if you can make one large enough, you're shikigami can be as dangerous as any of our powers, especially if you make them from my paper bombs."

A look of understanding dawned on Douji's face. "Oh. Okay, it'll be our little secret." He took his hands apart and the shikigami went limp. He picked them up, flattened them out and put them back into his pocket before going back to folding cranes.

Now that the matter of Douji's shikigami was settled, the espers returned their attention to the mecha. It seemed to be the same as the one in Hiroshima, a giant mechanical samurai. Sora was trying to repair damage that had been done during its last use in World War III as well as installing a nuclear energy cell using radioactive isotopes that had been collected from the local area. It wasn't quite as impressive the second time, after Hiroshima, it was getting pretty routine. Still, Sora was working just as fervently, this mecha was needed for the resistance and he felt the need to get it ready before Kodama and his mutants caught up with them.

While Sora was working on the mecha, Zokushou continued to gather intelligence on the situation with Kodama and the Jinmenji forest.   She took her time trying to map out the forest as best as she could and make a plan to get to Kagoshima and Kodama. Kodama seemed to be in a different league than the other New Wave Elite, and she wasn't sure where the espers stood in relation to Kodama. He couldn't be allowed to keep control over Kyushu with Nagasaki and the mecha so close to being within his reach, but at the same time the espers were a valuable resource in their own right and she couldn't afford to lose them either. This would be an important operation and they would only get one shot, so they would need to get it right.

Only a few days after they had arrived in Nagasaki, the battle came to them. A group of three outsiders arrived, two men and a woman, each one appearing to be pure muscle. They began a rampage through town, the security guards were hardly prepared for the fight and were dispatched quickly. Once word got to the espers, they knew that it was up to them. They approached the attackers carefully, trying not to draw attention to themselves so they could get the first strike. Keisei signaled the attack by throwing a paper bomb at the woman and setting it off. "Kayakujutsu, ignite!" At the exact same time, Kichiku punched the ground to create a fissure trapping one of the men, while Hidariude used an electric attack on the other one.

At first the onlookers cheered thinking the invaders were stopped, but then they all just got back up. The one

Kichiku had trapped punched straight up through the ground and pulled himself out. The other two just seemed to shake off the burns, bulged their muscles some more and made another go at the espers. The espers fought back with everything they had and held their own, but even they were surprised to find that the invaders were still fighting, their initial attacks should have done the trick.

The man fighting Hidariude, apparently their leader, gloated as he fought; proving that he could take on his opponent without even losing his breath. "You must be the ones from Seventh Moon the boss was telling us about. To be honest, we thought you'd be stronger, but clearly you are no match for the power of Jinmenji fruit! It's the ultimate super fruit and it makes us super strong. Maybe if you try some of the fruit you'd stand a chance too!"

The espers pulled back, trying to find a tactical advantage from different terrain inside the city, but just as they were starting to get away the invaders attacked them with vines that actually grew right out of their bodies. "Nothing can beat the power of Jinmenji!" The invaders boasted again.

Hidariude sliced through the vines, Keisei burned them, and Kichiku tore them apart with his bare hands. The invaders threw more vines at the espers, but the espers kept one step ahead and kept cutting back the vines as they approached the source and attacked the invaders directly.

Suddenly something happened that shocked both the espers and the invaders. The wounds that the espers had caused to the invaders started growing over with bark, and then the growths continued growing and spreading across their bodies. The vines they had been trying to use as weapons started growing around them and drawing them together. Within minutes, they had actually become a tree.

"Well, there's a new piece of intel we didn't have before." Sora commented on the bizarre turn of events.

Zokushou looked at the tree. "This is bad, they know where we are and how to get to us. But it appears they do have some weakness, we just don't know what this is. Espers, go back to the shrine and get some rest, as soon as we have this analyzed, you're going to Kagoshima and putting an end to this."

Chapter 15

The next morning the espers returned to check on the tree and found that it had almost doubled in size. Everyone else stayed far away from it, they were afraid of this monster tree. The espers touched the tree and used their ESP to examine it and figure out if there was any way to stop it. Finally they reached a conclusion and knew what to do, a proper funeral for the mutants that the tree had grown from. Keisei pulled out four slips of blank paper from her kimono along with her ink and ink brush. She painted the kanji of the four kami from their shrine, one on each slip of paper, then handed them to their corresponding esper. Hidariude took the ofuda of Kyutsume, Kichiku took the ofuda of Nyudo, Douji took the ofuda of Shinryuu and Keisei herself held on to the ofuda of Bakeneko. They each stood on a different side of the tree, Hidariude on the west, Kichiku on the north, Douji on the south, and Keisei on the east. They each placed their ofuda on the tree and held them in place with their right hands.

The espers then proceeded to pray in unison. "You three warriors who lost your lives here last night, we mourn your death with honor. We pray for your souls to find rest, and be released from the demon tree Jinmenji. In the name of the sacred kami, we release you." With this the each removed their hands at the exact same time and the ofuda burst into flames. Because of the ritual they performed together, the flames of the ofuda continued to burn through the tree and did not stop until the tree was completely burned away. The espers could hear the cries of the three souls they freed which left in peace, as well as the demon spirit of the tree itself. These cries were not audible to anyone else as they only resonated in the spiritual plane which only the espers could detect. Even though no one else knew what was going on, it was clear once it was over that the tree had been effectively destroyed as it was completely reduced to ashes right down to the roots.

Zokushou showed up on the scene after it was over. "Good job. Now I need you to go to Kagoshima." She handed Hidariude a map. "This will help you to find your way there, though much of the path has been overgrown with the trees. Unfortunately it's all we've got. Burumba says every time they try to send out anyone on reconnaissance they either die or come back close to death. I'm hoping your abilities can get you farther."

"Thanks for the map." Hidariude replied. "We can use our ESP to find our way around. Kichiku and I are familiar enough with Kodama we can trace his energy."

Zokushou was impressed. "You think you can sense him from here?" She had no idea what their range of abilities was.

"Well, probably not all the way from here." Hidariude admitted. "But since Kagoshima is on the southern coast of the island, if we just keep due south, we should start getting a reading before we actually hit the coast and we'll zero in on him there."

Zokushou sighed. "I wish I could say we had a better plan that that, but we estimate that if you don't start out for him today, Jinmenji will overtake Nagasaki before we can make another strike against him. You are our last hope."

The espers made their last preparations for their journey. They would have to go on foot because the roads were overgrown and under the watchful eye of mutants that would most certainly hinder their progress even more if they heard the engine from the truck or the motorcycle. Kichiku was getting Douji ready to come along when Zokushou interrupted.

"Douji will stay here where it's relatively safe." Zokushou told Kichiku. "I don't want him distracting you."

Kichiku was about to protest when Sora stepped in to take Douji. "That's right little buddy, you'll help me finish the mecha." Sora gave Kichiku a look that reminded him that they needed to keep Douji's powers a secret and they couldn't justify taking him on this mission without exposing that secret.

Kichiku reluctantly gave in and hugged Douji goodbye. "Don't worry Douji, we'll be back for you, I promise."

Douji tried to hold back tears, but this was the first time that Kichiku had left him since they left the Shrine of the Golden Dragon. "You'd better be. I'll pray for you."

The espers nodded back at their friends and left Nagasaki for the forest of Jinmenji. Very soon after they entered the forest they quickly noticed that all of the trees looked the same. They tried to feel out the energy of the trees and could sense that the trees were connected. In fact, it was all one tree. There were a few nodes where trees had grown like the one back in Nagasaki, but most of it was just the one tree that had expanded across the island. The good part of this was that because it all connected back to the original tree, they could simply trace the flow back to Kagoshima, and hopefully, Kodama.

As they followed the flow of energy through the trees, they also kept a lookout for any anomalies that would signify the presence of mutant attackers. The strangest thing they noticed though, was that when a mutant did appear, it did not have a significant difference in energy. Usually each individual had a distinctly unique energy, but these mutants did not even feel like they were different from the tree, they were more like waves of identical energy rippling over the tree network than separate entities. Still, when the energy ran against the normal flow or even when the energy spiked a little, they would give themselves away and the espers would change direction to avoid them.

The espers made some good progress sneaking between the trees. Between genetic engineering and training under Ryu, they had incredible endurance and without Douji's short legs slowing them down, they were able to get almost halfway across the island before nightfall. They weren't overly tired at this point, but they knew they would need to be at full energy to fight Kodama so they couldn't take any chances. They doubted that the mutants could see in the dark so in the very last twilight they dug in at the roots of the tree and huddled together, eating rice cakes and dried vegetables and then sleeping.

They took turns watching, each one for a third of the night while the other two slept.

The next morning they ate quickly and got moving just as the first rays of dawn cracked between the leaves. A group of mutants found their temporary nest after they had left. They could see crumbs of rice and felt the ground. "Still warm." One mutant grunted. "They couldn't have gotten too far." The mutants were back up the tree in a flash and kept up the pursuit of their quarry.

The espers could sense the mutants catching up to them. They knew the mutants were keeping up somehow and at the rate they were moving, they would get them soon. The fact that the mutants shared energy with the trees was an advantage for the attackers as was the fact that they would have the home field advantage. To try and make things easier the espers would need to find a location where they could fight at their best. The espers realized the mutants' connection with the tree would give them an advantage in the upper branches, so they dropped to the ground. The mutants pounced on the espers thinking they were catching them off guard.

Hidariude drew his sword and released his long cyber blade and in one movement sliced through two mutants at the same time. Green blood spurted from the wounds. Despite their wounds, the mutants tried to fight, but as the wounds grew closed, the scars were wooden. The mutants were stiff and slower because of this, so Hidariude kept slicing them as they tried to come at him. They quickly realized they couldn't fight up close so they started growing vines to use against Hidariude. However, this aggravated their wounds even more and they quickly turned completely to wood.

Kichiku was attacked by one massive mutant who already had twigs sticking out before he went for a full attack. Kichiku punched him squarely in the center of his abdomen with such force that he slammed into the tree. The mutant didn't even stand up, he just touched his hands to the tree and roots grew up around Kichiku's feet. Kichiku punched the ground cracking the earth around the roots only to find that the roots were still firm beneath the ground. Kichiku grabbed a hold of the roots and yanked them so hard that the mutant attached to them was lifted into the air and as the mutant was pulled close to Kichiku he leaned back and kicked the mutant with his bound feet. The mutant could not move again, the wounds beneath his skin were turning to wood and his muscles were stiffened. Within minutes his skin broke and gave way to bark.

Keisei drew her war fans from her kimono and began to fend off the mutants. The mutants had very poor fighting abilities and relied entirely on their heightened strength, agility and rage. Keisei used this against them by luring them into fighting each other or running into the tree. Some well-placed swipes from Keisei's fans did cut the mutants drawing green blood. One used vines to take Keisei's fans and another captured her by dropping vines from above and yanking her up by a pulley. Keisei did not want to use her paper bombs because she knew that if she did, the heat energy would pass through the tree network and alert others to their presence. But she was desperate right now because her comrades were occupied with their own opponents at this same time. She had no choice, she pulled an emergency paper bomb from her sleeve and ignited it, burning the vines holding her captive. As she dropped to the ground she threw more paper bombs at her enemies and detonated those as well. The mutants proved to be more flammable than the ones they found in Nagasaki. Keisei looked closer and realized that twigs were growing on these mutants and had caught fire like raw kindling. Keisei continued to focus her pyrokinesis and pushed the fire straight through the mutants' bodies. She hesitated just long enough to retrieve her fans before they too burned up.

After the battle, the espers regrouped. "These mutants are cannon fodder." Kichiku commented. "The fruit of Jinmenji gives them more power, but the price is that the tree ultimately reclaims them. The process seems to be accelerated as people use the power, which means that every time a mutant enters battle they are on a suicide mission."

Hidariude was infuriated. "Kodama is no better than Toromi, he's just passing the buck on to his subordinates and sacrificing them to protect himself!"

Keisei put her hand on Hidariude. "We have to hurry, my paper bombs sent a heat wave through the trees, and Kodama will know where we are."

"Let him come!" Hidariude screamed out the challenge into the forest. "It's time that he paid for what he's done!"

Hidariude was driven by anger and adrenaline and began a mad run through the forest. More mutants came at him and he just sliced them down, nothing could slow him down. Keisei and Kichiku did everything they could to keep up with him. By the time they saw the mutants Hidariude cut down, the mutants were in no shape to fight and Kichiku and Keisei found themselves following in Hidariude's wake of destruction. They were very concerned that Hidariude was going to become the very monster he was trying to stop. There was no time to slow him down now, but he was going to need a lot of help when this mission was over.

As the sun began to set, they felt the flow of energy in the trees begin to swell. They didn't think they had reached Kagoshima, but then they realized it wasn't the tree itself, it was Kodama. He stood before them now, tall, wild hair, muscles bulging, in his Seventh Moon military uniform. Hidariude paused to catch his breath and Kichiku and Keisei flanked him to protect him in case Kodama tried a sneak attack. Kodama looked extremely calm as he greeted his enemies. "You've made quick work of my underlings, you do not disappoint. I must admit I am impressed, when I heard rumors of your powers, I thought it was an exaggeration, but it seems that you are actually even stronger than I was told. I'm sure you're wondering how this forest provides so much power, and I might as well tell you, it's the least you deserve for getting this far. Jinmenji is yet another fine product of New World Enterprises, combining all of the super fruits of the pre-war days. Pomegranate, acai, goji, durian, gingko biloba, cranberry, orange, apple and guarana, all providing immense energy, strength, and other health benefits. All of these impressive dietary traits were combined into a banyan fig, and it's seed was planted in Kagoshima. I planted it after I was vaccinated. You see, the banyan can be a very nasty tree and with all of the other traits added into its gene code, it became a very powerful plant, and it's nastiest side effect is that the fruit contains tiny virulent seeds and spores that start growing inside anyone that eats the fruit. Over time the tree grows out from the host's body and kills the poor human. Only I have immunity to this, which means only I can truly gain the full benefit of the fruit. But there is a good reason for all of this death, you see, each time a tree kills a person, the energy flows back into the tree making the fruit that much more potent." At this point he stopped to pluck a round purple fruit from the tree and eat it. As he licked the juice from his lips he laughed. "Delicious."

It suddenly dawned on Hidariude that Kodama was indirectly feeding off of the people of Kyushu Island. This caused him to be enraged so he drew his blades once again and attacked Kodama head on. "You monster!"

Kodama calmly caught each of Hidariude's blades in each of his hands and then kicked Hidariude in the chest. "Perhaps I should also mention that it was in my plan all along that you would wear yourself out fighting my underlings. Your senses are dulled, your muscles are sore, and I am fresh and ready to fight!" He threw Hidariude to the side. "Next."

Kichiku and Keisei tried to coordinate their attack. Kichiku came in from the front and struck Kodama with both hands. Kodama blocked and they grappled and wrestled. Keisei used this moment to jump behind Kodama and attack him before he noticed. She punched, kicked and clawed him. Kodama just laughed. "Is that the best you can do? The girl is tickling me!" Kodama head-butted Kichiku, knocking him down, and then spun around flinging Keisei into the tree in a movement to fast for her to react to. "Pathetic."

Keisei put up her two fingers. "Kayakujutsu ignite!" The paper bombs exploded into a great conflagration. For a moment she smiled at her success. But that moment was short lived when she heard someone behind her.

"That was close." Kodama said. "If I hadn't torn off those paper bombs you stuck to me and run over here I could have been a goner."

"How did you...?" Keisei stuttered unable to fathom how Kodama had not only outrun the explosion, but somehow gotten behind her without her seeing.

"Behold the power of the miracle fruit of Jinmenji!" Kodama squealed with sadistic glee, then kicked Keisei across the forest.

By now Hidariude caught a second wind and engaged in battle with Kodama again. Now his mind was clearer and he was more focused on the battle at hand. He performed his signature combination attack; tiger claw, punch with hand blades extended, a slash with his long blade, and then a follow-up with his sword. To his surprise, Kodama blocked the attack effortlessly. He attempted a few more permutations of the combo to see if he could catch Kodama off guard, but to no avail. Finally, in desperation, Hidariude unleashed an electric attack. Kodama actually seemed to absorb the electric attack and redirected it at another tree trunk.

"Tingly!" Kodama said with another maniacal laugh.

Kichiku tried to assist Hidariude by punching the ground causing a tremor. Kodama dodged the attack by leaping into the air right when the tremor hit and landed on Kichiku. They resumed grappling and Hidariude joined them trying to fight him on both sides. Kodama proceeded to block both warriors with little effort.

Keisei returned to the fray, trying to hit him with her war fans. They had such little effect Kodama completely ignored her. Suddenly she became filled with rage, remembering how she had been ignored by her masters on Seventh Moon when she was younger. She would not be ignored now, she dropped her fans and hit Kodama with her bare hands and feet. Still Kodama was able to block her attacks as well as Kichiku's and Hidariude's without any effort at all.

It was frustrating for the espers that Kodama was reacting so fast. He didn't have the same senses and reflexes that the espers had, but he had enough raw energy to be moving fast enough to stay ahead of them. What they were witnessing just seemed impossible.

Kodama yawned. "I'm bored." He went from passive blocking to hitting each esper hard enough to propel them away from him into the trees around him.

Keisei had placed another paper bomb on Kodama, but this time she coordinated with Hidariude and Kichiku. Each got into position and quickly threw their best attack at Kodama. Hidariude crossed his blades and unleashed an electric bolt. Kichiku punched the ground unleashing a tremor that caused the ground to rise as it approached its target. Keisei pulled another paper bomb out and threw it at Kodama. "Kayakujutsu ignite!" The paper bomb exploded into a flaming streak as it flew towards Kodama. All of these attacks occurred at the exact same time, in perfect sync.

When the dust settled, Kodama still stood. He had managed to somehow deflect or block all three of the attacks and remained unharmed. "Was that really the best you could do? Well, I guess not, you are tired from fighting my underlings. And the other soldiers on the way here. You're spent, and that was your final attack this is over." Kodama was right, they could not move. They were exhausted from their journey and the fighting, and they had put the last of their energy into that attack. They couldn't believe this was how it was going to end. Kodama collected them and dragged them up to the canopy and dropped them each, one by one, into giant pitcher plants. "Since you didn't eat the fruit of Jinmenji, I'll have to let the tree absorb your energy this way. Then I will be that much stronger and I can go retrieve that kid."

Kichiku realized he was breaking his promise to Douji to come back for him. "I'm sorry Douji."

At this very moment, in the Suwa Shrine in Nagasaki, Douji could hear Kichiku's voice. He could sense that his friends were in trouble. "No! Hidariude! Keisei! Kichiku-san! I won't let you be hurt!"

Sora panicked because he and Zokushou were just bringing Douji home for the night and there was no way for him to hide Douji's sudden golden glow from Zokushou. He knew Douji was sensitive, but he didn't realize that he could pick up what was happening from this far away. But there was no stopping what was happening.

Douji transformed into the golden dragon Shinryuu and flew out of Nagasaki. He started towards the forest, and his body began to grow longer. He wove between the tree trunks, wrapping his body around every single tree in the forest. After coiling around the entire forest covering the island of Kyushu, he raised his enormous head right above where Kodama was with the espers in pitcher plants. He reached a huge three clawed hand in among the trees and plucked up his friends. Now that they were safe, he opened his gaping maw over Kodama took a deep breath and unleashed a furious blast of energy. "DIVINE WIND!"

Kodama did not stand a chance, he was in the direct line of the blast. The energy spread across the island, the explosion consumed the entire forest. Nothing survived the blast, Jinmenji and Kodama were no more. Having spent all of his energy, Shinryuu dissipated leaving Douji, Kichiku, Keisei and Hidariude to fall on the ground.

Seichei, Baz, and Aka arrived on the scene to see the four espers unconscious. Aka picked up Douji. "They're as good as dead, thanks to Kodama. He was right, it is a good strategy to let someone else do all the hard work and then just finish up." With Douji tucked under Aka's arm, the three left for their return trip to the space port.

The espers remained unconscious until the arrival of Zokushou and Sora. Sora shook them awake. "What happened? Are you guys okay?"

Kichiku was the first to respond. "Where's Douji?"

"That's part of the problem…" Sora replied sheepishly.

Zokushou gave them a moment to regain their senses, and then she railed right into them. "Why didn't you tell me about the child? What was that thing?"

The espers were still a bit confused. "What is she talking about?"

Sora sighed. "Douji transformed and…" He gestured at the wasteland around them that used to be the forest of Jinmenji. "He did all of this."

Suddenly the espers were shocked awake by the realization that Douji had done something that had exceeded even what they knew him to be capable of.

Zokushou could see that they were more awake now. 'Again I ask you; how did this child get this power?"

"He's like us. He was created by Seventh Moon. Only his powers are more extensive than ours. He was genetically engineered to be perfect and he has been chosen as the Yoshiromi of the Golden Dragon Shinryuu. What you saw was his true divine nature. We are his guardians and we stay with him to help him control his power and prevent incidents like that, but when we are in trouble it seems to set him off. Seventh Moon has been after him ever since they located him in the Kanagawa

Raid three years ago. He was the only survivor, and it's up to us to protect him."

"Well you failed!" Zokushou admonished them. "Maybe if I had known we could have taken the necessary precautions, but now it seems they have him."

"Seventh Moon captured him?" Kichiku screamed in horror.

Sora and Zokushou nodded.

"We have to find a way to get him back."

Chapter 16

Sora had brought Zokushou in the mecha and gathered the espers into the passenger compartment. They were going to use the mecha to try to catch up to Douji as Sora had explained that the mecha was the fastest vehicle they had. They were amazed by the roomy compartment in the robot's torso just below the cockpit. It was big enough for four people to sit comfortably and had a fiber optic monitor that allowed them all to see what was going on outside. They observed the landscape speeding by in a blur as the mecha quickly bounded across Kyushu, past Nagasaki, and leapt across the Kanmon Bridge back to Honshu Island.

"We're headed to the NWE launch pad." Zokushou explained. "If they're going to take Douji back to Seventh Moon, they will have to go there first and we'll cut them off at the pass. If you're wondering about this passenger compartment it was intended for infantry transport. With large scale mecha warfare, it was assumed that a small squad could be taken behind enemy lines without anyone noticing. I guess we're still using it that way."

In moments they were speeding past Hiroshima and then the Sakuma Dam. Zokushou became concerned as they passed the Sakuma Dam because she didn't see the mecha. "The Hiroshima mecha was assigned to Sakuma Dam. There aren't a lot of places to hide and we intended for it to be visible so that we could intimidate enemy forces. There's no sign of it, what the hell happened?"

"Do you think it was destroyed?" Hidariude asked.

"No, the parts would be lying around if that were the case." Zokushou answered. "I fear it could be worse, it may have been captured by the enemy."

Within just a few hours they were back to the Tokyo region and found the launch pad. Sure enough, the Hiroshima mecha was there. "It may not be the enemy, Commander." Sora suggested. "Something may have happened that caused the pilot to move without being able to inform anyone. Remember, we haven't reclaimed the airwaves, and the cellular networks are still down outside Tokyo, so there's no way for him to contact the resistance for updates. Fortunately, I should be able to contact him through a close range radio." Sora turned on the radio to transmit to the other mecha. "Hello Hiroshima this is Shuurikou on the Nagasaki. Come in Hiroshima."

The answer they got was the Hiroshima turning around to fight the Nagasaki. It had its guns out and fired off a few rounds. Sora was quick enough to dodge the bullets. It tried to shoot again, but it had already run out of bullets. It dropped its guns and drew its swords. The blades were made of plasma, essentially huge welding torches designed to be wielded like swords. The energy source was the nuclear reactor that ran the mecha, which tended to produce excessive energy which could be transferred to the blades and released as plasma. This was a very difficult technology to control as its range increased so sword length blades were as far as it had gotten and was far too dangerous to be wielded by humans and so had only been implemented as a mecha weapon where it was practical to release nuclear exhaust. Shuurikou had applied the same technology to the Nagasaki, modeling it after Hidariude it had one blade that it could hold in one hand and another that was projected directly from the left arm. Both blades were drawn to duel with the Hiroshima.

"I really wish I didn't have to do this." Sora lamented. "I put so much work into restoring these things, I hate destroying them."

"Maybe we don't have to." Zokushou suggested. "Do you three think you could help me take the mecha back?"

The espers thought quickly, then Hidariude answered. "I wouldn't be much help here, I can't produce enough voltage for my lightning blade to take down the mecha. But Kichiku's quake palm could disable the mecha long enough for Keisei to get to the cockpit and take out the pilot." Kichiku and Keisei nodded.

"Then it's a plan." Zokushou said. She opened the hatch and jumped out with Keisei and Kichiku. Kichiku landed first hitting the ground with enough force to shake up the Hiroshima. Without wasting any time, Keisei took Zokushou by the hand and bounded up the mecha's leg to the hatch for its passenger compartment. Zokushou opened the door and Keisei jumped in.

Inside she found four slashers and saw a fifth in the pilot seat above. She quickly threw a paper bomb on each one then swung herself back outside with Zokushou. "Get back! Kayakujutsu detonate!" After the explosion, the mecha stopped moving with its pilot disabled. Keisei cleared out what was left of the robots and Zokushou took the controls.

"Nagasaki come in, this is Hiroshima. We have secured the mecha." The victory was short lived though, a rocket went off behind them from the launch pad. They didn't have to discuss it, the espers could sense Douji's presence on the rocket, and they were too late.

The first idea they had was to storm the launch pad and look for another jet to follow Douji and his captors. The espers cut down the security robots and found the base controllers. "We need a jet now!" Hidariude demanded with blades drawn.

The controllers were stunned but managed an answer anyway. "I'm sorry but that's impossible. That was the last jet, there isn't another one here or anywhere in Japan. We would have to wait for another jet to return from Seventh Moon."

"When will that be?" Hidariude asked, brandishing his blades again.

"We have no idea. They send jets according to their needs and don't let us know until they launch from Seventh Moon."

The espers returned crestfallen and reported back to the others. "What now?" Sora asked sadly.

Everyone stopped to think, mostly lost in despair. But they weren't going to give up and finally Hidariude came up with an idea. "Sora, do you think you could repair an old jet if we could get you access to one?"

This was a matter of pride for Sora. "I can repair anything!"

"Then we're going to Kanagawa!" Hidariude exclaimed.

The espers climbed back in the Nagasaki and the two mecha picked up all of the broken robots and grabbed a few more spare parts from the hangar, then proceeded south to Kanagawa. It didn't take very long to reach their destination. They stopped at the lake at the foot of the mountain where the Shrine of the Golden Dragon stood. Here the mecha waded into the water and lifted out the jet that Hidariude and Keisei had arrived in over two years earlier and set it down on the bank.

Sora took a look at the jet, damaged from the crash, covered in lake weed and waterlogged to top it off. "Well, you certainly know how to challenge me."

"So do you think it's beyond repair?" Hidariude asked.

"I didn't say that." Sora replied. "I just said it would be a challenge. This is going to take a while, but we don't have a choice, this is the only way we can get Douji back. No matter how long it takes we have to try."

Sora began work on the jet. He seemed to have everything he needed with parts from the robots that he could rework into parts for the jet and some tools that he always carried with him in case of emergency. Zokushou assisted him as needed and they started to make quick progress.

The espers felt somewhat useless just watching the repairs. They decided to go back to the shrine to reminisce and pray. The shrine looked exactly the same as they had left it only a few weeks ago. It was very somber for them, they had always known they would never see Ryu alive here again, but they never imagined they would return without Douji. It felt twice as empty missing two of their family members.

Their first stop was the main shrine. They opened the seal together and entered the shrine. They gathered before the statue of the golden dragon and bowed to it. "Oh great Shinryuu, forgive us for failing to guard your Yoshiromi, Douji. He is very near and dear to our hearts, we really want to get him back and we ask for your help in our plan to retrieve him. Our friend Sora is repairing a spacecraft in order for us to return to Seventh Moon. Please aid him in his efforts and grant us safe passage to and from the Seventh Moon."

After praying directly to the golden dragon, they each took some time to pray at their respective branch shrines. This was a somewhat more futile effort since they now knew that they were the reincarnations of these deities and were therefore praying to themselves, but they were desperate and sought guidance from their past lives. Try as they might to remember their past lives they received no wisdom from eight hundred years ago. However, they did find themselves being drawn to another part of the shrine grounds, the three cherry trees that Ryu had planted.

The cherry trees had always been Ryu's special spot. He always tended to the trees and never let them come to help him. He said they were a special pet project he had taken over from his late wife Sakura who had started them as bonsai in memorial of the three lesser kami and the guardian priests who kept vigil at the shrine. Sakura had taken the trees to Seventh Moon as a sort of portable shrine to remember her home when she was far away from it.

The cherry blossoms had just reached full bloom when Ryu had died here a few weeks ago. Now the cherry blossoms were just reaching the end of their lives and started to drop off the tree. Keisei noticed the first petal fall and as a wind picked up, a pink rain of cherry blossom petals began to surround them. As the cherry blossoms swirled in the air, three figures seemed to manifest. Two of the figures they did not recognize though they seemed to strongly resemble a woman and a man not entirely unlike Keisei and Kichiku. The third figure however was surprisingly familiar.

"Master Ryu!" All three espers exclaimed together. "Is it really you?"

To their surprise, he actually answered them. "Yes my children. Allow me to introduce you to my master, Muramasa Sasuke." Ryu gestured toward the man who looked like Kichiku. "Also, I would like you to meet my wife, Masamune Sakura, your mother."

Sakura bowed. "I am honored."

For a moment nobody moved. Hidariude had remembered Ryu's spirit presenting himself earlier and understood that he might be seeing his father again, but to see his mother was more than he could bear. Kichiku had also never known his mother so to see her was a very emotional experience. Even Keisei who had never known family before couldn't believe what she was seeing.

Sakura wiped a tear from Keisei's face. "It seems my son has found as beautiful and worthy a wife for himself as his father did. I never had a chance to raise my children, but if I had a chance to have a daughter, I would be proud to have one like you. You honor the legacy of the miko of Bakeneko."

Keisei was speechless. She had lived her entire life alone, growing up being treated like a worthless piece of meat, always wishing she had a strong mother to protect her and teach her how to be a proper woman. It was not until this very moment that she felt that she had truly beaten the odds and become a worthy woman. "I never knew my mother, but I could only hope I could have had a mother like you."

Sasuke simply nodded to Kichiku. Somehow they all seemed validated by the appearance of the ancestral kami. "How is this possible? How are you here?"

Ryu answered. "We could not simply leave just yet, our work is not quite done. We knew you would need us so we wait here. We are in another world now, but there is overlap here in this grove of cherry trees, here we can be with you in this world and you can always come here to seek our guidance. Beyond these trees we see the world of the afterlife, and in my case, I always see where the Shinryuu Masamune is. Yes Hidariude, that means I have seen everything that has happened since you took the sword from this shrine, including what happened to Douji."

The espers now hung their heads in shame. "We're sorry we failed."

"You did not fail." Sasuke interrupted. "You fought with all of the effort that could be expected of you. You simply faced a superior enemy, one of the one hundred and eight yokai."

The espers were confused by this statement, though they realized there were one hundred and eight soldiers in the Seventh Moon army and they were curious if there was a connection. Hidariude was the one to ask the question. "Who are the one hundred and eight yokai?"

"They are a very important part of why this shrine is so important. You see the golden dragon Shinryuu appeared here for a reason, to warn of an army of one hundred and eight yokai. His champions that he chose here were the only ones who could stop the yokai with the dragon's power. The shrine was built as a nexus to allow the Shinryuu's power to be passed on to Kyutsume, Bakeneko and Nyudo to be the paragons of Japan's three warrior classes, the samurai, the ninja and the monk. In the century just before Shinryuu's appearance, Japan was attacked by invaders from mainland Asia across the sea to the west. The invaders were defeated by awful weather attributed to the seasons. Truth be told, the storms that defeated the invaders were no mere coincidence, they were the work of the dragons of sea and sky protecting Japan. Unfortunately, this also meant that many of those who were defeated by the dragon's efforts remained buried beneath the waves, their spirits wrought with unrest seeking yet another attempt to attack Japan again and finish their unfinished business. As it would happen, there were wicked spirits here in Japan that also sought to wreak havoc upon this land. Among them were the nine claws of Kyutsume."

"What were the nine claws of Kyutsume?" Hidariude asked. "I thought they were my blades."

"Yes and no." Sasuke answered Hidariude and continued the story. "The eight smaller blades Kyutsume carried were in memory of the eight warriors he killed in battle before he lost his own arm and was forced to retire. However, despite his attempts to honor those spirits and put them to rest, they conspired against him from the afterlife. They took possession of his severed arm and saw to it that it was reattached to the armor that Kyutsume left behind when he gave up the life of a samurai. Kyutsume had taken his kote to act as a replacement arm, but he had left the rest of his suit of armor with his clan when he began to wander as a ronin. The armor had been passed down through the past few generations and became one hundred years old just as the other eight reunited the arm with the armor. This became Tuskomogami, the ninth claw and leader among the leaders of an army that would exist only to seek vengeance upon the living who had discarded them. They marched across Japan to the west coast calling every yokai promising to give them the power to do all their wicked hearts desired. By the time they reached the sea, ninety-nine yokai had joined them and using the dark arts they cast the evil spirits into the soulless corpses of the invaders. The ayakashi, the drowned ones, rose from the sea and the one hundred and eight yokai marched back across Japan, an unstoppable scourge for that which is already dead cannot be killed again. The only way for these abominations to be stopped was for the demon spirits to be extracted from their bodies. No mere mortal could do this, so Shinryuu had to imbue his champions with the power to do the impossible, to defeat an immortal army."

Again, Hidariude was confused. "So what does this have to do with our war with Seventh Moon?"

"Everything." Sasuke replied. "There is a reason that the kami reincarnated as you in this life. Han Toromi has disrupted the Ki of this shrine and broken the seal Shinryuu placed upon the yokai. When he had Gaki steal the Yoshiro of Kyutsume, the spirits sealed by the ancients were released. The one hundred and eight soldiers created on Seventh Moon were soulless abominations. As such they were the perfect vessels for souls without bodies and the one hundred and eight yokai took their places. The kami had to do something about this, so they claimed you three to have the power to fight the ancient war again. Douji and Hime of course are the keys, Douji is of course the Yoshiromi of Shinryuu and Hime bears the soul of one of the demons that the kami displaced during the cycle of reincarnation twenty one years ago."

This seemed to be a lot to take in so they had to think about this. Hidariude thought a bit quicker and had more questions. "There are one hundred and eight successful genetically engineered individuals from the first generation of Seventh Moon. If the three of us displaced three of them, and Hime is one of those, then what happened to the other two?"

"That we do not know." Sasuke answered. "We only know that your enemies are not merely genetically engineered, they are possessed by demons. You three are truly the only ones who can stop them."

Now Hidariude turned to Ryu. "Why didn't you tell us about this before?"

"Honestly, I did not know." Ryu replied solemnly. "We knew the legend, but I had no idea that the demons had actually escaped. It was only recently that we were even able to determine that this was the case at all. The legend told that the kami exorcised the demons and defeated the army, but we were only holding vigil for the heroes, the truth that this vigil actually sealed the spirits was a secret lost in time. But as I told you, we are in a different world now. We can see things that could not be seen where you are. Sasuke found an anomaly as soon as he crossed over to the afterlife, but it has taken all of these years to determine just what it meant. Even as we figured it out, we didn't bother to explain it to you because by then you seemed to already have the situation under control. But now you are here in our world and we are concerned about Douji. He is the yoshiromi of Shinryuu and a part of our family. At this time, Shinryuu is actually right here at the shrine, which means that Douji is unconscious on Seventh Moon. He is in grave trouble. The power that Han Toromi seeks is not something he will find but if he is allowed to continue his search Douji will suffer."

"Well this has been informative, but how exactly does this help us?" Hidariude asked. "We may understand the situation better, but we still need a way to Seventh Moon to get Douji back. How can we do that? Can you help us fix the jet?"

"Actually we have been working on that. It's hard to explain the influence we have from this side, though miracle seems to be the appropriate word. In fact, Sora should be bringing you the good news any minute now."

Sure enough Sora was running up to them right now. Before he could get close enough to see the materialized kami, they dissipated back into petals. Sakura mouthed "I love you" and Ryu said "Fate brought you to us here, fate will bring you back together again." With that the three espers found themselves alone again.

Sora was almost out of breath from running up the mountain as he reached his friends. "Good news guys, the jet was in better shape than I thought, we're ready to go."

The four went back down the mountain to the jet. Sora started to give them directions on how to operate the jet. Hidariude patiently listened until finally he said "I flew this thing to Earth once, I can get it back to Seventh Moon."

"Are you sure?" Sora asked, suddenly a little doubtful and considering that his friend might be acting hasty.

"We have to get Douji back. Unless one of you has more firsthand experience operating a spacecraft, we don't have time for any more preparations. We need to go and we need to go now."

As they all boarded the jet, Hidariude had to stop Sora and Zokushou. "You have to stay here. We need to do this on our own."

Zokushou was about to argue, but Sora stopped her. "We understand. This is way out of our league, we'd just be getting in the way. We'll hold down the fort here. Just come back safe okay?"

"That is the idea." Hidariude said as he closed the hatch.

Sora and Zokushou backed away a safe distance as Hidariude fired up the jet. In minutes they were headed back up into the stratosphere.

"We're coming Douji."

Chapter 17

Hidariude, Keisei and Kichiku rested on the trip until they arrived at Seventh Moon, they knew they would need their energy for this mission. As they got close, they could sense Douji's presence and they were all awake. They docked, landing the jet inside an empty hangar on the edge of Seventh Moon. When they did, the dock automatically recognized the jet and extended a conduit to allow them to disembark.

The espers entered the station expecting to be greeted by security guards, either genetically engineered soldiers on duty rotation or robots such as slashers. To their surprise there were no such security measures. The corridors were completely empty. Not one person seemed to be anywhere around.

As the espers continued to follow Douji's energy through the corridors they began to find broken robots with their parts strewn across the ground. Even worse, they saw the soldiers and other Seventh Moon personnel in rooms along the way, but none of them were alive. Something terrible had happened and it seemed everybody was dead. If it weren't for Douji's life force still going strong, they would be afraid that he had been one of the victims. Every time they noticed a soldier they remembered what they had been told about the demons and said a prayer for the soul to find peace so that the body would not be reanimated. They weren't sure if it was helping, but it was all they could think of to do.

"One hundred and three." Hidariude had been counting the bodies of the soldiers as they prayed for them. "If we count the New Wave Elite we defeated on Earth, that's one hundred and three demonic soldiers accounted for. That leaves Baz, Aka, Hime and two others unaccounted for."

Just moments after Hidariude finished speaking they found the lab where Douji was being kept. There were three guards, Seichei, Baz and Aka. Baz and Aka were sitting on the ground while Seichei stood at attention. Douji and Hime were inside tubes suspended in fluids intended to suppress their powers. Hidariude drew his sword and extended his cyber blade, Keisei pulled out her fans, and Kichiku balled up his fists preparing for a fight, and entered the room.

None of the three soldiers moved. "Really, you're going to fight us?" Aka said listlessly.

The espers could sense that the three were not up for a battle right now. The espers did not drop their defenses, but Hidariude could not help taking this moment to ask the big question. "What happened here?"

Seichei answered the question. "Ever since the robot support units were implemented, there has been tension among the genetically engineered soldiers who feared they were going to be replaced. We noticed tension rising when we were last here to train a group of soldiers to work with robots to hunt you down. Those soldiers didn't want to work with robots and were clearly not too comfortable with us. Even Baz and Aka, being cyborgs, seemed to irritate them. We left about a week ago to resume our task of tracking you down ourselves when other soldiers were coming in for training and home security duty. None of them seemed to be comfortable with the growing numbers of robots that were being manufactured to back them up. It seems that this was a matter of pride that the soldiers found unforgivable and they finally decided to destroy the factory. However, the robots were programmed to recognize such violent threats as treason and retaliate. As the soldiers fought for their lives, the robots came to be perceived as a threat and more soldiers were recalled, each of them being dragged into the war as well. It wasn't long before every single soldier ended up here, excluding of course the ones who were assigned to deal with you as you quickly dispatched them on Earth. All of the civilian personnel got caught in the crossfire during the war between the soldiers and the robots, so now everybody is dead. It would seem we are all that is left."

"So now what are you going to do?" Hidariude asked.

Seichei coldly answered. "We have only been given orders to bring Douji here and to guard him and Hime until they have recovered. So we here we wait."

"Really?" Hidariude asked. "What if they do not recover? What if no one comes to help? You'll just stay here forever?"

"Where else do we have to go?" Seichei replied.

"Besides Han isn't dead." Aka added. "He'll come get us and we'll figure out what to do next then."

The espers were surprised. "Han survived this all somehow?"

"Yeah, we last saw him over a week ago just before he went in for some sort of operation and he's been recovering in his quarters ever since." Aka answered off-handedly, sounding bored. Suddenly he seemed to snap out of his funk. "I wasn't supposed to tell you that." Aka sprang into action running across the room to try to stop the espers from escaping. Baz and Seichei followed him to assist.

Despite Aka's assumption that they would leave to go after Han, the espers had no intention of leaving Douji. Kichiku charged forward to get to Douji, punching Aka with both hands when he got in the way. Aka blocked while transforming into his larger form to counter Kichiku's muscles. Baz tried to assist Aka, but Keisei interrupted by blocking her with her fans. Seichei quickly calculated that he must engage Hidariude to prevent him from assisting his allies and attacking Baz and Aka so he extended his cyber blades and threw himself into the fray.

Hidariude, Keisei and Kichiku did not want to risk harming Douji so they refrained from using their psychic powers and kept to simple hand-to-hand combat. Seichei and Hidariude began dueling with blade against blade as they had so many times before. Keisei was kicking Baz and defending with her fans. Kichiku and Aka were grappling, neither seeming to make any progress in their battle. All three pairs just seemed to be locked in a struggle of equal powers.

At the height of their sparring, Douji sensed that once again his friends were in trouble and struggled to break free of his container to help them. At the same time, Hime was resonating with Douji and her power began to surge as well. Both children began to glow, their light filling the containers so that they looked like lamps. Finally the surge of energy caused the capsules to explode releasing the two dragon children. The explosion was so forceful that the walls were blown apart and each pair of combatants was cast off into different directions.

When the light from the explosion subsided, each pair of combatants found themselves greatly separated from the others in the station. For a moment the espers each considered trying to reach each other again, but their respective opponents did not give them time to consider this option. This was the time to settle their rivalries. Separated from each other there was nothing to get in their way, none of them could rely on their allies and they did not have to worry about their friends getting hurt. It was time to pull out every trick they had and go all the way.

In the residential quarters, Seichei proceeded to attack Hidariude as if nothing had happened, hoping that his opponent did not recover as quickly. Hidariude brandished his blades and parried Seichei's attack. It seemed far too familiar, they had fought this battle too many times. Even without his ESP, he could predict Seichei's every move simply by remembering what he had done the last time. Similarly, Seichei could also predict Hidariude's actions since he was purposely fighting with a style that limited Hidariude's options. He kept his blades very close together to protect himself, preventing Hidariude from striking any vital parts. When Hidariude tried to maneuver around Seichei's blades to attack him from outside his protective shield, Seichei would follow with his defenses. Seichei was an impossible opponent because he was programmed to mirror Hidariude and there was no way to win using traditional techniques. Hidariude realized he only had one option; he pulled back, crossed his blades and unleashed an electric attack at Seichei.

Seichei dodged the attack, which was not a surprise in itself. What did surprise Hidariude was that he could actually detect fear. He had never seen Seichei express fear before, or any other emotion for that matter. He was a robot, programmed to function without emotion, to sacrifice himself if need be. But for a brief moment, in spite of his complete lack of emotion, Seichei actually showed fear on his face and exuded enough fear for Hidariude to sense it. As Hidariude realized this surprising anomaly of emotion, he also realized a mistake he had made that made this even more interesting; Seichei was immune to his electric attacks. The first time they had ever fought, Seichei simply absorbed the electrical attack, and now he was mortally afraid of it. Suddenly Hidariude remembered something else, Keisei had all but destroyed Seichei in that encounter and Baz and Aka had been beaten almost to death twice over. How did they survive?

"Transform Seichei." Hidariude challenged his opponent.

"What?" Seichei replied.

"The first time we met you transformed into a mass of metal blades." Hidariude began to explain. "Since then you have not transformed. Now that I am using my electrokinesis, you should level the playing field by transforming and using a power that I do not have."

Seichei stood without making a move. His hesitation was all the answer Hidariude needed.

"You can't transform can you?" Hidariude taunted Seichei. "Keisei broke you in that first battle. The only reason that you came back from that was that your body is one hundred years old, my guess is that particular day was the magic day. That day you received a soul, Tsukomogami."

Seichei attacked Hidariude in a fit of rage.

Hidariude blocked calmly. "I'm right aren't I? That's why you're afraid of my lightning blade. Just as I am the reincarnation of Okazaki Kyutsume, you are my rival from eight hundred years ago, Tsukomogami, the ninth claw of Kyutsume and leader of the one hundred and eight yokai."

"If it satisfies you, yes, you are right." Seichei responded. "Our souls have waged war for centuries across worlds, from the heavens of Togenkyo to the deepest hell of Jigoku. Indeed it began in Japan between the torn bodies of Okazaki Kyutsume. But the war ends here, the cycle of life, death and rebirth has brought us back to this plane of existence, let us finish this battle once and for all!"

*   *   *

Meanwhile, elsewhere on the Seventh Moon, Keisei was preparing for her confrontation with Baz. Their arena was fitting, the harem chamber. This was a place they knew all too well, and was known only to the girls and the men who took them from this place when they needed them. The chamber was made of gold, studded with jewels and draped in velvet, though not for the girls' pleasure, only ambiance for the men. Behind the velvet drapes were chains that held the girls to the wall, making sure they knew no freedom. Baz taunted Keisei. "It seems that fate has brought us here to face our beginnings and bring an end to it once and for all." As the two girls looked each other in the eye, they each saw the personification of their past and all the troubles that went with it. Today they would end their sorrows and their rivalry.

Keisei held her fans in a defensive stance, preparing for Baz's first attack. Baz opened her hands and shot a blast of fire at Keisei. Keisei redirected the fire away focusing her pyrokinesis through her fans. This created an opening for Baz which she used to kick Keisei in the head. Keisei was ashamed of herself for allowing this attack, but there was little she could do about it, there was simply no way to defend against both attacks at the same time. Keisei could only counter-attack by rolling with Baz's kick and using the momentum to launch a kick back at her. Now they were even with one blow each and at close range, too close for fire blasts, it was hand to hand combat now. Keisei felt more confident about close range combat

274

because she felt she had developed more skill at this than Baz had. The trick was to keep her close and not let her get far enough away that she could use her hand cannons.

Baz knew Keisei was a superior fighter and kept trying to back away, but Keisei wouldn't let her get away. Finally Keisei had Baz backed up against the wall with fans crossed against her throat. "Are you ready to give up now?"

"I'm not even your enemy Keisei." Baz replied. "We're just a couple of slave girls. We grew up here together. We're like sisters."

"Then why have you been hunting me and my family?" Keisei demanded.

"Because I was following orders and I did not understand what I was being asked to do." Baz answered. "I don't even know what I'm fighting for anymore." As a tear dropped from Baz's eye, Keisei actually felt sorry enough for her that she began to drop her fans. In a second, Baz's expression changed. "Oh that's right I remember now, I'm fighting for my life." Baz kicked Keisei then pushed herself off the wall in a somersault over Keisei's head. She continued to roll away from Keisei, stood up ran a few steps and turned back to face Keisei. Keisei raised her fans again ad this time Baz blasted her with her ice and froze her fans. Baz punched the fans shattering them. "Let's see you defend against this!" Baz taunted Keisei while preparing another blast of ice, but her system malfunctioned and nothing came out. The freezing mechanism hadn't been repaired properly after all and it was no longer an option. In this moment of hesitation, Keisei struck back and regained the upper hand.

Keisei kept up with her furious flurry of punches and kicks, though Baz began to block and finally countered by grabbing a hold of Keisei and throwing her by her own momentum behind herself. "You say you are fighting for your life, but what plans do you have after you have defeated me?" Keisei asked Baz. "Do you expect Seichei, Aka and Hime to defeat Hidariude Kichiku and Douji? And if they do, what is next? You can't expect to return to your old life here on Seventh Moon, there is no life left here."

"Han Toromi will have a plan, he will rebuild, he will find a way." Baz protested.

"We will put an end to him too." Keisei returned. "His days of tyranny over us and all of the rest of the world are over."

"No, you can't!" Baz screamed. "I love him!"

Keisei was shocked, she couldn't believe this. "I guess you were wrong before when you said we weren't enemies. I can't imagine why you would want to be with that man after all that he has done to us, but if you insist on siding with him then we are enemies."

"Han Toromi will rule!" Baz retaliated. "Seventh Moon will rise again and I will be his right hand! If you must fall for that to happen, then so be it!"

Keisei drew two paper bombs one for each hand and began her incantation. "Kayakujutsu..." At this same moment, Baz put her hands out to release afire blast from her hands. Her freezing system failed, but the flamethrower system was still working fine. "Ignite!"

Keisei released her fire at the same instant as Baz did. Their flames met exactly halfway between them. Now it was a matter of which would hold out longer, Baz's flamethrowers or Keisei's pyrokinesis.

*   *   *

Kichiku found himself in a training room with Aka. Aka decided to try getting the jump on Kichiku by retracting his cybernetic over-muscles and tried to use his smaller form's higher speed to get the first strike before Kichiku could regain his senses. Kichiku did manage to regain his senses faster than Aka had hoped and blocked the attack. Aka rebounded, picked up some speed and came around for another attack. Again Kichiku blocked the attack. Aka continued with his speed, punching Kichiku repeatedly, and Kichiku blocked every strike effortlessly. After a while, Aka's punches slowed down but the force increased as he transformed into his larger form with more muscle. Kichiku could still block these attacks and with Aka's speed being reduced, he was finally able to find an opening and hit him back. As Kichiku threw his first punch, Aka retracted his muscles again so he could use his smaller size and higher speed to evade Kichiku.

"I'm impressed with your fighting style Aka." Kichiku said to his rival. "I see you have learned to use your both your strength and your speed alternately."

"It took me a while to get the hang of it." Aka replied. "Thanks for noticing." He then resumed attacking Kichiku.

Kichiku resumed blocking and countering with such little effort that he could still carry on the conversation. "However I have noticed that you still have one weakness."

Aka snickered. "And what weakness would that be?"

"You have impressive speed in your natural form that allows you to evade me while striking quickly. In your cybernetically enhanced form, you have enough strength to be my equal." At this moment Aka pumped up his cyber muscles as if on cue. Kichiku countered the transformation by striking him with his palm at the precise moment Aka was in mid-transformation. "However since you must switch between the two states, you leave yourself vulnerable during the transformation. The burden of your cybernetics slows you down but until they are fully extended you can't use your full strength."

Aka caught his breath while he tried to force his transformation to complete. Kichiku used this moment to punch the ground and split it beneath Aka. Aka fell in and Kichiku clapped his hands together, closing the fissure around him. "It is over, surrender."

"Not a chance." Aka pushed back on the crevice walls to free himself. He couldn't quite get free at first, so he shrank himself back down to his smaller form and squeezed out, throwing himself into the air and performed a back flip, landing on the ground in front of Kichiku. At the same time he transformed back to his muscular form and grabbed a hold of Kichiku before he could make another move. Kichiku started grappling with Aka and they found themselves locked in a struggle of strength. Now it was time to prove whether Aka's cybernetics were truly a match for Kichiku's natural muscle.

*   *   *

Douji and Hime were still in the lab. Hime was in such bad shape she looked like she had already lost. Having developed psychic abilities without the sense to control them and repeatedly turning into a dragon had taken its toll on her. Her skin was discolored, her hair was stringy and her eyes were sagging. And yet, despite how worn her body was, she continued to exude an immense amount of energy. Somehow since Douji had defeated her a few weeks ago, she had become so unstable, she had actually become radioactive. She had so deteriorated that she couldn't even speak, she just growled at Douji while her mind tried to settle on some sort of attack. Finally she just threw a ball of pure energy at Douji. It was so sloppy and unfocused that it took no effort at all for Douji to avoid it.

Douji looked as healthy as ever, and under normal circumstances this would be enough for him to fight and defeat Hime with ease. Unfortunately, Douji still did not have control over his powers. At this moment he had managed to gain conscious control of his powers for the first time. With no experience using his powers, he was utterly confused, looking upon Hime in a deep purple haze through his own golden glow. He could not understand what was going on, seeing them both in this unfamiliar place.

Then it all came back to him, partly remembering what his friends had said and partly absorbing their memories psychically. As the memories flashed through his mind, he not only realized where he was, but what he was. "You're...like me."

Hime continued to attack Douji.

Douji dodged her attacks as if she was in slow motion, his senses and reaction time had been so enhanced by his current shintai state. "What...have they done to you? What have they done to us?"

Hime snarled again and threw more raw energy at Douji.

Douji simply slapped the energy away as if it were nothing. "I...feel sorry...for you. You have been given so much power, but you don't understand it so you misuse it. My family...we use our powers to come together. But the way you use your powers, you drive each other apart. You are so different, you are our opposites, the yang to our yin."

Hime still was not listening, she just grunted and reached out to hit Douji with both of her hands.

Douji took Hime's hands in his. "You believe that if you focus on your goals you will succeed because you are not distracted by concern for the well-being of others. But what you fail to understand is that this will be your undoing. We are stronger because we fight for each other, we fight as one."

A surge of energy came through Douji consuming Hime's aura, finally restoring her more stable condition from before their first encounter. She suddenly looked healthy and young again, but this transformation too took its toll and she fell unconscious in Douji's arms.

This same energy resonated in Kichiku as he overcame Aka and brought him to the ground. Aka's cybernetics gave way under the pressure and he reverted to his original form, defeated.

At the same time, Keisei also felt the energy and overcame Baz. The flames did not burn Baz, but there was still enough force from the blast to knock her into the wall. She collapsed unconscious and out of fire, defeated.

Hidariude also felt the energy and was able to produce an electric charge through his blades strong enough to repel Seichei. Hidariude retracted his cyber blades and pointed his sword at Seichei. "Surrender, it's over."

An all too familiar voice came from behind Hidariude. "No, it's not over, not yet."

Hidariude turned from his immobilized opponent to see none other than Han Toromi.

Chapter 18

"Now I am become Death, Destroyer of Worlds."
- Bhagavad Gita

Hidariude was immediately overcome with anger. Standing before him was the man who was responsible for all the hardship in his life. This man was responsible for World War III, the death of his parents, and almost started World War IV. Without a moment's hesitation he raised his sword and brought it down on Han Toromi's head.

Hidariude's sword was blocked by another blade. Han Toromi was holding his left arm up, a cyber-blade extended from his forearm. Desperately, Hidariude let go of the sword with his left hand, pulled back, extended the cyber blade and stabbed at Han's stomach. Again, the blade was blocked; Han now had a cyber-blade from his right arm to deflect the blow.

"Do you like the improvements I made to myself?" Han said to Hidariude with an eerie calm while he held Hidariude's blades away from his body. "It seemed like you were having so much fun with these I thought I'd get some myself. I know you're thinking it's going to take more than some cyber blades to be your equal. Well, these are only the most recent additions, I've also been undergoing some gene therapies over the years. After all, what's the point of ordering all these experiments if I can't benefit a little from them personally? Would you like a demonstration?"

Han released his hold on Hidariude and let him attack again. Again Han blocked both blades as they came from completely different angles than before. Hidariude tried to catch Han off guard with a sweep kick, but Han simply jumped and somersaulted over Hidariude. As he landed, he tried to strike at Hidariude again from behind, but Hidariude turned with the momentum of his sweep kick and raised his own blades to block Han. Han had his feet against the wall over Seichei and pushed off forcing Hidariude backward along with him. As he landed with his feet firmly upon the ground he turned one blade to hold both of Hidariude's off while spinning his other blade around underneath to stab Hidariude in the stomach. Hidariude managed to free one blade to deflect this blow, leaving them in the reverse of the position they had started with.

"Very good use of your ESP." Han observed coldly. "But what if I simply react to you without thinking of my own plans? Can you predict a battle plan that I haven't even thought of yet?"

"Then all you can do is block until I get tired." Hidariude answered.

"Very well then, a battle of endurance, first one to falter loses." Han challenged Hidariude.

Hidariude raised the stakes. "First one to falter dies."

"Then it's a match." Han laughed.

They broke away from each other and began to duel. Hidariude struck at Han from one angle and was blocked and then from another angle, blocked again. He switched around the angle of the blades in every way he could think of, but he could not get ahead of Han. "Did I forget to mention I also had a specially designed therapy just for dealing with you? I managed to get a sample of your brain matter from you cerebellum that retained your fighting skills. Over the years we did a number of tests on you to improve neural interface and among them we found that specific part of your brain that retained muscle memory. I made it into a prion and injected it into myself. Unfortunately I couldn't test it on anyone else since it only works with one who has this specific type of cybernetics and I just didn't feel like inviting anyone else into our club. So, in short I can fight as if I had trained alongside you my whole life."

After a few rounds of fencing, it seemed that traditional fighting was all but futile. Hidariude got desperate, crossed his blades and unleashed a lightning blade attack against Han. To Hidariude's surprise, Han simply blocked the attack with his left blade, absorbing it and then released it from his right blade. Hidariude narrowly dodged the reflected attack. "You see, I thought of everything! I came to this battle prepared!"

As Hidariude and Han continued their duel, Seichei started to recover enough to move, the bolts of electricity in the air waking him up. He considered helping Han, but as he pulled himself up, he realized his battle with Hidariude had weakened him too much, he would only get in the way now. Besides, it appeared Han had a good handle on the situation without him anyway. He pulled himself up and stumbled down the corridor toward the dock and away from the battle.

Meanwhile, elsewhere on the Seventh Moon, each of the other espers was picking up the bodies of their unconscious and defeated opponents. Hime was unconscious, and Baz and Aka had been adversely affected by the shockwave from Douji. Aka was completely immobilized, Baz was in somewhat better shape, still being able to use her arms, but she couldn't move her legs. They would each be able to recover eventually, but right now they were at the mercy of their rivals. Douji, Keisei and Kichiku each understood their counterpart and pitied them. They had merely been pawns in this war, each forced to do something against their will. They simply had not had a strong enough will to oppose Han as the espers had, but perhaps now they could get chance to redeem themselves, if only they could save themselves from Seventh Moon now. They all headed to the dock, sensing the continuing battle between Han and Hidariude.

Hidariude had resumed dueling by the blade. His electric attack had proven ineffective, and it was more dangerous to him to use. Dueling may not have been much more effective, but at least he knew he could endure it. As they continued to clash blades, Hidariude tried to maneuver Han around Seventh Moon to try to find an area that would give him a strategic advantage. The ground seemed to be the only variable Han hadn't totally prepared for. Hidariude attempted to strike Han with both blades simultaneously again, but Han just blocked and pushed back hard enough for Hidariude to be thrown down the corridor. Hidariude let himself be thrown so that he could turn a corner, run down the corridor and hide for a moment so he could surprise Han.

Han was on to Hidariude though, he went down the same corridor searching for Hidariude. "Come out come out where ever you are. Playing hide and seek, like when you were a child. An effective enough training technique I suppose. But remember, no matter how many times you played that game, no matter how many hiding places you found that you think nobody else knew about, I built this place!" Right then Han turned the corner, leading with his cyber blade, striking the wall where Hidariude stood. Hidariude dodged just in time and rolled with the momentum, trying to slash at Han's legs as he went. Han blocked the first strike with his other arm. Hidariude used his other blade to try hitting Han again from his far side. Han ducked to avoid the attack. Hidariude pulled back preparing for another attack. Han knew instantly that Hidariude was taking a moment to plan, a moment he didn't want his enemy to have, so he went in for the attack with both blades forward. Hidariude blocked, with both of his blades pushing Han's blades apart and creating an opening to kick him in the stomach. Han curled up his body, but it was simply a countermeasure, guarding himself against another similar attack. Hidariude tried to run again to find better ground, but Han pursued relentlessly. They came to a stairway and Hidariude tried to get down as fast as possible. Han ran downstairs staying on Hidariude's heels the whole way. Hidariude realized running wasn't getting him anywhere so he threw himself over the railing and started dropping down the stairwell.

"You won't get away that easily." Han taunted as he threw himself over the railing too. They were both in free fall now planning to drop all the way down the stairs to the bottom, hoping to find something to break their fall near the bottom. Han decided not to wait for the bottom to make his move, as he fell he kicked off of a wall and forced himself down the hole even faster. He now fell upon Hidariude with both blades again, but Hidariude sensed him coming and turned around with his blades out to parry, counter and strike back. They ended up bouncing off of the stair railings and clashing the whole way down. Finally they landed at the bottom of the stairwell, each had managed to break momentum enough to land safely, and parried each other's strikes enough to have avoided harm at each other's hands.

"Well played cyber samurai." Han taunted Hidariude. "Do you realize where we are now? We're at the core of Seventh Moon. The entire station was built around an asteroid, mostly good soil for farming which forms the ground of the greenhouse area, but there was also a part which was made of radioactive elements. The radioactive material was sealed off and used to make the generator that powers this entire station. You see, that's where we are now. Here is where the station gets its power; beyond the doors on this level are the generator and control panels for everything on Seventh Moon. You can end my entire operation from here. Of course, without power, you and your friends will not be able to escape and you will all die here too. Quite the dilemma then, defeat me once and for all or leave here alive. What will you do?"

"Shut up Han!" Hidariude screamed while coming at him with both blades. Hidariude hated Han's attitude, he was so sure of himself. He had just pointed out a weakness that Hidariude could take advantage of and at the same time pointed out it would be a suicide mission to attempt anything.

"So you choose to live." Han commented while parrying Hidariude's attack. "You would rather continue to fight this futile battle than take the easy way out. Admirable, but foolish. A true hero would put more concern on the Earth and get me out of the way, even if it meant sacrificing himself."

"What are you getting at Han?" Hidariude asked during a moment when their blades were locked.

"What I'm getting at is that you seem to be fighting with this noble ambition that you're better than me, but how many did you kill to get here? I know you killed my soldiers in Japan, I know you used skills you have learned as a warrior, and powers that I gave you as a former New Wave Elite. You are a killer, changing your reasons doesn't make you any better than any of my other soldiers. You're simply defective, that's why I had to replace you."

They broke their hold and prepared to duel again. They continued to trade blows, blade against blade over and over again. Han just laughed through it all. Hidariude could sense that Han was becoming particularly sadistic. In the past Han was egotistical and a megalomaniac, but now he had gone from being selfish and neglectful of others to actually enjoying actively bringing pain to others. Hidariude then realized what the reason must be. "You are the one hundred and eighth demon aren't you?"

"You can call me Akuma, the demon king. I remember once being told a legend that when the demon generals known as the Nine Claws of Kyutsume called the demons from around Japan, there were four that were too powerful for them to manage. They were particularly nasty obake, shape shifting demons; a rabbit, a dragon, and an oni who had sacrificed his muscles to become the fastest of his kind. They were each the equal of the one who had claimed to be the leader of the ayakashi, but when they boasted of their supremacy, Akuma came to challenge them. Indeed, he was stronger than the four, as he was the true king of demons, and he took his rightful place as the leader of the ayakashi, allowing the other four to be his generals, demoting the other eight generals to be lieutenants of their leader. Of course I don't really believe in all of that mythical metaphysical mumbo jumbo, but it has been said that the devil's greatest success is getting people to believe he doesn't exist."

As Han spoke, Hidariude could finally see Han for what he truly was. Beneath that human façade, Han was in fact the king of demons. "When you genetically altered yourself, you opened yourself for demonic possession. You gave up your soul to become a demon."

Hidariude saw an opening for just a second. Hidariude had blocked one of Han's blades with his sword and Han tried to stab at him with the other. Hidariude feinted and allowed the blade to pass him and strike the wall so he could use his own cyber blade to pierce Han's heart.

Han stumbled back. Hidariude drew back his blade. "It ends here Han. Your reign of terror is over."

Han touched the wound with his hand. He started to laugh, that sick sadistic laugh again. He tore at his shirt and pulled it back to show the wound. Right before Hidariude's eyes, the wound was healing itself. "I thought of everything, including regeneration. A little bit of starfish DNA, a little bit of sea sponge, and viola, I'm immortal. If I did trade my soul for this, I'd say it was a good trade. How are you going to defeat someone who is immortal? You never stood a chance!" Seventh Moon shuddered beneath their feet and then they felt lighter. Their hair began to float in the air. Han laughed again. "It seems when I hit the wall a moment ago I cut some power lines involved in the gravity emulator. I guess we'll be going back up the stairs the way we came."

As they drifted back up the stairwell, Han attacked Hidariude and they replayed their battle from before jumping off the stairs, clashing at every flight, effortlessly jumping back up the stairs with no gravity to hold them down. Hidariude quickly adapted to the new environment, but unfortunately Han seemed to be adapting just as quickly. "It's not so hard to fight when you know you can't die. But then you wouldn't really know that since you're still mortal. I suppose you still want to fight to defend your life since I can still kill you, but it just doesn't seem to matter much to me anymore.

You are going to die, no matter how much you fight it. On the other hand, it really is amusing to watch you squirm, so go on, entertain me. Dance for me my little puppet, dance!" Han laughed again even more maniacally as he continued to clash with Hidariude.

*   *   *

Keisei, Kichiku, Douji and Seichei all met the dock with Baz, Aka and Hime in tow. The espers looked suspiciously on Seichei for a moment. Seichei waved a hand signifying surrender. "Don't worry, I'm not going to fight you. Three healthy espers against one damaged android, I'm done for. I'm aborting all of my combat protocols and defaulting to simply protecting my team mates. All I can do now is get them safely away from here and back to Earth. I deduce that since you brought them this far you'd settle for getting them on board a jet so we can return to Earth."

The espers nodded. "We have to wait for Hidariude." Keisei added.

"I don't know if that is a practical condition considering the current situation, but since we are at your mercy, I don't really have a choice. I must get us back to Earth. For now let's load them into the emergency medical bay."

In the back of the jet was a grouping of beds for anyone who had been injured during a mission. They strapped Baz into a bed on one side and Aka into the one on the opposite side of the jet, with Hime set to rest along the back. Seichei prepared to take the helm since he had the best interface with the system. Kichiku and Douji strapped themselves into the back row of seats with Keisei sitting in front of them with an empty seat to her left reserved for Hidariude when he got back.

Then they felt the shudder, their hair began to float and the only thing holding them in place were their seat belts. "We lost gravity." Seichei explained. "I don't know what they are doing down there, but they seem to be damaging the vital systems supporting Seventh Moon. I'll try to wait for Hidariude, but there's no guarantee that the station will hold up until he gets back."

The espers closed their eyes and entered a deep trance trying to focus their senses on Hidariude, praying for his victory.

*   *   *

Hidariude could feel his friends praying for him. It gave him strength to keep fighting against Han, even more than before. "You just don't understand Han, you fight for yourself. You think making your body indestructible makes you immortal as the gods. But my strength does not come merely from within me, it comes from my friends, my family, from all those who count on me. Yes, I killed, but I killed to protect the ones I love, and I felt remorse for the loss of those lives. You gave me blades to destroy, but these are holy blades, meant to defend the innocent from those who would do them harm. I kill only as a last resort to end the reign of destruction that another creates, and when all other destroyers have been stopped, then my blade can rest again."

For a moment, time seemed to stop. Deep inside Hidariude's mind he felt the warm glow of something familiar. For a brief moment he saw Kichiku, Keisei, Douji, Sasuke, Sakura, and Ryu. Those who were still alive longed for him to join them, those who were dead smiled upon him with the hope he would not join them too soon. Ryu stepped forward from the ephemera, taking Hidariude by the hand. "Let me take it from here."

Hidariude's cyber blade retracted as time began to move again. Ryu's spirit now had control of Hidariude's body. He gripped both hands around Shinryuu Masamune and opened his eyes. He looked at Han Toromi with deep focus, and readied his weapon to strike with full force.

Han laughed. "Well, haven't we suddenly gotten confident taking me on with just one blade." Ryu came in and started with a flurry of blows. Han tried to block and parry but it seemed that his opponent's speed had doubled and he could barely keep up. "What is this power?"

"Don't you recognize it? Or has it been that long since you have seen me?"

"Who are you?" Han asked, suddenly showing fear for the first time since the battle began.

"I am Masamune Ryu."

"How is that possible? You died! I killed you!"

"This is true immortality, the everlasting soul. To live on in people's memories, of those you love, to make a positive influence on the world worth remembering.

Those who fear death enough to cheat it are those who know they will be forgotten and lost to time. Now, Akuma, I send you back from whence you came."

"And just how do you intend to do that?"

"With a technique I was never able to teach Hidariude, because it is only for those who have entered the spirit world. I call for Shinryuu!"

The kami began to manifest as Ryu performed a brilliant sword dance that bewildered Han Toromi. During the dance he maneuvered around Han's blades and cut his arms severing the blades. Finally he finished stabbing Han through the heart, but it wasn't just the blade this time. The golden dragon followed the blade through the wound, taking the demon soul with it. A glorious light filled Han, pouring out from his mouth, nose, ears, eyes and every other orifice. His body was disintegrated from within. Ryu placed the sword back in its sheath and closed his eyes.

Hidariude opened his eyes, once again in control of his body. As Ryu's spirit left him he felt the call of his family and ran to the dock. He felt the presence of his family on the jet, along with their rivals. He also understood the situation and climbed aboard. As soon as the hatch was sealed and the cabin pressurized, Seichei started the launch. Hidariude buckled in next to Keisei and grabbed a hold of her hand as they took off into space back toward Earth.

"It's finally over."

Made in the USA
Charleston, SC
29 July 2014